Dances

AND

Delegations

THE AFFAIRS OF LOVE AND COURT BOOK ONE

JENEVIEVE HERNANDEZ

authorjenevievehernandez.com

Book Cover by Jillian Elyzabeth @jillianelyzstudio

ISBN ebook: 978-1-965713-03-7

ISBN paperback: 978-1-965713-02-0

For my Mom.

You're one of my biggest supporters, and my best friend. You're my role model and confidant, and the best mother ever. I love you!

CHAPTER ONE

Sighing, I brush my hair over my shoulder, my straight hair flowing down my back.

"Carmen, this is your first event as a member of the club. You need to be on your best behavior. You know how the ladies are there. They're going to be all over you, and you need to act like you belong there. You do belong there, you know." Mother says, brushing my shoulders and adjusting the dress she picked out for me.

"Of course, Mother." I say, giving her a smile as she blows me a kiss, leaving my room and making the walk to her and Father's wing of the house.

If I listen close enough, I can hear my brothers down the hallway in our small communal lounge room, just a few steps from the staircase that leads to our wing.

They're laughing about something, and I envy them. While I'm trying to not be stressed out about being the youngest person there, they're both laughing and enjoying their evening.

Matteo has been a member of The Enchanted Ivy for years at this point, and Santiago a few. And then there's me. The youngest of the Alvarez children, and the last child to become a member of the ultra fancy country club that my parents frequent.

What used to be an exclusive club for some of the most

rich people on the east coast, has become more of a social event hoster that throws enough parties and events to send a normal person into an introvert meltdown.

With gossip, dancing, light alcohol, and plenty of scandal seeping through the walls of the club, it's the perfect place for the rich to flock.

It's a place for the powerful to be… people.

No paparazzi or photographs are allowed on the premises, which creates the relaxing atmosphere that everyone is looking for. The Enchanted Ivy has it all.

While I've heard stories from my brothers about the parties and events that are thrown by the club, tonight will be my first time experiencing it for myself.

Also knowing that my first year at school starts tomorrow sends a thrill running down my bare arms.

Unlike most schools, Blackstone's first year starts at sixteen, and ends at eighteen. So while you may be labeled a freshman, it's not like you haven't been attending school. And since Matteo has already graduated both high school and college, and Santiago is in his last year, my parents have always planned for me to attend Blackstone.

Taking one last glance in the mirror, my golden features highlighted with the makeup I'd applied, I smile to myself.

Most of the childish features my face still holds are covered, and everything is highlighted to show off my sharper features.

None of the freckles that line under my eyes, reaching out to my hairline, and my eyelids are visible, and I take a moment to admire the flawless application of the products.

"Carmen, it's time to go." Santiago says, knocking on my

open door and stepping inside. Santiago's hair is slightly lighter than mine, and tonight, it's combed and gelled to perfection, with his tuxedo fitted to his exact shape.

"Okay, I just need to fasten my shoes." I say, gesturing down at the black heels that have raised my five-foot height three extra inches.

"Wow, I almost didn't notice those." He says with a chuckle.

I give him a sharp look, knowing that he's teasing me about my height.

Everyone in my family is taller than me, and no one misses a chance to tease me about it. Usually, I wouldn't mind, but I'm wearing three-inch heels, so maybe the jokes could be laid off for one night?

Seriously, I'm—well, Mother—making an effort to give myself a more "adult" height.

Sitting down at the vanity, I raise my ankle, fastening the straps and brushing the black fabric of my dress down as I stand.

"Matteo went ahead to the car, and Father and Mother went ahead. Their driver was able to make it here a few extra minutes early, and they—Mother—wanted to make sure everything is ready." He says, extending his arm to me as we reach the stairs.

I take it graciously, knowing that one wrong move will send me plummeting down the two flights of stairs.

A chill runs through my body as the early September air hits us, and I envy Santiago's tuxedo jacket. We're inside the warm car within a few minutes, and I'm glad to see that the heated seat function has been applied to my chair.

Matteo looks up as I position myself across from him, and he looks me up and down before speaking.

"Carmen, you look nice. Did Mother decide your apparel?" He asks, a deeper question in his voice.

I refuse to huff in annoyance, and instead, I just nod. I know what he's going to say. That someone my age shouldn't be wearing this make of dress, the color, and so on.

I'm the first to admit that it's slightly out of my comfort zone with the sleeveless element, but I'm not going to admit that to anyone, especially not Matteo or Santiago.

All either of them see me as is their baby sister.

And, while that may be nice and loving, they never see me as a young lady, rather just a child with an adult—if you'd call it that with my height—body.

"It's… nice, Carmen. Aren't you cold, though?"

Thankfully it's dusk, and the light can't betray me by showing the light goosebumps that flood my arms.

"No, I'm good. And, I'm sure the club will have a few heating elements?" I respond, purposely moving the question to him.

Matteo nods, and turns his gaze to the tinted windows.

Our driver has been silent, and I feel a rush of embarrassment at the thought of him overhearing our mini-argument.

Yes, he's worked for us for years and has probably heard way more scandalizing things than a sibling quarrel, but it still sends embarrassment flooding through me.

Watching the city lights shine around the car

The driver pulls on the smaller road that houses the club

property, equipped with a large, multi-story building, swimming pool, gardens, restaurant, and a multitude of other things that show off the wealth of the club and its members.

The gated driveway is accompanied by a few security guards, and after our driver gives him the identification he needs, we're waved through and driving up the long concrete driveway.

I've only been here a handful of times, mostly with Mother as she comes to pick up something from the office, or to meet with a planner.

Matteo offers me his arm as I step out and I take it, feeling my wobbly ankles on the heels.

I've walked in heels hundreds of times before, but this is different. I shouldn't be this worried about being here, but if I act a certain way, I know that I'll never hear the end of it from my parents.

"Carmen, make sure you don't do or say or do anything that could potentially have you seen in a negative light. You know how some of the people here are."

I don't linger on his words, but I know they're the truth.

These people are all influential and have the type of money and power that most people can't even fathom, being seen in a negative light probably won't work to my advantage in the future.

The doors that open into one of the many large rooms intended for gatherings swings open, and the sound of laughter, clinking of glasses, and music greets me.

"Oh, Carmen, you're so grown up!" A woman to my left says, the woman next to her agreeing.

Mother rushes to us, and Santiago appears from behind us,

standing on my other side.

"Oh, my three angels, you look beautiful together. Matteo, thank you for escorting Carmen in here. You're free to mingle, I'm going to keep her with me for most of the night." She says, gesturing for him and Santiago to be on their way.

"Are the multiple rooms that are active during these events?" I ask Mother, noticing how some people disappear down the hallways and into some of the rooms.

"Oh, yes. This is the main one, but some of those house the game rooms—don't worry, we don't condone gambling—and various other things. Of course there's multiple restrooms on each of the floors." Mother says, squeezing my arm lightly as a woman with golden skin a shade or two lighter than mine approaches.

"Oh, you must be Carmen. I heard something about a new member here, but there wasn't enough conversation around it, so I wasn't sure who it would be." She pauses, looking me up and down. "Camila, I can't believe I didn't know that your Carmen was our new addition, forgive me." The woman says, reaching out to pat Mother's hand before flitting away to join another conversation happening a few feet away from us.

"That was Mrs. Valentino, Carmen. You need to watch out for her backhanded comments like that. I mean, she pretty much insulted me to my face. Making it seem as though I haven't discussed your addition thoroughly. Well, it's not like she's doing much better with her son. He's years behind your brothers in this world. Your brothers have plans for their futures. I haven't heard so much as a peep about him. He's a member here, you know." Mother says, venom in her words and voice.

I nod, realizing just how little I know of this small world that exists within the walls of the building.

"Let's introduce you to these ladies. Be on your guard like I told you. Don't show any weakness in front of anyone here." Mother says, a bright smile forming on her lips as she calls a greeting to the cluster of women in front of us. Their evening dresses all shimmering under the chandelier lights.

You'd think we're going to war with how much Mother is preparing me for.

CHAPTER TWO

One of the club owners is giving a speech regarding bookings for events, and as I allow my eyes to wander, my eyes lock with a boy standing near the back of the room.

His dark, golden brown hair is in loose waves and his even more golden eyes are looking directly at mine.

Peeling my eyes away from him for only a split second when the speaker drops her microphone, I turn my attention back to where he was standing. Only, he's no longer there.

I don't see the boy anywhere, but the mental image of him lingers like smoke in my mind.

"Carmen, do come and grab a bite with me." A woman says, tapping my elbow and motioning at the banquet tables that line one area of the room as soon as the speech is over.

I follow her, waiting for her to introduce herself. I'm not really sure why she's asking me to come with her, but standing around with nothing to do is less appealing than this.

"I'm Lorelei, by the way. I've been on the board just as long as your mother, you know? Camila is a good friend of mine." She says, adding a small pastry to her plate.

"Oh, how lovely." I reply, not knowing what else to say, standing awkwardly behind her.

"Well, aren't you going to find something to eat? Surely you want a little something." Lorelei asks, looking at my empty hands.

"I'm-"

"Do go fetch yourself a plate and something to eat. These events are rather long. You'll regret it later."

Taking her advice, I add a small pastry to my plate, only to look up and find her gone.

As the night progresses, I'm haunted by the gaze of the boy from earlier, but his face never appears throughout the crowds of people I meet all night.

When the event starts slowly winding down around midnight, I've practically given up hope of seeing him again. And when we leave two hours later without seeing him, I almost wonder if he was a figment of my imagination.

I fall asleep on Santiago's shoulder on the way home, and I vaguely remember him walking with me up the stairs and leaving me at my bedroom door.

CHAPTER THREE

Our driver that will be taking us to school every day doesn't say anything, rather, he just looks in the mirror every few minutes, presumably to make sure I'm still awake.

While I'm extremely tired, I do have to thank Blackstone for not having extremely early classes. Classes start at ten, making the morning only a little bit more bearable.

The only noise in the quiet car is Santiago is next to me, studying one of his textbooks, not paying me any attention. The gentle scribbles of pencil as he takes notes is both relaxing and irritating. Since this is his last semester of high school, and he hasn't let any of his grades dip below perfection, I'm not surprised by his commitment to being ahead.

Our driver pulls through the iron gates and exits the car to open my door, taking in my navy skirt and white collared shirt, my tie swinging as I climb out. I give him a smile as I walk, glancing down as I walk through the security doors into the building, smiling at my shoes.

The white crew socks that are paired with the black shoes really finish my outfit.

Well, everyone's outfit.

It's the school dress code, the boy's code only varying slightly with khaki pants instead of a skirt. So while I like to imagine that it looks amazing on me, it's not unique.

Walking to the locker that I equipped with all of my necessities last week, I scan the faces of students and faculty that pass me, looking out for any familiar faces. Not finding any, I turn to my locker, typing out the code and opening it.

My first few classes go without a hitch, but as I'm walking to my final class of the day, across the center of the school and at least two hundred feet away, a familiar head of brown, wavy hair, and golden skin is watching me.

It's the boy from last night. Our eyes meet, and it's like I'm in a trance.

I don't know why I didn't consider the fact that he probably attends Blackstone. It makes sense that he would.

I pause, my mouth slightly open as if I'm about to speak. Which is strange, considering he's so far away that it's almost impossible for him to hear me.

I'm pulled away from whatever moment we were having, when someone from behind me bumps me off balance and sends me tumbling to the floor.

Embarrassed, I gather the notebook and pencils that fell, when someone crouches down to help me. Santiago.

"Carmen, what happened? Here, up." He says, helping me to my feet and brushing off my skirt.

In a daze, I turn to where the boy had been, only he's nowhere in sight.

"What are you looking for? And why were you on the floor?" Santiago questions, snapping his fingers in front of me as if he's worried I hit my head.

"Oh, I don't know. Someone bumped me." I say absently, still looking for the boy.

"Did you hit your head, Carm?" He asks, only half teasing.

There's concern in his voice, but I can tell he's trying to mask it.

"I- No, I didn't, I'm just tired. Let's get to class." I say, pulling away from him and walking into my last class of the day. Looking back just as the door closes, I see him watching me curiously. It's not often that I'm not one-hundred percent honest with him and Matteo, and I'm pretty sure he can tell that I'm not being completely truthful.

I don't pay that much attention as my teacher speaks, rather, I spend the forty-five minutes wondering who the boy is. I know I can't ask anyone from my family. Matteo and Santiago will just bristle and tell me that I need to focus on studies rather than boys, and my parents… I shudder.

Mother will want me to stay as far away as possible from a son of her enemies—I say the word enemy lightly—and Father will no doubt repeat anything I tell him to Mother, and maybe add in something about how there are certain social lines that we shouldn't cross.

As in, fraternize with the child of someone that competes with my father in business.

Although I'm not sure who his parents are, I'm sure his parent's work is somehow related to Father's.

Most everyone at the club—from what I've heard at least— runs in the same business circles as him.

The bell chimes, signaling to us that class is over, and while everyone gathers their things and packs it into their bags, I pick up my unopened bag, having not even taken out a pencil and paper.

All of the way to the car I keep my eyes out for the boy, but he's like a ghost.

Santiago is already in his seat, and gives me a quick acknowledgement as I climb in, and I have to wonder if he's going to bring up earlier again.

I don't have to wonder for long, because as soon as we're on the road, he turns to me.

"What actually happened earlier? It's not like you to be just… pushed over. It's especially not like you to just sit there. You didn't even get up. Is someone giving you a hard time?" He asks, watching me carefully for any reaction.

"No, nothing happened. Someone must have just bumped me. I was thinking about class and wasn't paying attention. It was probably my fault for not paying attention."

"Carmen, you'll let me know if something is going on, right?" Santiago finally says, not seeming to buy my story.

I don't really know why I thought I would be able to keep something from him. Matteo and Santiago have always been able to read me like a book. "Yes, Santi, I will. You know that." I say, giving him a hopefully convincing look.

He peers at me one more time, his long lashes blinking slowly as if I'm going to do something in the minuscule amount of time it takes to blink.

I turn and watch as the city fades into the suburbs, and finally to the business boulevard—that's what us kids that live here call it—mansion after mansion, with more space in between each "house."

Each mansion has a large amount of property attached to it, giving the privacy that is hard to find in a house mere feet away from each other.

Santiago and I both hurry up to our wing, retreating into our rooms as soon as we arrive home, and I sigh, changing into shorts and a tank top, flopping on my bed.

After my first day at school, and last night's event lasting for hours, I fall into a deep sleep, awakening somewhere in the early morning hours.

Swinging my legs over the side of my bed, I take a sip of water and pull on slippers. I skipped dinner since I was asleep, and now I'm paying the price.

My clock reads two thirty-four in the morning, the glowing numbers the brightest thing in my room. Deciding to go downstairs and find something to eat, I make a mental note to be as quiet as possible.

As soon as I'm out of my door and near the top of the steps, I bump into a plant, making a light clattering noise as it knocks against the wall. I suck in a breath, and hope that Matteo and Santiago are sound asleep. They're the only people that could have heard me, seeing as we're the only people living in this wing of the house.

The hardwood stairs are slippery against the house shoes that I'm wearing, causing my pace to be extremely slow. After only slipping once, I've made my way down the stairs, only stopping once I've reached the first floor.

"Carmen! What are you doing?" A whisper-shouts from behind me, causing me to release a small yelp.

Matteo is looking down from a few stairs above me, wearing the expression of a protective older brother, mixed with the look of a frustrated parent. If it weren't directed at me, it would be quite an amusing expression. Most twenty-one year olds are out and about at this hour, and here Matteo is, looking frustrated that he was awoken from his sleep.

He walks the last few steps down, his tall frame looming over me. "Were you sneaking out?" He asks, looking me up and down, a slightly horrified expression playing across his face.

"What? No. I'm getting a snack." I reply, my jaw hanging open in horror at the thought of him thinking I'm sneaking out. "And, why do you care what I'm doing?" I demand, looking him up and down.

"Why do I care? A million reasons. Go get your food, I'm going back to my room." He says with a huff, turning and walking back up the stairs. What a conversation.

I make my way into the large chef's kitchen, opening the cabinets and pocketing a few items.

True to his word, Matteo is back in his room, the only indication that he's still awake is the small amount of light that seeps under his door and into the hallway.

Why didn't I notice that earlier? I would have made much less effort to be quiet.

CHAPTER FOUR

The next few days go smoothly, but I don't see the mystery boy at school. Either he's avoiding me, or our schedules are wildly different enough that we have a low probability of seeing each other. Frankly, I don't know which one is the truth, but both are frustrating.

"You're all aware that tomorrow night is a garden party for the club, right?" Mother says as we eat our breakfast.

The French toast that's being served smelling of cinnamon and sugar wafts into the air as I cut into my slice, and I look up at the sound of her speaking, both Matteo and Santiago doing the same.

"There is?" I ask carefully, wondering if she'll elaborate. Isn't this announcement a little bit late?

"Yes, Carmen, why else would I say that?" Mother says with an exasperated huff.

After breakfast is over, the day drags on, and my night is near sleepless, anticipation rushing through my veins.

Will I see the mystery boy again? Will I talk to him?

As the evening looms, I prepare for the party, Mother nowhere to be found.

I assumed that since she'd had such an influence on everything that I'd done for the last party, she would do the same for this one, too.

Sliding on an off the shoulder, knee length dress, I admire the cream color that allows the tiny floral print to blend into it. It's breathtaking, and suits me so well.

I run my hands through my hair, sliding a cream colored bow into it, securing it with little pins on the back of my head. While I know some people might see it as childish, it complements the outfit so well that I can't resist placing it in my hair.

The makeup I do is simple, only highlighting my natural features and lightly bronzing my neck and shoulders.

My clock chimes, letting me know that it's time to be leaving, and I make my way downstairs, Santiago waiting by the door for me.

Outside of the window, I see Mother and Father's limousine pull out of the gates, and we hustle to our limousine, Matteo waiting patiently.

"Matteo, why were you up the other night?" I ask, the silence too much after ten minutes of being on the road.

He looks up, the motion lazy as he answers. "I wasn't. I heard you knock into something and didn't know what was going on. I woke up and was investigating it."

"What? What happened?" Santiago interrupts, looking between the two of us as if he's missing out on the largest secret.

"On Monday I woke up to Carmen clattering her way down the stairs, and went to investigate." Matteo explains.

"Monday?" Santiago says, as if he's considering something.

"Carmen *was* acting strange on Monday, you know." He muses, giving Matteo a look that I can't decipher.

The conversation is dropped as we pull in the gates of the club, and I breathe a sigh of relief.

The driver opens the door, both Matteo and Santiago exiting first. Santiago offers me his arm as I step out, and I take it only for a moment.

Classical music hums through the air, and I can already imagine the scene we're about to enter as we walk into the gardens. The scene doesn't disappoint, with the twinkling lights and flowers decorated everywhere, it feels like I've walked into a new world.

All of the women are in dresses somewhat similar to mine, although mine is a little bit more girlish than most.

I hear the faint nose of music drifting from the main building, and I wonder if there are people in there as well. Maybe there's a separate party? Or some people are choosing to gather in there?

I greet Mother and the group of women she's with, but I don't stay with them for long. Conversations of which flowers should be used for the next parties, and what colors the lights should be is both boring and draining.

Grazing my fingers across one of the bushes of flowers, and I wonder how upset anyone would be if I strolled through the garden. I don't hesitate for long, remembering that I'm a member of this club, and have all of the rights to explore the large garden. Or, at least I hope I do.

The hedges come well above my head, and as I walk through the pathways, I breathe in the fresh, floral scent of the gardens around me.

After walking for almost ten minutes, I stop in what must be the center of the garden, an old-fashioned swing hanging from a large tree, and a bench in the middle.

I've roamed much past where everyone is gathered for the party, and well into the gardens, now. As I sit on the swing, the sturdy ropes holding the wood and cushion hold my weight easily, and make me feel comfortable enough to want to swing.

"Most people don't stray this far from the party." A voice calls out in the dusk light. It's the boy.

I jump at the surprise voice, but immediately still myself. "Why not?" I ask as the boy approaches me.

His golden skin is even more beautiful in the lighting that gently streams through the tree. "They prefer to stay near the gossip and drinks." His voice is rich and smooth, and I'm surprised at how I want to hear him continue speaking, if only to hear the sound again.

"Then why are you here?" I ask, raising an eyebrow at the irony in his words.

"Simple. I'm not a gossipy old lady, and I'm not of age to be drinking." I giggle at his words, the bullet-point reasons amusing.

He chuckles, his shoulders moving slightly as he does so, but his tuxedo never moving. It's fitted seamlessly to him, and I wonder how many times it had to be refitted for it to fit him that perfectly.

"Ah, I see. Good reasons, I guess."

"And what about you? Why would such a new member be straying from the party?" He asks, stepping closer, genuine curiosity in his voice. His light brown eyes searching mine as he speaks.

"The same reasons as you." I say, flitting my eyelashes.

"Good answer, Miss Carmen." He says, a twinkle in his eyes.

"How do you know my name?" I ask, stupidly forgetting that just about everyone knows who I am, thanks to my parents spreading the word like a wildfire.

"I'm Alessandro," he says, reaching out and offering to shake my hand. At least, that's what I expect him to do. Instead, he gently raises it to his lips and brushes a feather-soft kiss across the back of my hand.

It's not even that cold, but a chill still rushes up my arm.

"Alessandro, how nice. I'm betting you're Italian, then?" I ask, pulling my hand back and draping it across my lap. If his slight accent didn't give it away, the name alone does. I'm not surprised that he has an accent, since I have a slight Spanish accent.

My parents have always traveled back and forth between here and Spain, so it wouldn't surprise me if his parents do, too.

He chuckles. "You'd be right, Carmen."

Smiling because I'm enjoying the easy conversation that rolls between us, I bite my tongue right before I ask if I saw him at school on Monday. Refraining myself from asking, I tell myself it was obviously him. It must have been.

"How long have you been attending these parties?" I ask, looking him up and down, taking in his nice physique and handsome clothing.

"Almost two years." Alessandro answers, looking me in the eye as he answers.

From my position on the swing, I'm about eye level with him, and I have to wonder what our height difference would be if I were to be standing.

As if acting on impulse, I swing my feet lightly to slide off the swing attempting to slide forward. Only, Alessandro must see this as me trying to swing, because he puts his hand on the rope beside me, his long fingers dangerously close to my arm.

"Would you like to swing?" He asks, a twinkle in his eye. It's on the tip of my tongue to decline, but something in me insists that I say yes. I nod, and the twinkling in his eyes intensifies.

He stands behind me, careful to only touch the ropes, pulling the swing back before giving it a gentle push.

A giggle escapes me as I float upwards, and I hear Alessandro from behind me release a laugh at my excitement.

"Carmen? Are you back here?" A voice calls out. Matteo's voice. I look behind me, wondering if Alessandro heard him, but he's gone, just like the night I first saw him.

"Yes, Matteo." I call out, sliding off the swing as Matteo rounds the hedges.

"What are you doing back here, Carmen?" He asks, walking towards me, curiosity in his gaze.

"I was exploring the gardens. Is that not allowed?" I reply, taking a step towards him.

It's almost dark, and I squint as I walk, the evening light hanging on by a thread.

"By yourself?" He asks, looking behind me as if he suspects someone to be accompanying me. Which, he wouldn't be wrong for assuming, since Alessandro had been here mere seconds ago. "Let's get back to the party, you shouldn't be wandering in the dark. You don't know your way around here and could get lost." Matteo says, gesturing for me to walk ahead of him.

I release a small sigh, but walk ahead, knowing he's not going to just leave me out here.

CHAPTER FIVE

I see Alessandro at school once on Monday, but he either doesn't see me, or chooses to not acknowledge me.

Instead of spending my time thinking about him, I focus on my studies, knowing that rather soon Mother and Father are going to want business plans from me. They've both been adamant about us Alvarez children having large plans for life.

The only problem is, I don't have any ideas for businesses, and it's pretty clear that Matteo will be taking over Father's business when he steps down. My feathers aren't ruffled by that, since most business things don't interest me all that much.

I need to find something that my parents approve of soon, because the modeling idea I brought to them a few months ago was deemed 'unreliable'.

Another week goes by, nothing happening except Mother's planning for an end-of-summer party at the club.

The day of the party is precisely two weeks after the garden party, and even though it's been a short amount of time, the weather has already cooled down by a few degrees.

When we arrive, the party is in full swing, couples are dancing, others are mingling in small circles, and some are standing near the dessert table.

The atmosphere is darker than before, only the chandeliers providing light, but it doesn't bother me. Rather, I enjoy this even more.

I slip out of the main room, turning down one of the long hallways, curious as to where I'll end up. Just like my little escapade in the gardens, I have no idea where I'm going, just knowing I'm going to explore.

Music hums from one of the cracked doors I find after a few minutes of exploring, and I walk inside, the scene surprising me.

There's a group of people a few years older than me, spread across the room in groups. Some are sitting on couches, others surrounding tables with games.

Slowly stepping back, knowing that this isn't really my scene, and I don't know any of these people, I feel embarrassed for even walking in here at all.

My black corseted top dress swishes, the billowing skirt spinning around my legs as I take another step back, backing right into a... person?

I turn to see Alessandro behind me, his broad chest having been what I walked right into. "Alessandro?" I ask, as if there's another boy here that resembles the definition of stunning.

He smiles. "The one and only."

I grin, having to look up to meet his gaze. Alessandro looks to be close to six feet tall, a stark contrast to my mere five-foot height.

"What are you doing back here?" I ask, wondering how he's found me for a second time.

"Searching for you."

"Why?"

"Simple. To give you a tour." He says, clasping his hand

around mine before walking to the door. Heat races up my arm, stemming from the hand that he's holding.

I don't catch the look he gives the other occupants of the room, but I catch a few nods across the room. What was that about?

He peeks out the door before he leads me into the desolate hallway, as if he's playing hide-and-seek. I'm even more curious than I was before.

"Miss Carmen, prepare for the tour you've been hoping for." He says before tugging my hand and running down the hallways and up the stairs.

"How are you so sure I want a tour?" I ask as we stop in the second-story hallway.

"Because no one just wanders during these parties unless they're searching for something."

"And just what am I searching for, Alessandro?"

"Knowledge about the club grounds. Everyone who joins wants it." Alessandro says with a smirk. "With all of the land that surrounds this place, and enough hallways and rooms to be a castle, it's only natural to be curious." He's right.

"You're right. I do want to explore this place. Lead the way." I say, glancing excitedly into his eyes.

Alessandro smirks, his eyes twinkling as I place my hand in his.

"Before we get started, if anyone finds you and asks what we're doing, remember that you're a member here, and have all of the rights to be on the grounds." Alessandro says, looking me right in my eyes as he says so, as if to make sure I remember.

"Okay, but what about you? Where will you be?" I question,

unsure on why this only applies to me if we're found.

His eyes twinkle again. "Nowhere in sight. Can you imagine the scandal if the two of us were found together?" He pauses for dramatic effect. "Alone."

I nod, knowing what he's insinuating. "Yeah, I guess so. Is that why you left the other night when Matteo called my name?" I ask as he leads me down the hall.

"Yes and no. Your brothers and I have a… strained relationship. No relationship, really. More of a dislike-to-dislike relationship if you'd want to call it that." Alessandro says, sounding like he's not exactly sure how to word it.

"Why?" I ask curiously, more than a little intrigued. It's not like Matteo to just dislike someone. Santiago, maybe, but not really.

"Let's just say our families have their differences, and that includes us." Alessandro says carefully, as if he's trying to consider his next words carefully. "Plus, there's a little bit of bad blood from Santiago since we're always vying for the top spot in classes." Alessandro says, a quirk in his voice as he opens doors and tells me the uses of each room.

"And Matteo? Also, aren't you seventeen? Why would you be in Santiago's classes?" I question.

"I'm ahead a year in school. As for Matteo, I think it just stems from Santiago having a large dislike for me. Also what I said about our families' businesses being too similar for there to not be high tension between us." He says as we reach the flight of stairs that will lead us to the third floor.

"What's your last name?" I ask as he leans against the railing, wondering just who he is.

"Valentino."

CHAPTER SIX

"Oh, I see." I say, remembering Mother saying she and Mrs. Valentino have always had their differences. I'm sure that also applies to Father and Mr. Valentino.

"Yep, the one and only. And, before this tour continues, I'm going to say no to the third floor. I'll never escape from that level of scandal." He teases, but I can tell it's for my benefit that we're not going to the third floor.

"So our families don't necessarily have it out for each other, but there's more than a little bit of tension?" I ask, leaning next to him on the railing. Who cares about this tour if I'm getting all of the secrets between our families?

"Precisely."

I nod, understanding. "But you don't have that tension with me, right?" I ask, looking up at his golden eyes as he answers.

"Of course not, Carmen." Alessandro replies, a glint of… something passing through his eyes as he speaks.

I smile, glad for his answer. "So how do you spend these parties, since you obviously aren't a gossipy old lady." I ask, walking in the general direction of the stairs. Alessandro takes a few long strides to catch up with me before answering.

"When I'm not with the daughter of my parent's 'enemy'? I tend to just stick to the sidelines." He says with a chuckle. The sound of it is like music, and I immediately want to say something so he'll laugh again, if only to hear the sound of it.

"Ah, so I've brought a whole new amount of enjoyment to your evenings, then?" I ask, looking up at Alessandro as he speaks.

"Definitely."

I smile, my cheeks flushing as he responds. "I'm glad I can be of service, then." I say, a giggle escaping me as I speak.

"I'm glad you needed a tour guide." He says.

"So where else are you going to show me?" I ask as we reach the staircase.

"The inside of the main room." He says seriously, a small twinkle still in his eyes. Why are we already going back?

"But we aren't done exploring." I point out, giving him a confused look.

"And we won't be able to if our families find out that we're spending time together. We need to be back at the party—separately, of course—and not make anyone suspect that we were gone." It makes sense, but I also don't want to be back around all of the women that are delivering snide remarks and backhanded compliments, either.

"You really have this whole thing figured out, don't you?" I ask, walking a single step down the stairs.

Alessandro smiles. "I've mastered the art of evading parties like this one. It's all in keeping up appearances, Carmen." He says, gesturing for me to walk down the stairs.

"Probably so." I reply, walking down the stairs and slipping into the hallway, Alessandro far behind me.

I'm arriving back into the main room just as my brothers are, and I silently thank Alessandro for suggesting we go back.

Any longer, and my guard dogs would have been searching for me.

I know I haven't done anything wrong, but I still feel uneasy about Matteo and Santiago knowing that I've spent time with Alessandro. I don't know their side of the story, but that's only because they haven't brought him up. And, if they're not going to, then neither will I.

A few more minutes slip by before Alessandro enters the room, and he makes himself discreet as he walks to the table that holds the desserts.

I watch him pick up a plate, adding a few desserts to it and making his way to the edge of the room where a few men mingle and laugh over their drinks. He doesn't join them, but he's close enough that upon first glance, he's with them.

I end up hanging out with a group of older women, their chattering about their grandchildren and their achievements easy to tune out, but also easy to respond to if one of them asks me a question. Why, yes, Janet, your little William really is the smartest boy in his fourth grade class.

I catch Alessandro's eyes on me every few minutes, and I suck in a few deep breaths, wondering if anyone else is catching him, since it's very obvious to me.

The party is coming to a close another hour or so later, and I breathe a sigh of relief knowing that I'll be home soon, far away from all of the tension in the room. Maybe I'm the only one that can feel it, but even so, it's enough to send my nerves on high-alert.

Alessandro gives me a wink as he exits the room, and I feel my cheeks erupt in flames.

The drive home is silent until Santiago speaks. "So, Carmen, now that you've experienced some of these parties, are they everything you hoped they would be?"

I look over at him, his sudden words pulling me out of a daze. I've been thinking about Alessandro, the image of his smile and golden eyes etched into my brain.

"Um, yeah. I think the whole thing is pretty cool, actually. Do you enjoy them?" I ask, genuinely wanting to know the answer.

I've always assumed that he and Matteo enjoy them, but I wonder if there's some nights when it's tiring or boring for them.

"They're okay. I mean, having everybody in your business twenty-four-seven isn't really fun, but sometimes there's something enjoyable to do at these parties." I nod, not knowing what else to say.

I want to ask why he hates Alessandro, but I bite my tongue, knowing he'll demand to know where I got that information from. I wonder if there's any other reason besides school and our families.

Once we arrive home and I've flopped down on my bed, my fuzzy pajamas warming me, I allow myself to dream of Alessandro.

The way he'd grabbed my hand and run down the hall, his eyes, everything.

I wrap my arms around my pillow, a smile plastered across my face as I replay the evening like a movie.

Our movie.

CHAPTER SEVEN

"Carmen, are you awake?" A voice from outside my door calls out. Matteo.

I roll over, wrapping myself in my blankets. Sunlight is streaming through the large windows that I forgot to pull the curtains over last night, bathing my room in golden light.

"I am, now." I call out, my voice muffled, not having the energy to roll my face out of the pillows.

I hear the door click open, and the sound of Matteo's slippers on my floors.

"Good morning." He says, the edge of my bed sinking as his weight presses it down.

"What do you want?" I ask, pulling my face out of my pillow and rolling slightly, looking up at Matteo.

"Santiago and I are going to drive into town and stop by Father's office. Do you want to come?"

"To a business meeting?" I ask, already not liking the sound of this.

"No, we just need to pick up a few papers from him and drop them off at the other office in town. His assistants are too swamped to do it, so he asked us." He says, reaching over and ruffling my hair as he stands.

"Yeah, sure. I'll come. Give me a few minutes to get dressed. Shoo." I say, rolling to the edge of my bed and barely swinging my legs over the edge in time to catch myself.

"Okay. Maybe if you and Santi behave, I'll buy you breakfast somewhere." He says, clicking the door shut behind him.

I quickly dress and wash my face, taking no more than ten minutes to get ready.

Sliding on my sneakers, I walk out to Matteo's car. He's already pulled it out of the multi-car garage, making the walk much quicker than I expected.

While I've never had a deep fascination with cars, I do notice small details here and there that pique my interest.

Sliding into the backseat and buckling, Matteo eases the car out of the gate and onto the road. "So, first destination on our little family expedition?" Santiago asks from the passenger seat as he slides his sunglasses on his nose.

"Office." Matteo says, accelerating his car. Santiago turns on music, and we drive in silence.

"Would Mother or Father have to come with me to get my license? Or since you're both adults, would one of you be able to take me?" I ask, breaking the silence that has enveloped us. I'm not sure why I'm asking this, since I haven't mentioned this to either of them yet.

The thought has been on my mind for a little bit now, since Matteo and Santiago both got their licenses when they turned sixteen.

Matteo reaches and turns down the music before asking me to ask my question again. I repeat it, this time with a little bit less confidence.

"Why do you need a license?" Santiago asks, not even bothering to respond to my question. I suck in a breath, knowing the speech I'm about to get.

I'm not sure why I didn't realize that this is what their response would've been. "That way if I wanted to go shopping or something I could drive myself."

Truthfully, I'm not really sure why I want one, but it might have something to do with the fact that no one in my family sees me as old or mature enough to be able to take care of myself.

"We have plenty of drivers that could drive you if needed to go somewhere." Matteo says, catching my gaze in the mirror.

"Well, yeah, but I want a license, though. Didn't you two both want one when you were my age?" I ask, feeling slightly frustrated. I know that their intentions are coming from a place of love, but I'd still appreciate it if they treated me my age, and not like an incapable child.

"We both did, but it was a little bit different. We had to drive to and from Father's office, and run small errands for him. You don't need to do extra things like that. It would be easy for a driver to drive you." Santiago says, the matter-of-fact tone in his voice stinging.

"Yes, but I want to drive myself." I say, knowing that this conversation is pretty much over.

Matteo seems to realize the direction this conversation is turning in, and instead of continuing on the 'Carmen doesn't need a license' path, he instead answers my original question. "We wouldn't be able to take you. It would have to be Mother or Father. We're not your legal guardians." He says, an apologetic tone in his voice.

"I'll have to ask them, then." I say, but we all know that I'm not going to. There's a note of finality in the conversation as I speak, and there's not any more words between us until we reach the office.

Matteo parks, and we all exit the car and enter the building. Stepping inside the elevator, Matteo pressed level twelve, but before it can spring into motion, a voice calls out. "Room for two more?" A somewhat familiar voice says, as two people slide into the elevator. I suck in a breath when I realize it's Alessandro, and a man that must be his father.

What? Why are they here?

"Well, hello, gentlemen. Oh, and miss Carmen, too." Alessandro's father says, noticing me in between my brothers.

"Hello, sir." Matteo says, reaching out for a handshake.

Santiago does the same, and I do, too.

His grip is softer than when he shook Matteo and Santiago's hands, and he gives me a smile as I pull my hand away.

Alessandro doesn't say anything, but I catch Matteo and Santiago purposefully looking in any other direction than him.

I lock eyes with him for a second, and his signature smirk appears. It disappears in an instant as Santiago shifts his gaze.

The tension in the air is so thick it can surely be cut with a knife, and it has me wondering when did elevators start taking so long?

"Are you here to see our father?" Matteo asks, breaking the uncomfortable silence.

"Oh, of course. We have a few things to discuss, and I figured I'd bring Alessandro along. After all, he'll be taking on the company one day. Best get training him now." He says with a chuckle, slapping Alessandro's shoulder.

He nods in agreement, but I can't help but wonder if there's something else under his expression.

"That's nice. Matteo and I have been doing business with our father for so long now that it's hardly training for us. I remember those days fondly." Santiago says. I almost elbow him, but I refrain. Is it really necessary to have to one-up Alessandro and his father right now?

I breathe a sigh of relief when the doors slide open. Everyone gestures for me to exit first, and I take a few strides to Father's office, feeling only a little bit strange, seeing as we're all going to the same place.

Matteo strides ahead of me and opens the door, Father's spacious office greeting us. He's seated at his desk, bent over a few papers, but looks up as our group approaches, and smiles at us.

"Wow, this is quite the party. If I had some notice, I would've bought a cake." He teases, standing to shake Mr. Valentino's hand.

Matteo takes the stack of papers from Father's hand, and we exit the office, leaving Father and his company.

"Well, that was fun." Matteo says as we enter the elevator.

"Shouldn't you not say things like that when there are security cameras around?" I ask, wondering if anyone is listening to our conversation.

"What do you mean? The elevators are camera and microphone-free." Matteo says easily, leaning against the wall as we descend.

"Really?" I question.

"Yeah. Father doesn't have things like that on most of these levels. A few of the lower ones have them, but it takes a lot to get up here. They just let us up since we're obviously his children, but you don't make it to these upper levels without an impressive title." Santiago says, sounding fully confident.

Matteo nods, agreeing with him.

"Wow. I guess I didn't know that." Once we're back in Matteo's car, he takes off in the direction of Father's other building.

This time, only he goes inside, and he's back within a few minutes.

"Since my two personal assistants were helpful, I think I can get them some sort of… reward." Matteo says, pulling into the parking lot of a donut shop.

I smile as he jogs inside and returns a few seconds later.

"I made an online order." He says proudly, sliding in the car. The smell of sticky sweet donuts floods the car, the smell only intensifying when Santiago opens the box and stuffs a donut in his mouth. Matteo does the same before handing me a plate.

We eat the donuts in silence, Mateo munching on his as he drives us home.

The events of this morning are almost enough to make me forget the conversation I'd had with them earlier. Almost.

CHAPTER EIGHT

"Carmen, I need you to come with me to a quick little meeting. Normally, I wouldn't need you, but I figured you might like to see the behind the scenes of planning an event." Mother says, her voice carrying through my open door and to me at my desk. "And, having you there would be the perfect thing to show the other ladies how wonderful you're turning out to be." She adds.

"Right now?"

"No, tomorrow. Of course right now. I need to be there by five, because Mrs. Valentino will be there at about five-fifteen. You know how she is." Mother says, her voice already fading, as she hadn't even entered my room.

I quickly dress and make my way to the car, knowing that Mother is already out there.

The driver pulls through the gates of the club property, and I wish for a quick meeting. The sooner we're past this, the sooner there's another party, meaning I'll be seeing Alessandro shortly.

"Carmen, remember that these women will do anything to have things their way, even if it ruins the party. Everyone wants to be heard, even if it's not for the greater good." Mother says as we walk into one of the club offices, the smell of coffee and tea accompanied by the scent of pastries.

"Of course, Mother. I'll be sure to point the attention of

the conversation to your ideas." I promise, knowing that I'll probably be silent the whole time, because when has Mother ever let someone throw her ideas to the side? Literally never.

"Oh, welcome, ladies. I was beginning to worry that something had happened." Mrs. Valentino says, sweeping her arms in a 'thank goodness' motion as we enter the room.

I guess Mother's calculations were wrong, because here Mrs. Valentino is, already here and already making 'well meaning' comments.

"No, everything went smoothly. I'm guessing there was less traffic than you expected? I seem to remember you saying you'd be here at five-fifteen. Thank goodness you were able to be here early." Mother replies cooly, striding past a few of the ladies and seating herself at the table.

I imagine that the reason there's not a seat at the head of the table is because Mother and Mrs. Valentino would battle it out for the seat every meeting. The thought of Mother becoming physical with someone over a seat brings a smile to my face, but I know that if it came to it, Mother would do just that to secure her place.

The real reason there's so much strife between the ladies is because everyone is equal here.

There's no *real* leader—besides the owners of the club that are practically non-existent—so that means the ladies are left to their own devices whenever they want to plan parties and events. Sure the club managers plan plenty of events, but if you're a member here, you get free reign if you want to host a party. The hefty fee that the members here pay is enough for the club to supply all of the staff and utilities that someone would need to host a party for half of the population.

"If everyone is ready, let's begin. I know that this is an impromptu meeting, but don't worry, it's just for a few details that need to be gone over for the party celebrating our lovely golf team. So, that means we'll need to be present–or, those of us that are on the board, of course–for the party." Mother says, looking over the women as she speaks. I don't miss the slight smirk she holds when mentioning the board, because both her *and* Father are members of the board that manages the golf team, and many of the women here aren't.

Well, except for Mrs. Valentino and her husband.

"Yes, yes, of course. Can we please get to the details that we're all here for?" One of the ladies to Mother's right asks, sounding bored. Mother gives a forced smile before jumping into the actual party details.

It sounds like it will take place indoors, but I'm sure no one will notice if I slip into one of the many rooms, or possibly even the gardens, to find Alessandro.

CHAPTER NINE

It's been a few days since the planning of the party, and the date has finally arrived.

I sweep my arms over my knee-length, pastel-colored dress, and I slide my feet into my shoes, feeling ready for the night.

Thankfully, the party is starting much later than the previous ones, meaning it'll be easier to miss an absent person. Also known as an absent Carmen.

I slide into the back of the waiting vehicle, and mentally call for Matteo and Santiago to rush. The sooner we arrive, the sooner I can meet Alessandro.

After they're securely in their seats does our driver start the drive to the club, his perfectly normal speed irritating me as I wish to be there sooner. It's absolutely crazy how excited I am to see Alessandro, considering the last time I saw him was a few days ago at Father's office.

When we finally arrive at the party, the dark sky is a stark contrast to the lights that stream through the opened curtains of the club building.

For appearances, I walk inside with my brothers, and after a few minutes, they disperse throughout the ongoing party.

I take this as my chance to find Alessandro, wandering down one of the many hallways in hopes of spotting him.

"Carmen?" A voice calls out from behind me. I turn,

surprised.

"Alessandro?" I say, watching the approaching figure near.

"The one and only. Sorry for following you back here, I was hoping I would see you tonight." He apologizes, falling in step with me.

"You hardly followed me. I mean, I'm barely down this hall. It's fine." I reply, glancing up and smiling at him. Alessandro smiles back at me, and for a moment, we're just normal teenagers who snuck away during a party. "So, what were your plans for tonight if you didn't find me?"

"Hang around the people that somewhat like me and leave early." Alessandro says with a smile. "I know, very interesting and exciting."

"Very much so." I tease back, a small laugh escaping me as I speak. "So, what are your plans now that you've found me?"

Alessandro doesn't speak for a moment, he just watches me with a twinkle in his eyes. "Whatever you'd like to do."

I smile at this, his gaze enough to send butterflies fluttering throughout my stomach.

"Carmen?"

I stir, my mind in another universe. "Yes, Matteo?" I reply, the fading of lights of the city flying by the car window.

"Mother wanted me to ask where you were all evening." Is all he says, and I drag my thoughts away from Alessandro. I should've anticipated this question.

Why can't anyone just let me live my life? Why can't I have

any level of privacy?

"I took a walk. The party was a little bit full, you know?" I lie, hoping he'll buy what I'm saying.

"Really?"

"Yes, really. Why else would I say that?" I reply, the worry in me causing my words to come out sharper than intended.

Matteo doesn't respond, rather he just rests his head on the seat and opens his phone, Santiago fast asleep next to him. Why's he so tired?

I feel a pang of disappointment in myself for being sharp with Matteo, and turn my attention back to the window. Why couldn't I have just been a little bit nicer to him. All he was doing was listening to Mother's instructions.

The image of Alessandro and I strolling through the hallways and laughing as we talked is enough to pull my mind out of the spiral it's in, and I welcome the memory.

CHAPTER TEN

"Carmen, do you want to come with us?" A voice behind me says, somewhere in between a whisper and a normal tone. I turn, the bustling hallways a good cover for Alessandro's voice.

"Where?" I ask, people walking and chattering around us as we stand in the middle of the halls. It's been four days since I last saw him at the party, and it feels like an eternity.

"We're going to visit the aquarium." Alessandro says, the twinkle in his eyes almost blinding me.

"Um, I want to, but I ride home with my brother every day. I need to come up with an excuse or something." I say sheepishly, the students around us filing through the hallways, the parking like a beacon of light at the end of a school day.

"Oh, no problem then, I just thought-"

"No! I want… I want to come. Just let me think of something to tell him. Also, who is the 'we' you mentioned earlier?" I ask, stalling for time so I can figure out something to tell Santiago.

"Oh, it's me and a few of my friends. My friend–Cameron– is taking a girl on a date, and wants a wingman." Alessandro says sheepishly. Wait, is he insinuating that this will be a date? If he is, then I'm definitely in.

"Okay that sounds go- hide!" I say, grabbing Alessandro's arm and dragging him into a nearby closet.

"What just happened?" Alessandro asks, his chest pressed to

mine as the door shuts behind us His voice is surprisingly calm, as if it's a normal occurrence to be squished in a closet with a girl.

The closet is *considerably* small, and for a few moments it doesn't register that he's asked me a question. All I can think about is how close we are.

How close our bodies are. How close our faces are. How close are lips are.

I take a deep breath in, and look up into Alessandro's eyes, their golden color gazing intently in mine as he waits for an answer.

"Carmen?" Alessandro's words finally awaken me, and I tear my eyes away from his. I can still feel his smoldering gaze on me, but I do my best to keep my eyes away from his.

"I saw Santiago, and didn't want him to see us together. I mean, if he sees us talking then I'm randomly not going to be driving home with him, he's bound to be suspicious, right?" I say, hoping my reasoning sounds legit. Of course I'm not lying, but dragging someone of the opposite gender into a closet usually means something else. Something *very* different.

"Oh, um, okay. So what are you going to tell him when he asks why you're not going home with him? Assuming you still want to come. This sneaking around is probably a little bit… tiring. I would completely understand if you didn't want to come anymore."

"I think I'm going to say that I'm studying with a friend, then we're going to go shopping afterward. That way, when I call our driver and I'm not on campus, it won't look suspicious." I reply, looking up through the dim light to gauge Alessandro's reaction to my story. I catch a twinkling behind his eyes, but I can't figure out why. "Well, what do you think?" I ask, still waiting for his answer.

"I think I've really corrupted you." Is all he says, a smirk playing across his lips as he chuckles.

Thoughts swirl throughout my brain, and I almost forget that I still have a mission to complete before we can leave. I have to go lie to Santiago and make him believe I'm hanging out with friends that I don't have.

"You should stay here or something while I go find Santiago. I'll find you once he leaves, okay?" I say, reaching for the door.

"Yes, ma'am. I'll be here until you come back for me." Alessandro says, giving me a salute in the near-darkness.

I giggle as I step out the door, but quickly regain my composure and search for Santiago, knowing that he'll be somewhere by his locker exchanging the books he'll need for this evening.

"Hey, Santi, I won't be coming home with you, today." I say, approaching his locker as he shuffles his books around.

He stops what he's doing to look up at me with a more than confused face, and I feel heat creeping up my neck in worry. He's coming to completely see through my lie.

"Why not?" Is all he responds with, slowly continuing to move his textbooks.

"I, uh, I'm going to spend the afternoon with a friend. We're going to study, then go shopping. I'm going to have our driver pick me up later, so you don't need to worry about picking me up or anything." I say, cursing the uneasiness in my voice. Why can't I just be normal and speak through a normal sentence without stumbling over my words?

Because you're lying, my brain screams, answering my own question.

"And you've discussed this with our parents or something?" Is all Santiago asks.

Wow. He must be really preoccupied with something, because there's no way normal Santiago would be so easy to get past like this.

"Um, no, well, I'm going to. But I'm sure they'll be fine with it. I'm not going to be doing something they wouldn't approve of, so it'll be fine." I reply, my words coming out in a jumbled mess.

Santiago raises an eyebrow at me, but doesn't say anything as he straightens from his locker.

"Look, Carmen, I'm not going to be saying yes or no to this, but you better not get yourself in any trouble or hurt. And you better make sure that if Mother or Father ask where you are or what you're doing, you talk to them." Santiago says. Who is this new Santiago?

"Yeah, of course. I was just letting you know so you didn't wait for me. Have a good ride home." I say, giving him a quick hug and peck on the cheek. He gently ruffles my hair, but there's an emotion behind his eyes that I can't read. One that's full of tiredness, stress, and something else. Something that's distracting him from my obvious lies.

As he turns his back to me and walks to the parking lot, I give myself a mental fistbump for being able to keep my cool during our conversation. Well, cool enough that an extremely distracted Santiago wasn't able to pick up on my deceit.

Now, all I have to do is make sure he actually leaves, and then I can leave with Alessandro.

I wait five or so minutes before walking to the doors to check and see if our driver is still here, but after glancing through the lot and unsuccessfully spotting him, I make my way back to the closet to find Alessandro.

"You can come out, now." I say with a laugh, opening the closet door to find Alessandro leaning against the wall, his hands tucked into his pockets.

"Ah, I'm guessing you were successful in clearing your afternoon?" He asks, following me into the hall.

I turn as I walk, meeting his gaze with a smile. "Today was our lucky day. I guess something is going on with him, meaning he was way less interested in who I'm, spending time with."

"I'm sure that if he saw it was me, whatever problems he thought he was dealing with would be very minimal compared to his darling sister spending time with the sworn enemy." Alessandro says with a small laugh.

I reply with a laugh of my own, and I remind myself that Alessandro hasn't done anything to me that would cause me to avoid him. Unless Santiago and Matteo want to bring it up with me, they have no right to be angered by me spending time with Alessandro.

Technically, I have no idea why they despise Alessandro. They've never actually told me. It's only Alessandro that's filled me in, and of course it was his side to the story.

"Well, good thing he's never going to figure out, right?" I say, looking up at Alessandro as we walk past the ivy walls.

"So do you get dropped off, or do you drive yourself?" I ask, wondering if his driver would tell someone about us spending time together.

"Oh, I drive myself. I've got to get some miles in my car somehow." Alessandro says, reaching into his pocket to retrieve a set of car keys.

There are only a few other cars here, and I'm glad for the privacy. The less people that know that I'm spending the afternoon with Alessandro, the better.

Alessandro strides ahead to open the passenger door for me, sliding my book bag off my shoulder as I settle into the seat.

He winks before closing the door behind me, opening the rear door to set our bags in the backseat before sliding into the driver's seat.

As he presses the start button for the engine, a call rings from his phone. He answers, and after a few moments he hangs up the phone.

"Well, I'm sorry to say that we've been stood up. Apparently, the friends that were going to come with us decided to go home." Alessandro says with a slight grimace.

"We can still go, right? I kind of didn't just lie to my brother for nothing." I say, only half teasing.

I want to spend the day with Alessandro.

To be honest, it didn't even really cross my mind that his friends would be there with us. All I'd cared about was being with Alessandro.

"Of course. I was hoping that you'd be able to meet my friends, but it's fine. You're still up for the aquarium and shopping?" Alessandro asks, sliding on his sunglasses before shifting the gears of his car.

"We don't actually have to go shopping. I just said that as a cover for Santiago." I reply, making a 'don't worry about it' gesture.

"If you said we're going shopping, then we're going shopping." Alessandro says with a smirk as he pulls on to the road.

CHAPTER ELEVEN

"Wow, I can't remember the last time I was here." I say, stepping into the dimly lit hallway that's lined with the aquarium. The tanks wrap from one side to the other, extending over us in an ocean tunnel.

"Yeah, I haven't been here in forever. It's nice." Alessandro says, his eyes shifting from one side of the tank to the other, following the movement of the ocean life.

"It's so beautiful." I say, turning my attention back to the aquarium.

"Yeah, beautiful." Alessandro says from close behind me, his breath sending shivers down my neck and shoulders.

I have to wonder if he's referring to the aquarium around us, or… me.

It might be foolish to believe he's talking about me, but after our last few encounters it's fully within my rights to question his intentions.

I wrap my arms around my middle, feeling the effect of Alessandro's close presence, his nearness bringing both comfort and jitters.

The short amount of time I've spent with him has always left me feeling at ease, and I've never felt like he's out to get me or something. Alessandro just feels so…right.

A couple walks by and gives us a strange face, reminding me

of the few people that we've encountered who have looked at us equally as strangely.

I have to wonder if it's because of our school uniforms, or the fact that we've stayed in this section of the aquarium much longer than necessary. It's not like we have a whole entourage of students with us, so it doesn't appear that we're on some type of field trip.

We're just a boy and a girl dressed in the uniforms of the most elite high school in the country. Totally normal, right?

The jellyfish weave their way around each other in the dark water, their colors blending with the colorful coral that rests at the bottom of the aquarium, and I have a hard time pulling my eyes away from them.

I'm so mesmerized by the ocean life around us, that I'm not aware of how close Alessandro has moved towards me, the only indication being his hand slipping over mine. I try to not have an outward reaction, but the warmth and jolt of electricity that stems from Alessandro's grasp is enough to leave my brain frazzled.

Heat floods my hand and rushes up my arm, flowing through my whole body like a shockwave. Before I lose my nerve, I wrap my fingers around his, and tighten my grip on his hand.

Alessandro doesn't say anything, instead, we both look down at our joined hands, this moment feeling different than all of the other times we've spent together.

We stand for what feels like hours, but only seconds at the same time, neither of us moving as we both gaze down at our hands.

We've held hands before, but this is different. Those times were funny, and didn't feel like this. I can almost imagine a ball of energy shining from our hands, the electricity that's crackling from our touch building inside the ball.

Alessandro clears his throat and gently tugs my hand in a "let's walk" motion. And I follow. The feeling being so right.

The gentle sound of water is the only sound that surrounds us as we pass through the various inhabitants of the ocean. Neither of us has spoken since earlier, but the silence is so comfortable as we stroll without a concept of direction or time.

"Hello, what are we shopping for today? Do you need measurements done?" A cheery woman says as we enter the designer store that Alessandro picked out for us to visit.

"No thank you. If we need anything, we'll be sure to let you know." I reply, giving her a smile before turning to Alessandro. "So, what are we getting here?"

"Anything you'd like." He says with a smile, his full, white smile on full display.

"Me? I really don't need to get anything. If this is about me telling Santiago about going shopping, that was genuinely just a cover so that no one will be suspicious when I call our driver to come pick me up."

"I know, but surely there's something that you want." Alessandro says, pausing if he just realized something. "Wait, do you not have a driver's license?" He asks bluntly.

"Um, no, I don't. I mean, I'm going to get one soon, but I

don't currently have one." I say, cringing as I do so. Why did he have to ask that?

Alessandro nods, noticing my aversion to the topic. "Sorry for asking, by the way, I guess I didn't realize how that would come across. I think it's nice that you don't have a license. There's no law that states you have to start diving at sixteen." He says gently, obviously not having a clue on what to say.

"Well, apparently it does." I say, hopefully quiet enough for Alessandro to not hear me.

"What do you mean?" He asks curiously.

"I- It's nothing, really." I say, sliding my fingers over the material of a dress next to us. We've moved to the less-crowded area up on the second floor, and only the occasional shopper comes near us as we talk.

"Nothing?" Alessandro asks, a teasing tone light in his voice to mask his curiosity.

"Well, I haven't gotten my license yet, because my family is more than a little bit against it. It's kind of a sore topic with me, because it's a constant reminder that all my family sees me as is an incompetent child." I say, only now realizing how open and honest I'm being with Alessandro.

It's been like this with Alessandro since the moment I met him. Always telling him too much, and always sharing things that I don't even want to admit to myself.

"Oh." Is all Alessandro replies before speaking again. "Just so you know, I don't see you as an incompetent child, and no one else does, either. I mean, would you really be a member of the club, or one of the honors students if you were just an incompetent child?" He asks, his gaze focused on me.

"Well, I guess so. It just feels like whatever I do, I'll never be seen as anything other than someone who's unable to make their own decisions." I finally reply, glancing over to see a somber expression on Alessandro's face.

"I think we all feel like that sometimes." Is all Alessandro says, giving me a slight smile that leaves me wondering what he's thinking about.

"Are you sure I can't help you with something?" The sales attendant asks, interrupting the eye contact that Alessandro and I are holding.

"Yes, actually. Do you mind helping us find some shoes? I think we're in a slight rush today, and don't have time to browse all of your options." Alessandro says, his tone completely different than it had been mere seconds ago when we'd been speaking.

"Of course. What are we thinking?" She asks, giving me a smile as she asks.

I don't really *need* new shoes, but I guess that since we're really following through with this, I might as well buy a new pair that will match with the new cocktail dress that arrived yesterday.

I had it made with the intention of wearing it to the autumn party that Mother mentioned would take place sometime next month.

"Something to match a black cocktail dress, please. I'm thinking simple, but still full of character." I say.

She gives me a wide smile as she rushes to find something matching the description of what I've mentioned.

It must be so nice to work here. Sure, I'd rather be wearing the designer clothes that line every shelf in here rather than assist others in finding the perfect piece, but at least being here would be a step closer than I am now.

"So, you only need shoes? You're not going to let me spend real money on you?" Alessandro says with a teasing look, his golden eyes twinkling with mischief.

"Wait, you're paying for the shoes?" I question, giving him a confused look before continuing. "And, by the way, any of the shoes she brings will be rather expensive. I'm sure they'll be up to your 'real money' standards." I tease, looking up to see a wide smile appear on Alessandro's face.

"It wouldn't be a very gentlemanly decision to bring you on a shopping trip and not pay for it, don't you think?" He asks, both humor and seriousness laced throughout his words.

"I wouldn't know, seeing as I'm not the gentleman in this situation." I reply, looking up through my eyelashes to see a smirk play across his face.

"Of course. I wouldn't have it any other way. I'm glad to be your gentleman." Alessandro replies, gazing into my eyes as he speaks, almost as if he's waiting for a reaction from his words.

He doesn't receive one, though, because just as he finished speaking, the sales attendant returns with a small cart. The mini shelves on it have several pairs of shoes, each unique and beautiful.

"Let's do a quick review of what you do and don't like, then we can move on to sizing and trying them on." The woman says, seemingly happy with my impressed gaze on her small display.

"That sounds wonderful." I reply, giving her the go ahead to pitch each pair to me

CHAPTER TWELVE

"Thank you so much." I say as the glass doors close behind us. Alessandro had insisted on buying me two sets of shoes, and while plenty of people have bought me clothes or other accessories, something about Alessandro buying them feels different.

The evening glow that colors the sky is casting the perfect tint over Alessandro, making the gold of his eyes even more beautiful.

"Of course, Carmen. It was my pleasure. I have to ask, though." Alessandro replies, clearing his throat before continuing. "Will you be wearing them at the next party or event that the club hosts?"

I give Alessandro a smile that I can only hope appears secretive. "Maybe. We'll have to see. You should be on the lookout for them, though. I can't promise anything." I say, looking up through my eyelashes to see a smirk play across his lips.

"I'll be sure to watch for them." Is all Alessandro replies with, his smirk alluding to the fact that he pretty much knows I'll be wearing them.

"I think I need to be leaving. I'm surprised that there hasn't been a search for me yet, and it's best that I don't push my luck. I'm going to call our driver, and he should be here to pick me up, soon?" I say after a few too many moments of gazing into Alessandro's eyes.

"Oh, yes, of course. I'll wait with you, then leave once you've been picked up." Alessandro replies easily, gesturing at a cafe a few businesses down from where we are.

The cafe looks like something out of a cartoon, the playful lettering that reads across the sign gives the impression that it will be modern, but also mixed with the cozy coffee shop aesthetic.

"Are you sure? Aren't you worried about being seen with me? Won't that cause some major strife between our families?" I ask, confused by the finality in his words.

"Well," he says, reaching down with his right hand to carry my shopping bags, his left hand wrapping around mine. "That wouldn't really make me much of a gentleman, don't you think? Leaving the lady he's been accompanying for the afternoon all alone while she waits for her ride. That's basically the polar opposite of being a gentleman." Alessandro says as he leads me to the coffee shop.

I call our driver and request for him to pick me up near the entrance of the clothing store that Alessandro and I had previously been in, giving me the perfect way to leave Alessandro without my driver seeing us together. While I don't think he will go and tattle on me to Mother or Father, I also know that if anyone were to ask him about who I'm with, it's his job to be honest.

I can guarantee that any forbidden interactions between Alessandro and I will be forbidden if someone from my family discovers that we've done a lot more than simply converse at a party.

I'm far too deep in my maze of lies and excuses for me

to not be exempt from some sort of permanent barr on our growing relationship.

"Carmen, dear, don't you think it's much later than appropriate to be arriving home this late?" Mother asks as I pass her on the way to the staircase.

Leaving Alessandro had been much easier than I'd imagined, my driver seemingly oblivious to the fact that I asked for him to pick me up at one location, and I'd walked to him from a different one. He never asked me about it, and I never offered him any information.

"Sorry, Mother. We must have been there during rush hour, because there were so many people in the store." I reply, wanting the topic to be dropped. So what if it was a little bit later than she would normally allow me to stay out?

My parents don't necessarily have curfew rules, but if I were to be walking out of the house at two in the morning and got caught, then I'm sure they would send me to my room.

"We? I don't remember Santiago mentioning your friend." Mother questions as I start up the first step. I refrain from grumbling at her continuing to press the question, but I keep it inward and plaster on a smile as I respond.

"Yes, I went with another student. We shopped and then got hot chocolate at the cafe a few businesses down. Surely you've seen it, right?" I ask, asking another question before she can continue to grill me.

Once I'm inside my room and the door is locked, I try

on the shoes. I act as though I didn't try them on a few hours ago, but I'm hoping to feel the magic that the store must have weaved throughout their products. I walk up and down my room in rhythmic motions, practicing for the day that I walk the runway.

It will never happen, but I still cling on to the idea, especially when I'm wearing new shoes. Something about perfecting my runway walk in brand-new shoes gives me the same sense of what it might be like to walk the real runways.

For now, I can only use the floorspace of my bedroom for practice, but maybe on a day when Matteo and Santiago are gone, I'll be able to walk up and down the long hallway that has the entrance to every room on our wing.

I've been considering the idea of using one of the unused rooms throughout the house and having a mini photograph shoot in it. I mean, who would want to hire someone without professional looking photos in their portfolio?

It's a silly idea to continue practicing my modeling poses and walk, and an even sillier one to attempt photos.

Maybe, just maybe, I'll summon enough courage to ask again about modeling. After my parents assured me that I wouldn't make it in the modeling world, I lost confidence and almost abandoned the dream all together.

The new shoes are perfect for practicing my walk, and it's in small moments like these that I gain confidence in my dreams.

Maybe modeling isn't the dream that many have, especially when their families have more money than what they know what to do with, but it's *my* dream. Wearing brand-new clothes and showing off the designer's hard work and talent, it's what I want so, so badly.

I carefully slide off my new shoes, and I smile as I slip them into their box, carefully wrapping them in the protective paper that they came in. I'm not sure I'll ever wear these anywhere, the thought of them being damaged—or even worse, ruined—too great of a horror in my mind.

Alessandro bought these for me. He bought them without a second guess, perfectly sure of his decision to gift them to me. Yes, I've received so many more gifts, a few of which were more expensive than these, but these new shoes have a special place in my heart.

It's not about the shoes, I guess. Technically, they're just another pair of shoes that could adorn the walk-in closet that's attached to my room, but something about me spending the day with Alessandro and him seeing a vulnerable side of me is making me more emotional than I would usually be.

Until I wake up and realize that these are just another pair of shoes, I'm going to wear them with so much more care than I would ever give to my other clothes or shoes.

CHAPTER THIRTEEN

"Santiago, don't you think you're going to get in trouble for that?" I say in a voice that's only a little bit louder than a whisper as I place my hands on my hips. I hear him swear under his breath as he turns to face me, his face illuminated from the moonlight that's streaming through the window at the end of the hall.

"What are you doing awake, Carmen? Don't you have exams tomorrow?" Is all Santiago replies with, a dark, frustrated look deep in his eyes.

"Ye- wait, why didn't you answer my question? I asked the first question." I say, stepping closer, my nightgown swishing at my knees.

"Listen, Carmen, I don't expect you to know what's going on with me right now, but just stay out of it. Go to sleep, please. I need to get going." Santiago says, taking a few strides to the window that rests at the end of the hall.

"Going on with what?" I hedge, following him as he continues to walk.

I suppose the architecture of the house was rather smart. Father and Mother definitely planned for teenagers, because all of the windows in our rooms have essentially no way to just "slip out".

Yes, I'm sure if one of us were desperate enough to sneak

out, we'd figure something out. But, to be honest, sneaking out hasn't ever crossed my mind as something I want to do, and until now, I didn't think it was something one of my brothers would want to do, either.

"Going on with older brother stuff. Honestly, Carmen, you won't even notice that I'm gone. Go to sleep and get some rest for tomorrow."

Santiago says as he opens the window, the cool breeze of the night hitting my bare arms and legs, sending a chill through my body.

Instead of trying to convince him otherwise, I try a new tactic to get him to change his mind. To be honest, I'm not even sure why I care where or why he's sneaking out, but even if I don't know the reason behind my curiosity, I still want him to stay home.

"What would Matteo say about you sneaking out?" I ask, knowing I've hit a weak spot for him. Yes, he's a grown adult, but he has a weak spot for Matteo's approval. Which, if I'm being honest, I usually do, too. For both Matteo and Santiago. He turns at this, and I see something flash across his face.

For a moment, I compare this to when I 'snuck out' with Alessandro earlier, and how neither of my brothers would approve of it. At the thought of this, I feel a stupid smile rise on my face as I remember all of our time spent together.

"Why are you smiling like that? Who are you thinking about?" Santiago suddenly asks, swinging his previously outside leg back inside the window as he takes a closer look at me.

Shoot. Was I really just smiling like a fool over Alessandro? Yes, yes I was.

"No one. And, besides, you *still* haven't answered *my* question." I reply. My hands that were previously crossed over my chest to warm myself from the chill of the night rest at my hips again.

This boy. Accusing me of thinking of someone while smiling like a fool. The nerve. Even if he *was* right, that doesn't give him a right to call me out like that.

"Listen, Carm, I won't get in trouble if no one knows." Santiago says, taking a few strides to me. "And, no one will." He takes one last step to me and gives my cheek a quick kiss before climbing out of the window. What does he mean? Does Santiago just *assume* that I'm not going to tattle on him? He'd be right if that's what his plan is. He knows that I'm not going to wake up the house or something and send out an alert that he's left.

I bunch my fingers into fists before stalking back into my room. As much as I want to slam the door, I refrain from doing so. That would definitely wake up Matteo, and by then, he'd be on high alert and surely notice that Santi is gone. Or, he would just see the open window and inference from there.

Whichever it may be, Matteo would ask why *I'm* awake, and that answer is definitely not being answered.

"Hey, Alessandro! Wait!" I whisper-shout, grasping his wrist as he strides across the lawn of the schoolyard.

"Carmen? Wha-"

"Just come with me before someone sees us." I say, pulling

him into one of the alcoves that can be found at the older slide of the school building.

"Yes, ma'am." Alessandro says, pressed against me as we hide in the shadows of the brick wall. "So, was there something you wanted to tell me? Or did you just feel the need to be pressed against me in a small space? Again." Alessandro teases, his whisper so close to my ear that it sends shivers up and down my back.

"Well…" I say, pretending as though I have to think about it.

If I'm being honest, the idea of not even speaking and just staying silent with Alessandro close sounds nice. But, that's not why I brought him here.

"Well?" Alessandro teases again, a light chuckle escaping his lips as he waits for my answer.

"Well, I was just wondering if you wanted to plan on doing something together. I don't know." I say, suddenly feeling very scared of his answer.

Everything feels both unstable and completely complicated when it comes to Alessandro. At the same time, though, it feels as though he's the most stable thing in my life, and the least complicated part of it.

"You know what? We don't have to-"

"Carmen, I'd love to. What did you have in mind?" Alessandro interrupts, a tone that I'm not sure I've heard before creeping into his voice.

"I don't know. Whatever you want to do. I kind of didn't think that far into the future." I say, covering the last few words with an unnecessary laugh, feeling slightly self-conscious over the thought that I didn't come with an idea on what to do.

"I'm up for whatever you want to do. When do you think we should plan for? I have a very busy schedule." Alessandro says with added emphasis on the word 'very' even though he surely isn't that busy.

"Whenever you think. I did the hard work of trying to set something up. I'm going to leave it up to the gentleman to decide." I say, recalling our conversation in the store.

"Ah, I see how this is going to be. Well, Carmen, tell me a time that works for you, and I'll have something planned." He pauses before continuing. "Any day or time that you'd like."

"Any?" I ask, looking up through my lashes, to see his stunning face.

"Any." Alessandro says, meeting my gaze with a smirk.

"Tonight. Can you do around eleven?" I ask, the words tumbling out of my mouth before I have a chance to rethink them.

Alessandro's eyes flicker in surprise, but instead of asking questions, he just nods.

"Where would you like me to pick you up?" He asks, looking me up and down before looking into the mostly-emptied schoolyard.

"At my house, but not inside the gates. I'll meet you outside of the gates." I say, gazing into his eyes one last time before taking off and jogging to meet Santiago in the car.

Santiago has definitely been waiting longer than usual, and with the dark circles under his eyes that are no doubt from lack of sleep, I avoid eye contact with him.

Maybe he'll think that I've forgotten about our little

encounter a few nights ago, and won't be listening for my footsteps as I sneak out tonight.

CHAPTER FOURTEEN

What was I thinking earlier? Why did I think that it would be a good idea to tell Alessandro to pick me up at eleven? Apparently earlier-today Carmen had her whole escape route planned out and had no idea how difficult mustering up the nerve to do this would be.

Now, here I am, wearing a skirt and sweater, my purse securely strapped to my chest, looking out the hall window.

Apparently I'd forgotten that the balcony outside my window doesn't have some magical stairs that will lead me right into the passenger seat of Alessandro's car. I should have thought about my escape route better, especially since I just saw Santiago sneaking out a few days ago.

Why didn't I take notes or something?

Taking a deep breath, I open the window as quietly as possible, which, thanks to our cleaning staff, is pretty quiet.

Securing my foot on one of the flower trellis that lines this side of the mansion, I start my precarious descent to the ground. The things I do for Alessandro.

I guess what everyone says is true, that teenagers will do stupid things for someone of the opposite gender. Here I am, someone that's never even considered sneaking out, sneaking out to meet a boy. What have I become?

Only once I have both feet firmly planted on the ground do

I look up and feel proud of my accomplishment. That was a long climb. What was I even thinking, attempting that?

I don't have time to dwell on my bad decisions, because I still have to climb the brick wall that lines the front of our property. I have a better plan of action for this one, since I know where some of the best climbing spots are.

And, I know I just said that I haven't ever tried sneaking out, but that doesn't mean I wasn't ever an annoying little sister and always followed my brothers whenever they did daredevil stunts like challenge each other to climb the wall.

While it's been a long time since I was young and wanted to be wherever my brothers were, that doesn't mean that the wall is that different, right? Hopefully not.

Quickly finding a few places for me to climb, my skirt rustles against my knees as a cool breeze blows the night air. Here, at the top of the wall, looking out for the sound of Alessandro's car, I feel free. My hair billows around my face as it dances in the breeze, and I soak it in as I look up at the thousands of stars that adorn the dark sky.

Hearing the approach of a car engine, I quickly scramble down the wall, rushing to the gate, not wanting Alessandro to know that I snuck out to meet him. I'm not one hundred percent sure what his reaction would be, but I'm not just going to be admitting that I'm sneaking out.

Suddenly, panic floods through me as I imagine some random person finding me out here, all alone and vulnerable as I wait for Alessandro. What if Alessandro shows up and I'm not here, and he just goes home instead of searching for me?

Calm down. Hardly anyone drives down this road, seeing as

it's just a bunch of rich people that have big walls and security.

Security.

I don't dwell on the fact that there's a good chance this will show up on security, but I make a mental note to speak with the head of security tomorrow, and tell him that there's nothing to worry about.

How did Santiago manage to sneak past all of the security without being found out? If asking him didn't involve telling him that I snuck out, I would definitely be questioning him. You know, for research purposes.

Recognizing Alessandro's car as it slows, I breathe a sigh of relief and brush my hair behind my shoulders as I approach his passenger door. He quickly steps out and rushes to open the door, looking me up and down, smiling as he does so.

"Hi, Carmen." Is all he says before quickly entering his door and sliding the car into drive.

"Hi, Alessandro." I reply, looking over at him, the faint glow of the screen lights causing shadows to appear on his face.

"I hope you weren't waiting too long out there. There was a little bit of commotion back home. I know that I'm late." Alessandro says, glancing over at me with an apologetic look on his handsome face.

"Oh, no worries, it was fine. And, besides, you're only five minutes late. That's still perfectly reasonable." I say, crossing one leg over the other, my skirt fanning out on my leg and seat.

Truthfully, I'm rather glad he was a few minutes late, because if he had arrived at eleven like we'd originally planned, I would still be struggling to climb over the wall.

Sure, it wasn't as difficult as climbing down the side of the house, but it still had its own difficulties.

"So, do you have a destination for us?" I ask, looking over as he maneuvers us on to the highway.

"I do." Is all Alessandro says with a smirk, his eyes never leaving the road ahead of him.

While I appreciate his consideration for safety, I want nothing more than a clear, unobstructed view into his eyes.

"You do, but let me guess, you're not going to tell me?" I tease, somehow knowing that I'm right.

"Well, it sounds bad when you say it like that, but yes. You might guess it before too long, but I'm not sure. Just don't look in the backseat. I have things back there that would probably give away where we're going." Alessandro says, excitement easy to hear in his voice.

"Okay, I won't look, but I am allowed to guess, right? If I answer correctly, will you tell me?" I ask, curiosity coursing through my veins, leaving me feeling charged.

"Of course. Although, I will warn you, this is somewhat an obscure thing to do, so don't worry if you don't get it correctly." Alessandro cautions, playfulness in his tone.

"Okay, okay, but don't I even get a hint?" I say, looking over at Alessandro to gauge his reaction.

"I think that would be against the rules of the games, but if you get it wrong more than three times, I'll give you a hint." Alessandro decides, his hands steady on the wheel as he manages to continue our conversation while simultaneously maneuvering us on the highway.

I decide to not even try for rational ideas, and instead go for the most obscure things so I get a hint, preferably sooner, rather than later. While I'm not worried at all, I still want to know, pure curiosity driving me.

"The moon." I say as nonchalantly as possible.

"What?" Alessandro replies, confusion laced in his words.

"Our date, it's going to be on the moon." I repeat, feeling rather proud of how my response wasn't expected.

"Our date? Is that what we're calling this?" Alessandro asks, a new tone sliding into his voice. Oh my gosh, I did not just say date.

My cheeks heart with blush, and I'm thankful for the darkness that's masking it. "What do you think? Would you qualify this as a date?" I ask, turning the question onto him.

"I would think so. Only if both parties would qualify it as one, though." Alessandro says, a smirk spreading on his lips.

"Well then if our date isn't on the moon, it must be on the beach." I tease, adding emphasis on the 'date' part, if only to have a chance to say it again.

I'm on a date with Alessandro. A real, official date. Even if it didn't start out like it.

"I mean, I could make a small detour to hold our date there." Alessandro says, also adding emphasis on 'date'.

It hits me then that he's just as excited to be on an official date with me, and because of that, I'm even more giddy.

"No, I think wherever we're going will be just as fun as the beach, though. I don't really think that either of us will be home at a somewhat acceptable time if we go that far." I finally reply, looking over to see a grin on Alessandro's lips as he listens to me speak. Immediately, a blush heats my neck, flushing my cheeks, and I pull my sweater up a little bit higher, just in case

Alessandro can see the pink flames on my face.

The tension and electricity fills the car, and I wonder just what will happen tonight.

Alessandro only glances over for a quick second before turning his attention back to the road, and his smile only widens when he sees me.

"What's your version of acceptable?" Alessandro asks, trying to mask his words with a chill voice, but I can still hear the underlying curiosity in his tone.

"I mean, well, I guess I'm not sure. What about you?" I ask, suddenly realizing that I have no idea when I'm even going to be back home.

Alessandro takes a moment to respond, and I almost wonder if he even heard me. "I'm not sure, exactly. We shouldn't be out too late, though. I have exams tomorrow, and I think your class does, too?" He finally says, ending his sentence with a question.

"Yeah, I do. I didn't know you did, too. I guess whoever does the best in this test is the best in their grade, right? Since there are exams for each class?" I question.

"Yes. I think all day will be testing, and classes will get out early. Since this is kind of their 'first real exams of the semester' testing." Alessandro says, his eyebrows coming together as he speaks, as though he's considering something.

"Oh, okay. Cool. I guess you and Santiago will be vying for the top student of your class, then?" I ask, watching his eyes carefully for a reaction. We haven't really talked about our families when we're together, but after the first time we met and he told me our families don't get along I haven't really brought it up again.

"Yes. I guess we will be." Alessandro says, his words sounding completely measured and steady, as though he's choosing to not bring up their feud in my presence. I appreciate it, because I don't think I can handle harsh words towards Santiago. Matteo, too, for that matter.

While I know their feud, I don't want to ask him all of the details—at least not right now—surrounding their feud. I mean, I could, but I don't really want to hear the reasons on why I should or shouldn't be frustrated with either of them.

I'm aware it's selfish, but I still want to only see the good in both of them, and not be concerned with whatever their argument is.

"Since we'll get our scores back a few days after we test, maybe we can meet up and share our scores or something." I say, unsure of why I used that as an excuse to see him again.

"That might be fun. We'll have to see what day we get them back. I think there's supposed to be a party on Saturday, I think we should be able to see each other there, right?" Alessandro asks, looking over at me, the car lights around us on the highway blending into the background as I lock eyes with Alessandro.

I don't respond for much longer than I should have, because even after he drags his eyes from me, I can still see him in a different light than a few minutes ago.

It felt like time froze when we locked eyes, and we were the only people in the world. In the universe.

"Oh, I, uh, didn't know there was a party on Saturday. We'll definitely see each other there. I'll find a way to sneak away or something." I say, giving Alessandro a grin that he can't see.

His jaw clenches for a moment before he relaxes it, and curiosity flows through my veins as I wonder what his reaction was to. "I'll find you." He promises as he exits off of the highway and drives to our destination.

CHAPTER FIFTEEN

"Here we are." Alessandro says, parking his car in a small, gravel parking lot near the edge of what I assume is a city park.

"What is this place?" I ask, unbuckling and smoothing my skirt as Alessandro comes around to open my door.

"Um, you'll see in just a moment. I'm going to grab the thing from the backseat." Alessandro says as he swiftly removes a basket and a blanket. I raise an eyebrow, but don't say anything as he takes my hand and leads me to the large lawn, plenty of other people here already.

"What are we-" I start, before seeing the large projector that's aimed on a large, white backdrop. "Oh my gosh, I've always wanted to see something like this." I say, squeezing Alessandro's hand and looking up at him with a large smile. Watching an old movie that's being screened via projector has always sounded so fun.

"I'm glad. I was worried this might be out of your comfort zone, but I wasn't sure. Do you want to choose a spot to sit?" He asks, giving me a large smile of his own.

"Right here." I say without even considering his question.

"Okay, let me put this down then we can sit." Alessandro says, spreading a large, thick blanket on the ground, motioning for me to sit down before spreading a smaller blanket over my legs.

How considerate. While my skirt isn't that short, and has

enough extra fabric to fan around my legs, it still touches me that he thought this out so well.

Alessandro sits next to me, putting the basket that he had been previously carrying, between us. When he opens it, it has a mini charcuterie board in it, and water.

If I wasn't already sure that I really like Alessandro, this would definitely do it for me.

We quietly eat as a black and white movie from the fifties starts playing, the opening credits rolling as silence engulfs everyone on the lawn.

Around twenty minutes into the movie, Alessandro moves ever so slightly closer to me, and I take this as a sign to do the same.

We do this small dance for a few minutes, until we're right next to each other.

We're close enough that our legs are pressed against each other, and if I wanted to, I could lean my head against his arm.

Just as I make the move to do so, Alessandro wraps his hand around my waist, and I take this as my sign to lean against him.

I slow my breathing–the sound surely audible to Alessandro–so I can hear his breathing.

Once I can finally hear it, his breathing is much calmer than expected, but I wonder if he's doing as I am, and trying to get it under control.

"Carmen?" Alessandro asks, his voice coming out much more breathy than I would have expected.

"Yes?" I ask, not moving a muscle, continuing to rest my head on his arm and keep my eyes on the movie in front of us.

"I-" He takes a breath before continuing. "Never mind. I'll tell you later. Let's just watch the movie right now. Sorry." Alessandro says.

"This has been one of the best nights of my life." I say as I slide into the seat of Alessandro's car. He shuts the door behind me before quickly rounding the car and entering his door.

"Me too. I really had an amazing time." Alessandro says with a wide smile, his hands sliding over the wheel as he backs out of the parking lot.

While we're not technically celebrities, it felt so nice to be out in a public space and not worry about being seen together. With our parents being as famous—and rich—as they are, there are definitely some people who keep close tabs on them.

When we were at the aquarium, we were still in school uniforms, and blended in. And with the store, celebrities and other people similar to us visit there often. This is our first real date out in public. Well, as public as the middle of the night is.

I yawn as we pull on the road, and when I glance at the glowing numbers on the car screen, I gasp at the time. It's two in the morning.

"Whoa, what's wrong, Carmen?" Alessandro quickly asks, glancing over for a brief second before returning his gaze to the road ahead of us.

"Oh, it's nothing." I say, feeling mildly embarrassed by my reaction. I was the one who suggested meeting at eleven. I shouldn't be surprised by how late it is.

"No, what's wrong?" Alessandro presses, sounding both calm and controlled, while simultaneously being unsure and slightly worried.

"It's stupid. I just saw the clock and was surprised by the time. I guess I didn't expect for it to be two in the morning when I saw it." I say somewhat sheepishly.

"Oh, well I guess it is rather late. Sorry about that. I wasn't thinking when I planned this out." Alessandro says, quickly running a hand through his hair as he frets over the time.

"It's not like you can control time. And, if we're both being honest, I am the one that chose the time for us to meet. Also, I wouldn't trade this evening for a little bit of extra sleep. Or, pretty much anything, actually." I say, surprising even myself with my statement.

Alessandro's muscles soften at this before he speaks. "Do you really mean that?" He asks, looking over for a split-second before dragging his eyes back to the road.

"Yes, of course. Why would you be able to control time?" I ask, confused.

"No. I meant the part about trading our date for anything." Alessandro says with a smile, reaching down and picking up my hand.

His touch sends nerves racing up my fingers and throughout my arm, but I don't move my hand away. Instead, I wrap my fingers around his, Alessandro's fingers flexing for the briefest of seconds before wrapping them even tighter around mine.

"Of course I meant it." I finally say, the words echoing in my ears.

The traffic that accompanied us on the drive here is nearly nonexistent, and now it's just us on the road, the lights of the city flying by in streaks of light as we drive. Time passes by too quickly, and soon enough we're nearing my home. I wish for the night to never end, and for the ability to stay in this moment of peace and excitement for much longer.

When we reach my house, Alessandro parks his car where I

instruct him to, and he quickly opens his door and rushes to my side, opening the door and extending his hand for me.

"So, how are you going to get back in?" Alessandro asks, breaking the mini-silence that's between us, and I startle only slightly at his words.

"Oh, I'm going to…" My words trail off as I realize how scandalous it sounds to say that I'm going to climb the wall. If being out this late together wasn't enough, I'm going to admit that I snuck out? What have I become?

Alesandro seems to put two and two together, and gives me a half horrified, half amused face as he realizes that I climbed the wall. "Did you really climb the wall to meet me?" He asks a few seconds later, looking it up and down before doing the same to me.

I blush and meet his gaze as I nod, gauging his reaction as I admit to sneaking out and climbing a freaking wall to meet him.

"I, I don't know if I should be horrified that you snuck out to meet me, or if I should feel special because you snuck out to meet me." Alessandro finally says, a laugh escaping him as I smile at his words.

"I mean, I definitely feel both, so I think you have the right to do the same." I say with a giggle, noticing how Alessandro's eyes flash in the moonlight when he laughs.

Our laughter fades after a few more seconds, and when I look over to meet Alessandro's eyes, I'm surprised to see his intense gaze on me. I don't look away from him, and in the moonlight, I feel brave.

Taking a step closer to Alessandro, I step close enough that we're both in the shadow of the wall. My skirt swishes as I step past him and lean against the wall, feeling the hard stone through my sweater. It chills my bones, but with Alessandro's intense gaze, I hardly feel a thing.

Alessandro takes a step closer to me, his long stride leaving him directly in front of me, and in any other circumstance with another male, I would feel threatened. But here? I feel safe and comfortable.

Smiling as I clasp my hands behind my back I lean ever so slightly to Alessandro, feeling both unsure of what's happening, but also curious.

Alessandro takes another small step closer, his body only inches from mine, and I allow my eyes to drop to his lips.

What would happen if I kissed him? I only have this thought for maybe two more seconds, and then I don't have to wonder.

Suddenly, Alessandro's lips are on mine, his hand coming up to cup my cheek as he kisses me. A small gasp escapes me, even though I was pretty much expecting it. What I didn't expect was the feeling of electricity flood my body, and to dismantle my senses.

I press myself closer to Alessandro as we kiss, and wrap my hands behind his neck. Curling my hands around his silky-soft hair, I almost wonder if this is real.

Is this a dream? Am I actually kissing Alessandro? Are his hands actually moving to pull me even closer?

As if Alessandro can hear my thoughts, he pulls back, stepping more than a few feet back, his breathing sounding both breathless and surprised at the same time.

"I- we- you should probably get home right?" Alessandro finally says as he meets my gaze, his eyes looking ablaze.

Instead of answering, I look up to study the height of the wall. Maybe I just never noticed, but I'm almost one-hundred percent sure that it has never been this tall.

How am I supposed to get back over this thing when I'm both tired and exhilarated?

"Probably. Although, I'm going to be brutally honest and say that I'm not really sure I can go back." I say somewhat sheepishly.

Alessandro looks at me slightly confused before realizing that I'm talking about the wall.

"I can help you. What do you need?" He asks, finally coming closer to me.

"I guess you can help me get over the wall. It was definitely shorter on the other side." I say, my logic not even sounding somewhat coherent.

"I can give you a boost if that's what you mean. Here, put your foot in my hand." Alessandro says, putting one knee on the ground as he cupping his hand for me.

"Um, what about my skirt?" I blurt out, clapping my hand over my mouth as the words escape my lips.
Alessandro frowns for a second–probably confused–before his eyes shift, as though he realizes the meaning behind my words.

"Oh, that. I'm not going to look or something, I swear." Alessandro says, looking up at me with sincerity in his eyes.

"Okay, then. But don't drop me or something. I don't think a broken bone will add up with the whole 'I was asleep all night' story that I plan on telling everyone." I say, placing my shoe into Alessandro's cupped hand.

"Don't worry about that. I have you." Is all he says before lifting me much higher than I'd expected.

I grip the top of the wall and with Alessandro's help, and soon I'm in a sitting position on top of it. I cross my legs at the ankle as I dangle them over the wall.

"You can look up, now." I say, looking down to see

Alessandro stand and turn his gaze to me.

"You should-" Alessandro starts, just as I speak, too.

"I had a really great time with you." I say, gazing down at him as the breeze ruffles my hair, Alessandro's doing the same.

He smiles and gazes up at me, and I wonder just how bad it would be if we sat out here for another hour.

"I did, too. I want to do this again, you know?" Alessandro says, looking up with sincerity in his eyes.

The moonlight is bathing the world around us in a milky glow, but Alessandro is crystal clear.

"It's like we're the only people in the universe out here." Alessandro says, taking a step backward so he can see me better.

I let my hands prop me up on the wall as I watch him, my eyes and body tired and weary.

"I know what you mean. Technically, most everyone is asleep right now, so we kind of are." I say as another breeze ruffles my hair and sends goosebumps down my exposed neck and legs. A small shiver runs through my body as the cool air hits me, leaving me even more eager to go to my warm bed.

Well, I would prefer to spend more time with Alessandro, but our time is up. Even I know that.

"You should get home." I say after a few more seconds, giving Alessandro a small smile as I swing my legs to the other side of the wall.

"Good night, Carmen." Alessandro says, turning to walk to his car.

"Good night, Alessandro." I say, taking the jump to the ground.

CHAPTER SIXTEEN

"Carmen, since you and Santiago will be leaving school a little bit early, why don't we plan a quick trip to the club? I need to visit with Renee, and she said she'll be out there this afternoon." Mother says I'm making my way out of the door.

"Sure. I'll ask Santiago for you. He's already waiting for me outside." I say, closing the door behind me.

"Hey, Santi, Mother wants us to come with her later to the club. She has to meet someone." I say, sliding into my seat, not even glancing over at Santiago as I buckle the seat belt.

I'm surprised Mother didn't comment on the amount of makeup that I'm wearing, and I don't even want Santiago to have a chance of spotting the overuse of concealer under my eyes. Even I have to admit that it's much more than normal for school.

After making my way back inside last night, I had barely felt awake enough to change into pajamas.

I'd fallen asleep immediately, and this morning when I looked at myself in the mirror, I almost didn't recognize the girl staring back at me.

She was wearing a full smile and happy eyes, and… dark circles. Yes, dark circles under my eyes that were practically screaming 'oh, look, Carmen snuck out and was out until three in the morning'. My makeup had only done so much to conceal the tired look that my face was trying to tell the world, and now my plan is to avoid Santiago for as long as possible.

Simple, right?

"Okay. I guess I can go up there with you two." Is all Santiago replies with, his head leaned against the window as he watches the world around us blur while we drive.

Should I ask him if he's okay? Santiago hasn't done anything really out of the ordinary, but he's also not acting like the normal Santiago that I know.

He looks… drained.

I'm not sure what that's about, but I don't know if he would tell me if I were to ask. He's always opened up to Matteo way more than he ever has to me.

Deciding to leave it up to Matteo to sort out, I turn my attention to last night. What even happened?

I can see everything in perfect clarity, but also in a certain fuzziness, too. It's like the perfectness of my night is too much for my brain to comprehend, and it's still catching up.

Whatever it is, my brain will never be able to conjure up a memory that's as perfect as it was in the moment. Never in a million years will I be able to live that night in exact clarity, because never in a million years will my emotions and excitement ever be that charged and new.

Never again will I be experiencing my first kiss with Alessandro, but if that's what kissing him feels like, then the feeling might come close again.

"Renee, how lovely to see you, I've missed you these past

few parties. Surely it isn't that old knee acting up, again?"
Mother says, sitting down next to a woman I don't recognize.
She looks to be about seventy, and has more eyeliner and
lipstick than most girls at school would even wear.

"Of course it is. You know how it's been recently." Renee
says, gesturing under the table that she and Mother occupy.

Santiago and I are still standing near the table, unsure as to
what Mother would like us to do.

"Carmen, let's get out of here." Santiago says quietly next to
my ear, his breath tickling my neck.

"I was hoping you'd say that." I say, turning to walk next to
him as he starts walking in the direction of the restaurant.

It's a longer walk away than anything on the property, and I
remember Mother saying something about how it needed to be
located a good distance away from the clubhouse, since it's not
'aesthetically pleasing'.

I'll admit that the small restaurant doesn't really fit in with
the 'look' of the club property, and it does look better farther
away from the pool, garden, and clubhouse.

As the leaves crunch underneath us on the path, I'm starting
to appreciate more and more how private the club is. From the
location to employee number, it all makes for a much more
secluded and relaxing atmosphere.

"What do you think you scored on your testing?" I ask
Santiago as we sit down at one of the outdoor tables, the smell
of autumn filling the air as a breeze rustles leaves.

"One-hundred." Santiago says cooly, his eyes sliding over
the menu as he settles on something to eat.

I glance over the menu and settle on a soft drink, none of

the meals sounding appealing enough right now.

"What about you? Are you confident in your submissions?" Santiago asks a few minutes later, looking up from his drink, genuinely curious in my answer.

Instead of giving him a response, I almost ask about his results, and if they'll be better than Alessandro's.

I want to ask him all of these things, but I refrain from doing so, because to his knowledge, I don't know anything about his and Alessandro's differences. I wouldn't be surprised if he's still under the impression that Alessandro and I haven't even spoken, yet. And as of now, that might still be the best impression for him to have.

It's not like I was sneaking out to visit his enemy, spent most of my night alone with him, and kissed him.

At the thought of kissing Alessandro, my mind trails off for a minute, and I'm only brought back when I hear Santiago's voice.

"-Carmen, are you okay?"

Blinking my eyes rapidly, I realize that I haven't even responded to his question, and I've been staring off into space for who knows how long.

"I, um, yeah. I guess I'm just a little bit tired." I say, a light yawn escaping my mouth.

"Did you not sleep?" Santiago questions, an eyebrow raised as he studies me.

Oops.

I definitely wasn't supposed to say that.

"Yeah, of course I did. I'm just tired because of the testing. Aren't you?" I reply, trying to sound calm and nonchalant.

"I mean, I guess so." Is all Santiago replies, taking another bite of his food as he moves his eyes away from me.

I really need to be more careful when I'm talking about anything that surrounds Alessandro, otherwise I'm going to have a giant slip-up like the one that almost just happened.

CHAPTER SEVENTEEN

"There's a party tonight at the club. Do you know if you'll be going?" Alessandro asks as we stride down one of the near-empty hallways in school.

Yesterday, after the testing, Santiago had found me immediately, and I hadn't had a chance to meet Alessandro. Now, I'm in between classes, and we shouldn't run into Santiago for at least another thirty minutes, because his class is still running.

"Yes. Mother already let me know that we'll be going. You're going to be there, right?" I ask, looking up at him as I speak.

"Of course. My mother would never miss a club party." Alessandro says with a laugh, although there's true sincerity in his voice.

"Same."

"Will you meet me tonight? I'm not sure where, but I think we should be able to get away for a few minutes." Alessandro asks, stopping in front of his locker as he speaks, unlocking the latch.

"I mean… I can see if you'll fit into my busy schedule of speaking to old ladies that want to decide my future." I say, leaning against the locker next to his, looking up and smiling as a smirk plays across Alessandro's face.

"That *does* sound rather busy. I wouldn't want to interrupt and steal you away for the evening." Alessandro says, leaning his shoulder against his now-closed locker.

"It is. Especially when they all talk about you as though you're not even there." I say, trying to sound like I'm making a joke, but even I can hear the truthfulness that bleeds into my voice.

Something washes over Alessandro's face, but before I can decipher what it is, a bell from a nearby classroom sounds, and we both quickly split ways, a wistful look passing between us as we walk away from each other.

Tonight.

I just need to survive until tonight, and then I can see Alessandro without the impending school bell splitting us whenever we have a free moment together.

I cross my legs at the ankle, my black dress barely making it mid-thigh, and in my sitting position, it feels *much* shorter.

Mother insisted that I wear it, because tonight is more of a party than some of the other ones we've attended- whatever that means.

"What are you both doing tonight?" I ask curiously, both Matteo and Santiago sitting across from me and staring out the opposite windows.

"Not much, I guess. Why?" Matteo responds, looking me up and down to view the dress I'm wearing. I don't miss the dissatisfied look that flicks across his face, but since he didn't say anything, neither will I.

"I don't know. I guess I don't see either of you very much when we're at the club." I say, Santiago finally looking over to meet my gaze.

"We never see you, either." Santiago says somewhat suspiciously. Probably because I'm spending all of my time with Alessandro.

"I guess we all have our social circles." I reply cooly, deciding to just drop the question.

Neither of them really answered, and I have to wonder if it's because they both just find groups of people to spend time with, or if either of them is spending time with a *certain* person.

Whoa, neither of them have a girlfriend, and I would definitely know if they did. Neither of them would keep that from me.

As the driver pulls through the gates, I unfasten my seatbelt and prepare to step out of the car.

"Here." Matteo says, offering me his arm as I slide out of the vehicle. I take it and stand, but I'm surprised when he doesn't drop it after I've stood.

"Make sure you're careful, Carmen." Is all Matteo says as we walk into the party, his voice echoing in my ear as he and Santiago disperse within the party.

The lights are dimmer than I expected, and while the music isn't exceptionally loud, it isn't exactly background music.

I step into the main part of the room, my eyes searching for Alessandro as I walk. Looking over my shoulder in hopes of seeing him, I'm unfortunately only met with people that are chattering over the music, drinks in hand.

Another song comes on, and I take a step forward without

paying attention, and accidentally run directly into someone's chest.

"Oh my gosh, I am so-"

"Excuse me. I should have seen you coming." An unfamiliar voice says, and I look up to view the face of the man I bumped into.

"Oh, no, it was my fault. I'm so sorry." I say, studying the man's face. Upon my second inspection, he doesn't *look* to be a man. He looks eighteen, possible nineteen.

"No, don't worry about it. I wasn't paying attention, and stepped right into you. I should be the one apologizing." He says, reaching his hand out to clasp mine in a handshake.

"I'm Emilio. And even though we met rather awkwardly, I hope that we can move past that." Emilio says, his grip mildly tight on mine.

"Carmen. Nice to meet you, Emilio." I reply, giving him a polite smile.

Even though Emilio seems nice, I'd much rather be spending every precious second of my night with Alessandro. Who, speaking of which, is still not anywhere near.

"Are you spending your evening with anyone? I'd love to get to know you." Emilio asks, looking hopeful.

I inwardly cringe. This is *not* happening right now. "Oh, yes. I actually have plans, so I'm afraid I'll have to leave. It was nice meeting you." I say giving him a last smile before quickly turning, determined to find Alessandro.

As the music changes, I turn my head instinctively, and I gasp when I see Alessandro. He's on the balcony that overlooks the room, leaning against the railing, watching me.

I quickly shuffle through the crowd to make my way up the stairs, the sound of laughter and music fading the farther I climb the stairs. To my surprise, the balcony is empty, and Alessandro has vanished.

What? I spin in a full circle unsure of what just happened.

"Car-" I turn in the direction of Alessandro's voice, his figure almost invisible in the low light and deep shadows.

I take a few steps to him, only stopping when I'm inches away from him.

"Hey, why were you hiding? I'm not sure if you noticed, but I was *seriously* struggling there." I say, my words only partly teasing.

"Sorry about that. I guess I didn't think to give you a location to meet me. That's why I was waiting at the balcony." Alessandro says apologetically. He takes a breath before speaking again. "I almost went downstairs when I saw that guy, though." He adds, giving me a grin that's somewhere between teasing and serious.

"It was a good idea to wait at the balcony, if only you had come down, though. It would have made that interaction a *little* bit less awkward." I say, leaning against the wall as I talk. I cross my legs at the ankle and watch as Alessandro listens to me speak.

"Why? From what I saw, it was…friendly, but not anything horrible. What happened?" Alessandro finally asks, taking a step closer to me as he asks, a few people in one of the billiard rooms laughing, reminding us that we're not the only people here.

"Not too much, but he wanted to spend the evening or something with me—whatever that means—and it was awkward to explain that I'm spending my evening with someone else." I say, looking down to my feet as I speak, feeling awkward all over again.

"What do you- oh. Yeah I understand how that might be awkward." Alessandro says, his face only looking sympathetic and not embarrassed by the direction of our conversation. "I do have one question, though." He adds, a small smirk playing across his face as he speaks.

Oh my gosh. Whatever he's going to say, I can already guarantee it's going to make me blush. "And what might that be?"

"Is it true you'll be spending your whole evening with me?" Alessandro asks, his tone both teasing and curious.

"Oh, I don't know. Maybe I'll spend it with my brothers while they discuss topics that bore me to *death*." I say, taking a step closer to Alessandro.

Close enough that there's less than a few inches between us.

"Or, maybe I'll spend it with the boy that can't seem to stop occupying my brain." I say, looking up to meet Alessandro's gaze.

"Do I really occupy your brain?" He asks, more shy than I expect.

"Of course." Is all I say, not denying it in the slightest.

"I'm glad." Alessandro says, his lips pressing into a half smile as he studies me.

"What about me?" I dare to ask, waiting for Alessandro's response.

"Definitely."

The thumping of the music bass around us starts to intensify as a new song plays, and my body moves ever so slightly as a result.

Maybe it's just because I'm new to this whole club thing, but the music is so overwhelming that it's almost impossible to think clearly.

"Let's get out of here. I feel like there are better places to have a conversation." Alessandro says, wrapping his fingers around mine as he gently tugs me in the direction of the glass doors that lead to the outdoor balcony.

As the doors automatically slide closed behind us, a small shiver runs up my exposed legs.

"Do you want to sit?" Alessandro asks, gesturing towards one of the outdoor sofas that faces the balcony railing.

"Yeah, for sure. My feet are rather tired, thanks to these shoes." I say, sitting down at the edge of the sofa, my crossed ankles doing nothing to ease the ache of my sore ankles.

"Here. For your legs." Alessandro says as his tuxedo jacket gently drapes across my legs, covering them from both the cold air, but also the chance of an accidental mishap.

My dress *is* rather short, and while I'm not going to be admitting that to anyone, I still know that sitting isn't the best idea for something of its length.

"Thank you." Is all I can manage, his thoughtfulness touching. How many times has this been that he's done something so caring and so…*right?* Too many to count, that's for sure.

"Have you been busy lately?" I ask, filling the silence with a question.

"Um, kind of. My father has been pressuring me to

accompany him to business meetings and stuff, but it's been hard to balance that with school." Alessandro answers, his response both honest and surprising.

"Oh, um, yeah, I guess that is busy. I get it though." I say, referring to my workload of school that seems to double in size every day. "It's not like I'm ignoring my school or anything, but the homework is no joke." I say, trying to lighten the mood.

"Definitely. If I weren't always vying for top student with your brother, then maybe I would slack off on all of my extra courses or advanced classes." Alessandro says with a chuckle.

His arm stretches behind my shoulder on the back of the sofa, and I contemplate leaning my head against his shoulder like I did the other night.

"You would?" I ask, honestly surprised by his statement.

"I think so. I mean, I'm kind of swamped with all of the extracurriculars. I should have read the fine print when I decided to make your brother my rival." Alessandro says with a chuckle.

"What, like there was a contract and all?" I tease, sliding my fingers over his as I speak. Instead of grasping them, I just trace the veins on his hands and wrists as he replies.

"Of course." Alessandro says in mock seriousness.

"I would love to be busy with school, if only because it meant that my job was the cause of it." I say, finally resting my head on Alessandro's shoulder.

"What do you mean?" He asks, confusion in his voice.

"Oh, it's nothing." I say, realizing that my words are coming out more honest than I'd like.

"Are you sure?"

"Well, I just mean that I'm not allowed to model, and that's what I *really* want to do." I finally say, looking up at Alessandro to gauge his reaction to my words.

I don't know what I'm expecting.

Maybe confusion, maybe agreement with my family, maybe maybe maybe.

"So, what do you want to model? Clothing? Makeup? What?" Alessandro asks, curious and interested in my answer.

"Oh, well, I guess mostly just clothing, but I wouldn't be against makeup or something. Why?" I reply.

"I'm just curious, that's all." Alessandro responds earnestly, the conviction in his voice, convincing enough. "If you don't mind my asking, why aren't you allowed to model? Is it a family thing? Or something else?"

"I… It's family I guess. There's not really anything else standing in the way. Well, besides the fact that I could be absolutely horrible at it, of course." I say, purposely keeping my eyes away from Alessandro's as I speak. I would be lying if I said that it's not slightly embarrassing that I'm not allowed to model, but It's not just the modeling part that embarrases me. It's the fact that I'm not allowed to make just about any decisions for myself.

"I see. I guess I relate to that, too." Alessandro responds. Out of the corner of my eye, I see Alessandro turn his head to face mine, and I brave the embarrassment and turn to face him.

"I'm guessing you're talking about your father's business?" I ask, curiosity burning in my voice.

"Um, yeah. It's a lot more than that, but I'm his only son–only child, too–so there's a lot of pressure on me from him and Mother to be the best son ever, and it's kind of a crushing weight, sometimes. You know?" Alessandro asks, a vulnerability in his voice that I'm not sure I've heard before.

"I guess since I have two older brothers, it might be a little bit different, but the pressure to be outstanding with everything I do is definitely there." I respond, biting my lip as soon as the words leave my mouth.

I'm not sure why I keep admitting all of this to Alessandro.

"That's probably pretty true. Your brothers are honestly kind of lucky, you know. If either of them wants a different path than what's expected of them, then there's someone else to take all of the pressure off of them." Alessandro says, sounding both defeated and bitter.

"Yeah, when you look at it that way, it does seem that way." I agree, hating how easily the words roll off of his lips. Alessandro sounds like he's thought about this before.

"But for you, I guess there's a different expectation, since you're a girl, and the youngest, right?" Alessandro asks, sounding both curious and apprehensive. As if he doesn't want to step past whatever boundaries he thinks I have.

"Definitely. I mean, I'm basically expected to be this perfect doll that does whatever my parents want me to do, which I don't like, but It's so much worse with my brothers. Do you know why?" I ask, a vulnerability that I haven't allowed my voice to carry in a long time.

"I don't. Why?" Alessandro asks quietly.

"Because they're *so* different from our parents. Yes, I know that my parents love me, but this is a different kind of love. They genuinely want me to be one-hundred percent protected and safe, but it's so different. It's not because they *want* me to be a doll, but because they see me as one to protect. I can't fully explain it." I say, taking a pause before continuing. "And the worst part is that I want to not disappoint them. I barely argue with them, but it's because they both make an effort to never be rude or unjust with me. Even if I completely deserve it, they'll both take the high road every time. They're *too* perfect to me. Matteo and Santiago are *too* perfect for me to ever let them down." I say, a silent tear sliding down my cheek as I admit this.

I hear Alessandro clear his throat as though he's trying to figure out what to say, and I cringe for the slightest second as I remember his feud with my brothers–Santiago especially–and how hard it must be to believe that they're perfect to me.

"I can't say that I've had the same experiences as you, but I do know what you're saying about being a doll." Alessandro replies, running his free hand through his styled hair, a few stray pieces falling and hanging down by his eyebrows.

Neither of us say anything as we gaze into each other's eyes, and I fight my breathing to keep it even as I continue to train my eyes on Alessandro's.

"I don't think I've been this honest with someone since… forever." Alessandro finally says right after his eyes dip to my lips before tearing them back to my eyes. It's almost like he's saying something–anything–to distract himself.

"Me too. I don't really talk about these things with anyone." I say, my hand resuming it's tracing on Alessandro's wrist.

The music that softly beats through the closed french doors blends with the gentle sounds of the night, and I take a deep breath and close my eyes.

"Are you tired?" Alessandro asks curiously, noticing my closed eyes.

"Oh, um, no. I was just relaxing. I feel like a weight has been taken off of my chest, and it feels nice." I say opening my eyes, a blush heating my cheeks as I realize how foolish I must look.

"So, you're not going to fall asleep and make it appear as though I've abducted you or something?" Alessandro says, a laugh following his words.

"Well, I don't think so, but there's always the possibility of it." I tease, leaning my head and resting it on Alessandro's shoulder.

As the music seems to fade into the background, I allow myself to only hear the breathing of Alessandro and I, the feeling soothing.

"It's getting late." Alessandro says after thirty minutes of silence between us.

"It is?" I ask, not wanting to believe him.

"Yeah. I wish it weren't though." Alessandro replies, pausing before speaking again. "Just so you know, I much rather it out here with you, than in there." He finishes, turning his head to face me.

"You do?" I ask, both believing him, but also needing to hear him say it again.

"Absolutely. Sure, these parties are fun, but I don't get the same high out of them that my parents do. It's all about status and accomplishments in there. With you, I feel like I can just be vulnerable." Alessandro admits, sounding both shy and truthful.

I turn, our eyes now inches from each other.

"Really?" I breathe, not believing him. I'm just…me. I

know that I'm nice and all, but someone that brings out his vulnerability? Someone that he'd rather spend time with when there's a party going on just a wall away?

"Carmen, I don't think you realize how much I like you." Alessandro says, his smile a mix of shyness and cockiness that I'm growing to look forward to.

"I…" I struggle for the right words to say, but come up with nothing. Instead of struggling to find the words, I do the next best thing, and kiss Alessandro.

CHAPTER EIGHTEEN

Alessandro sucks in a breath before kissing me back, the surprise of my kiss taking him aback.

I slide my hand behind Alessandro's neck and tangle his hair between my fingers, the softness of it taking me by surprise.

A thousand butterflies flutter and flit throughout my stomach, all the while warmth courses up and down my veins, the feeling electric.

Alessandro turns his body, shifting it so that we're facing each other, and runs his hand up my arm and throat, cupping my cheek and pulling me even closer.

I gasp before leaning even further into Alessandro's kiss, the feeling electric and warm against my lips. Alessandro pulls back just far enough to distance our lips, but not far enough for me to stop feeling the lingering of his kiss.

Alessandro doesn't speak, but I can see everything he's not saying, just by seeing his eyes. I don't say anything, either, rather I just tug Alessandro closer, using the hair that's still wrapped around my fingers to do so. Alessandro obliges to my not so subtle request, and kisses me, again.

I smile against his lips as goosebumps flood my neck and shoulders as Alessandro's finger gently moves along my jawline.

"I-" Alessandro starts, but is abruptly cut off when the sound of glass shattering rings from inside the building.

I pull away from Alessandro and turn my head in confusion, my ears on high alert as the sound of shouts and screams erupt from the club.

"What's-"

"Stay here, Carmen." Alessandro says, springing to his feet and rushing through the doors at a speed that surprises me.

I wait for what feels like an eternity before I can't contain my worry and curiosity. Going against what Alessandro requested, I stand and enter the french doors.

I don't know why I didn't realize that the sound of blaring music ended, but it's painfully obvious as I step through the threshold. No one occupies the second floor where I stand, and I feel like an intruder as I walk to the edge of the balcony and look down at the lower floor, where a crowd surrounds Emilio and...*Santiago.*

Oh my gosh.

I stifle a yelp as the realization that very few things could have happened to create the scene that I'm watching unfold.

"Someone get them both out of here! What a menace to our beautiful party." A shrill woman calls out, sounding both annoyed and slightly shaken.

"I agree! Why are we allowing these two *children* to ruin our event? How dare they." An older man says, his voice scratchy and angry.

"For everyone's information, *I'm* twenty years old. I'm not a mere child that can be scolded when I was clearly the victim in this situation." Emilio calls out, sounding as though he's wanting to garner the emotions of those around him.

"Oh, and I'm just-" Santiago starts, rage fueling his voice as he takes another step closer to Emilio. If it weren't for the hand that Matteo rests on Santiago's shoulder, I can almost guarantee that Emilio wouldn't be standing as calmly as he is now. Which, speaking of Matteo, where did he come from?

"I think Mr. Alvarez needs to leave the party. I'm not sure exactly what happened, but I do know that I heard his voice first, and we all know what a hot temper he has." A woman says, stepping closer to Emilio, taking his side.

Mrs. Valentino.

I feel my own fury hot in my pulse as more and more people move to Emilio's side of the room, seemingly all siding against Santiago.

While I don't know what he did or didn't do, I don't like this.

I turn to rush down the stairs, unsure of what I'm going to do, when I hear Father's voice ring out below.

"Now, now, they're both young. Obviously someone is to blame for this, but let's just get back to our party. Every parent knows that the show must go on, even if there's a temper tantrum happening." He ends his little speech with a chuckle. From the outside looking in, he looks calm and relaxed, but as his daughter, I can tell that he's furious.

I pause at the top of the step, the small landing not lit, and for a moment, I wonder if I'm still scared of the dark.

Oh my gosh, get a grip, Carmen. I'm sixteen years old. I don't need to be such a baby.

I take the stairs as quickly as possible, and just before I can turn the corner into the main room, I bump into somebody.

Ouch.

"Excuse me, sir." I say, looking up to see Alessandro's father.

He looks less than amused with Santiago and Emilio, but a soft smile appears on his face as he sees me.

"Not a problem. It appears that your brother over there has landed himself into a scuffle, eh?" He says, looking curious as to my answer.

"Um, I guess so. Excuse me, though. I need to check on him." I say, moving past him in what's hopefully a non-disrespectful motion.

"Of course." Mr. Valentino says, giving me a 'go ahead' gesture. I nod, acknowledging him before scurrying into the main room, only to *again* bump into somebody.

Jeez. What is with-

"Don't go over there." Alessandro says quietly, pulling me closer to the shadows that hug the walls.

"What's going on? And why can't I go over there?" I ask, knowing that I really *can* go over there, but Alessandro's words own a warning that sounds ominous.

He looks different than he usually does, but I can't quite place why.

"I'm not sure exactly what happened, but your older brother–Matteo–had to work past a lot of people to be there right next to them. Something's not right, but I don't know what." Alessandro answers, sounding confused and worried.

"This isn't like Santiago. Well, not entirely. Yeah he has a temper here and there, but nothing like this, I don't think. Did they fight or something? Is Santiago hurt?" I ask, failing to see over the heads of the many people that have gathered.

"I don't think it got that far, but it was close. From what

I've heard here and there, your brother was seconds away from punching him." Alessandro answers, his eyebrows furrowing as he easily looks over the crowd.

"Why-"

"Listen, let's send these boys on their way, and continue our party." Father calls out, his booming voice quieting the opinions of others around him, the room falling into silence.

"Or, we can just send the *problem* out of the party." Mrs. Valentino hisses, her defensiveness over Emilio intriguing.

"Do you know him?" I whisper, looking up to watch Alessandro.

His jacket.

We left his tuxedo jacket on the outdoor balcony. No wonder he looks different.

"Kind of? He's a new investor or something for Father's business, and that's why he's a member here. Apparently he's his father's right hand man, and is handling most of the paperwork and contracts with Father." He takes a breath before continuing. "Nothing is official yet, but he's—his father, I guess—pretty interested in owning stocks in the business."

"Then why isn't your father standing up for him?" The words tumble out of my mouth before I have a chance to filter them.

"Honestly, I don't know." Alessandro answers truthfully.

A few lowered voices carry from the direction of Santigo, and I see Matteo ushering Santiago towards the door.

"You should-"

"I have to go. I'll talk to you soon. Oh, and, your jacket is still on the balcony." I say, looking up to see Alessandro's understanding face. In the dim light, his facial features are shadowed and hardened, and for a split second I consider kissing him.

No. Not here.

"Goodbye, Carmen." Alessandro says softly, giving me a smile before I turn.

"Goodbye, Alessandro." I whisper, moving as quickly as I dare to reach the door.

I stumble multiple times, but by the time I make it outside, I can see Matteo and Santiago standing near a bench, both of their arms crossed as they speak in low, hushed voices.

"Matteo?" I call out, the idea of sneaking up on them feeling wrong.

"Carmen? Where did you come from? And where were you?" Matteo calls out, sounding both relieved and concerned.

"I, um, I just followed you out here. And I was in there the whole time, but if you haven't noticed, I'm not very noticeable at this height." I say cooly, brushing away any of his thoughts of concern. "Are you leaving?" I question, both deflecting his concern and answering my own curiosity.

"Yes, we're leaving. You don't need to come with us, but you're welcome." Matteo answers, looking me up and down before taking a step closer to me.

Thankfully, our driver appears, the headlights of the limousine shining across the pavement. "Come on, you two. Let's get home." Matteo says, gesturing for Santiago and I to climb in. I oblige, and Santiago does the same.

It doesn't slip past me that Santiago hasn't said anything, and a jolt of worry courses through me. Santiago has never been one to stay silent, so the longer he doesn't say something or question me, the more I worry.

"Why…" I start, the intention of asking why we're here too strong to ignore.

"Carmen, Santiago and that guy just got in a little squabble, and now he's being sent back. Nothing more, and nothing less."

"Nothing more? That guy is…" A few swear words slip past Santiago's mouth, but I choose to ignore them, in favor of knowing the truth.

"Santi-"

"I'm just telling the truth. He's a… I don't even know." Santiago says, his voice trailing as he clenches his jaw.

"What happened?" I question again, the curiosity inside me unsuppressable.

"He-" Santiago starts, but in a split second, he snaps his mouth shut. "He just said some things that made me angry." He finishes, turning his head to the window, signaling that this conversation is over.

"What did he-"

"Carmen, let's just leave the conversation alone. I think we all need to take a breather." Matteo says, not so subtly telling me that the conversation is over, and that I need to drop it. It's on the tip of my tongue to argue, but I settle for crossing my arms and turning my head to face the window.

Why won't either of them tell me what happened? I almost demand to turn the car around and go back to the party, because if I'm not going to be getting any information out of my brothers, then I might as well be spending time with Alessandro. And, if I were there, I would have the opportunity to ask a gossipy old lady to tell me what happened.

Watching the night rush past us, I rest my head on the cold, glass window, my breath fogging the world outside. What is Alessandro doing right now? Does he know what happened? Does he think that I abandoned him?

I allow my eyelids to lower, and before I know it, Matteo is gently shaking my shoulder, awakening me.

"It's time to get out. We're home." I nod, and as we walk into our home, Santiago ahead of me, and Matteo behind, I feel a pang of worry.

This isn't us, and it never has been.

"Good night, Santiago." I say, giving him a quick hug before he retreats into his room.

Santiago stiffens for only a split second before hugging me back.

"Good night, Carm. Get some rest."

I pull away from him to see Matteo watching us, meeting my eyes for a brief second before retreating to his own room.

Flopping down on my bed after closing my door behind me, I pull a pillow to my chest, and selfishly think of myself, rather than Santiago.

My conversation with Alessandro floods my brain, and I tighten my grip on the pillow as I remember how painfully honest I was with him.

Why did I tell him all of that?

To be fair, he *did* open up to me, too. The thought hardly comforts me, but I decide to let go of my worry. It's too late to go back in time and start over my conversation with Alessandro, and if I'm being honest with myself, I'm not sure I would.

Would I have been so brutally honest right at that moment?

Probably not.

But to say that I regret it, that would be a lie.

Why am I so confused, yet sure when it comes to Alessandro? Why do I know that I want him in my life, but feel self-conscious when I open up?

Is this normal?

CHAPTER NINETEEN

A text chimes on my phone, and my body jumps in surprise at the notification.

It's five in the afternoon, and I'm finishing my homework from Friday, my studying much more difficult with thoughts of last night plaguing my mind.

Opening my phone to see a message from Alessandro, I blink to make sure that I'm reading it correctly. We haven't actually messaged, even though we've had each other's phone numbers for a while now, so I'm slightly surprised to see his name above the chat.

The message that he sent asks if I want to do something with him tonight, and I immediately type back a 'yes' without even asking what we'll be doing.

Alessandro asks what time he should be here to pick me up, and just like the last time I left, I tell him eleven.

Sneaking out might not be the best idea, but until I tell my family that I'm spending time with Alessandro, it's best to not draw attention to myself.

"Are you sure this is a good idea?" Alessandro asks once we're both inside his car.

I—again—climbed the wall to meet him, and while Alessandro isn't going to tell anyone, he sounds unsure of my actions.

"Of course…not." I respond, my voice teasing, but my words truthful. "Just drive. We'll be fine. I'm the one who's snea- using the less-used path off of our property." I say, unsure of which one of us I'm trying to convince with my words.

"Okay, then, but you're going to tell me this time if it's getting too late, or you want to go home, right?" Alessandro asks.

"Oh my gosh, just drive." I tease, placing my hand on Alessandro's arm, my sweatered wrist resting on his.

Alessandro smiles in response, and slides his car into drive, the dark world outside of the windows slipping by in a blur.

"Do you have anywhere you want to visit tonight?" Alessandro asks, curiosity brimming in his voice as he speaks.

"No, not really. I kind of assumed since you asked me out, you would already have a plan." I say, feeling a blush warm my cheeks.

"Oh, I do. I was just wondering if you were expecting someplace in particular." Alessandro quickly says, reassuring me that there's nothing to worry about.

"In that case, no. I don't have any guesses or expectations, as long as I'm with you." I answer honestly, fully meaning my words.

Really, as long as I'm spending time with Alessandro tonight, then I don't care about where we end up.

I glance over when Alessandro doesn't immediately respond, and I'm immediately glad that did. His lips are pressed together in a shy, but happy smile, and I can almost swear that his ears are turning pink.

Do I actually have that effect on Alessandro?

A shy smile plays across my face and I look away as I realize that he has the same effect on me, too.

Returning my gaze to Alessandro, I meet his eyes as they slide over to me for a brief second before returning to the road ahead of us. The tension between us that circulates inside the car, is strong enough to erupt goosebumps along my arms.

And while my legs are slightly warmed from my tights and skirt—which only reaches just above my knees—they still flood with goosebumps.

"What do you do in your spare time?" The words tumble from my mouth as I try to imagine Alessandro doing something other than school and work with his father, and I just can't picture it.

"Um, this is going to sound…unexpected, but I like to paint. It's just a hobby, of course." Alessandro answers, sounding both shy and uncertain. As if he's not sure that's a good response.

"What? Really?" Alessandro paints? How come I didn't know this?

"Yeah. It's something that I've been doing for a few years now. I guess it became a creative outlet that let me forget about all of the other problems in my life." Alessandro responds, his hands tapping the steering wheel, no doubt an uncomfortable tic.

"I get that, you know? I really do." I respond truthfully, knowing that fashion does the same thing for me. "So, do you ever let anyone see your paintings?"

"Not in the past, but if you wanted to see them…I would be happy to share them." Alessandro pauses, before continuing. "That is if you even want to see them. They're not that great or anything, just a hobby." He hurries to say, as if realizing that I might judge him for them.

"Well, first, I definitely want to see them. And second, I'm sure they're amazing." I suck in a breath. "You're amazing."

Alessandro's ears turn an even darker shade of pink–not quite crimson–but instead of his shy smile from earlier, a cocky one is playing across his face now.

"I mean, you're not wrong." Alessandro responds, his voice full of ego and…curiosity? Almost like he's wondering what my response will be to this.

To be honest, I don't know what I *should* say.

"I'm never wrong." I tease back, loving the banter that is between us. "But really, though, I *do* want to see your paintings."

"I promise I'll show them to you sometime." Alessandro vows, exiting into a near empty parking lot, and the only sign of life is a fast food restaurant near the end.

What is this place?

"So, I hope you don't mind that I called ahead and already ordered our food." Alessandro says as he pulls up to one of the windows. A woman passes him two bags with food, and two drinks, Alessandro taking them and placing them between us.

"Not at all. I do want to know what we're doing, but I guess I'm going to figure it out, soon."

"Well, I was thinking that we could park and just…talk. I don't know, I feel like besides the other night, we haven't had a chance to just have a normal conversation. Isn't that what most people do?" Alessandro asks sheepishly, rubbing the back of his neck as he pulls into an open space. Which, isn't hard to do, seeing as there's not another soul–or car–in the parking lot.

"I'm pretty sure most people are able to have a conversation without having to look over their shoulder." I agree, smiling at him as I listen to my own words.

How did I even end up here?

Suddenly, I'm spending all of this time with Alessandro, and going against everything I know that my family would want me to do. Which is weird, because just a few weeks ago I had no intentions of doing anything of the sort.

"Here, this is quite possibly one of the most unhealthy foods I could give a…" Alessandro trails off before grinning. "A date. But, I hope you like it." He finishes, handing me a milkshake, fries, and hamburger.

"I mean, it's not *all* that bad." I say, unwrapping the burger and taking a sip of the cookies and cream milkshake. "Oh, how did you know that this is my favorite flavor?"

"It is? I kind of just…guessed." Alessandro says, grinning as he sips his own drink.

"What flavor did you get?" I ask, curiosity brimming in my voice. Without saying anything, Alessandro just extends his cup in a 'try it' gesture. And I do.

I wrap my lips around the straw, the taste of strawberries immediately entering my mouth, the flavor amazing.

Instead of only taking a sip, I quickly take two more before pulling away.

"Did you like it?" Alessandro teases as I swallow the remaining milkshake.

"Um, definitely. I didn't realize how nice the flavor is." I smile, looking up as Alessandro smirks.

"Try mine." I say without thinking. Raising my cup to Alessandro's lips, I wait for him to take a sip. He smirks at me before tasting mine, and I don't miss the devious look he shoots me before also taking three sips.

"Hey, this is mine." I tease, pulling my cup away. The only problem with my plan, is that the straw is still in Alessandro's mouth.

Oh.

"I believe that belongs to me." I say, my voice coming out breathy as I take the straw from Alessandro, my movements so quick that he doesn't even have a chance to remove it from his mouth.

Yep, I just did that.

I quickly slide it back into the lid, taking a sip of my milkshake to avert my gaze from Alessandro's amused face.

Do I think he meant for the straw to stay firmly in his mouth? No. But do I think that he could have not tried to take more than a sip of my milkshake? Yes.

Hypocritical, I know. But, at least I'm self-aware.

I finally bring my eyes back to Alessandro's, my lips still firmly planted on my straw. He hasn't moved an inch, and he's still giving me a smoldering look.

Oh my gosh.

I almost choke on the cookie piece that I'm swallowing, the gaze that Alessandro is giving me is more than intense.

Alessandro doesn't say anything, rather, he just reaches and gently takes my cup from my hands, and sets it in the cupholder, his eyes never leaving mine.

I watch him intently, never moving, never breaking eye contact.

Alessandro brings his hand to my cheek for a brief second, before wrapping it around the back of my head, pulling my lips to his.

CHAPTER TWENTY

I have to say, I kind of saw this coming, but I didn't expect it to happen *right now.*

Alessandro's kiss is soft, but definitely still passionate. Goosebumps erupt along my neck and shoulders, the feeling both warm and electric.

I raise one of my hands to slip my fingers through his hair, and twist strands of it around my fingers in a never-ending motion. As I do so, my fingers brush the back of Alessandro's neck, and under my fingers, I can feel goosebumps flood his neck.

I move my fingers in the same motion, the goosebumps rising every time. I smile into his lips, and pull him closer as a small shudder moves his body.

Alessandro brings his other hand to the other side of my face, and our kiss deepens.

I abruptly pull away when headlights shine through the back of Alessandro's car, the other driver becoming increasingly closer to us. Quickly turning my head, I gasp and drop my head, sliding down into the floorboard.

"What…?" Alessandro says, turning his head to watch the approaching car.

"*Drive!*" I whisper-shout, urgency flooding my voice as the car nears. The moment that we were just having is completely over.

"Okay, but wh-"

"That's my brother!" I say, not risking the chance that any headlights will expose me.

"What? Okay." Alessandro says, sliding the car into drive, gently moving forward.

"No, you don't understand, he probably saw us!" I say urgently, my mind racing as I mentally prepare myself for the excuses I'll have to use.

"Which one was it?" Alessandro asks, pulling to the edge of the lot as he waits for the oncoming vehicles to pass the exit.

"Santiago." I say, taking a breath in as I climb back into the passenger seat. "Why?"

"Don't turn around, but he appears to be following us." Alessandro says, a smirk playing on his face as he speaks, but truthfulness in his tone.

"You're lying. I'm going to turn and look." I say, my head moving as I speak.

"Okay, but he'll definitely see you, then." Alessandro says as headlights flood through the back window like before.

"You weren't lying." I say, my mind racing. "How did he know that we are in here?" I question.

"I actually don't know. It's possible he followed us, but I don't know. And, just to make the situation worse," Alessandro says, reaching over and checking my pounding pulse with his fingers, "it looks like there's someone with him. Presumably your *other* brother."

If Alessandro's touch on my wrist wasn't enough to cause an even faster pulse, the fact that *both* of my brothers are right behind us is enough to do it.

I guess it's time to plan my funeral?

"Oh, well that definitely makes the situation worse. Why are they here?" I ask, resisting the urge to turn and just make sure that it's actually him. Who am I kidding? The glimpse that I saw was one-hundred percent Santiago's car. There was no doubt about it.

"I don't know. They didn't follow you, because they would have pulled up sooner, right?" Alessandro muses, finally pulling onto the highway.

"I don't *think* they followed me, but I guess I don't really know." I state. "Are they still following us?"

"Um," Alessandro says, his eyes shifting to the mirror. "Yes."

"Fabulous. You might as well just find the nearest graveyard, because if they know that I'm with you…let's just say that I don't think it will go over very well." I say, reaching over to take a sip of my milkshake. If I'm going to die, I might as well finish my dessert, right?

"Sounds good." Alessandro says, adding more pressure to the gas pedal, causing us to speed up.

"How fast are we going?" I ask, trying to peer over to read the speedometer.

"Don't worry, we're still within the speed limit, just at the higher end. Which, your brother seems to be doing, now." Alessandro says with a chuckle.

"Is he really?" I ask. "And, do you know how hard it is to not turn around to see?" I lament, annoyance in my voice. I'm not really annoyed with Alessandro, rather the fact that we're practically in a car chase, because my brothers are so overprotective.

"Definitely so." Alessandro quickly replies. "Oh, I meant about the following us part. I can't say I've ever been in your position, though. I imagine it's frustrating." He chuckles.

"Oh, definitely frustrating. I know I was just telling you how perfect they are, but they're *really* annoying at moments like these." I say, taking another sip of my milkshake.

"But, to be fair, if I was one of them–especially Santiago–I wouldn't let my little sister date my enemy." Alessandro replies, genuine understanding in his voice.

"But what if your enemy was actually a good guy? And," I take a breath and try to erase the girlish smile that plays across my face, "did you just say that we're dating?"

Alessandro bites his lower lip and smirks as he continues to drive. "I didn't say *we're* dating, but I'm sure something could be arranged, right?" He says, all the while his eyes never leaving the road ahead of us.

"I think something could be arranged, but that might have to happen *after* my funeral." I tease, looking over to watch the laughter that bubbles from Alessandro.

"Okay, I'll make sure to do it after. What date is the funeral? I'll need to add it to my calendar. Someone as busy as myself needs to have it put on the schedule weeks in advance." Alessandro teases.

"Not months? Years?" I ask, giggling as I speak.

"Weeks was me promising to fit you in relatively soon. Don't worry, it takes most people *years* to be fit into my busy schedule."

"Ah, I'm honored. Hopefully you receive an invite to the funeral, because I don't think there's enough time for me to plan a guest list. It will have to be done by either Matteo or Santiago, and I'm not sure if they're too partial to you." I tease.

"You would *definitely* be correct on that. While Matteo and I have only had a few run-ins, he's too loyal to Santiago to ever like me." Alessandro says, the topic sounding less related to my fictional funeral, and more aligned with real life.

"Don't you think that your rivalry is a little bit…immature?" I ask, Alessandro speaking at the same exact time as me.

"Hey, they've finally let off. Granted, we're close to forty miles away from where we started." Alessandro says, quickly moving into the right lane.

"Really? That's great and all, but now we have another problem." I say, looking up from under my eyelashes I meet Alessandro's gaze.

"What's that?" He asks after exiting the highway and starting the drive home.

"Now, we have to get back before they do, because they could just go look and find out that I'm gone. Like, confirm their suspicions." I say, pressing my lips into a sheepish smile.

"Okay, well, that shouldn't be hard, but I have to ask." Alessandro says, expertly maneuvering us around other vehicles. "When you snuck out–don't even try to convince me that you didn't–did you not lock your door? Is there a key?"

"Are you asking me about my bedroom?" I tease, watching his face flush as I speak

"No- you know that-"

"Hey, I'm joking. I have to use a less *conventional* escape route. Until I study the logistics of sneaking out using my window–which looks terrifying, by the way–I'm using the hall window, which means there's not really any way to lock it." I say with a smile and a shrug, as if to say 'can you blame me?'

Alessandro just chuckles at my statement, and speeds up just slightly.

"Don't worry, one way or another, we'll get home before your brothers do. And, there's also a chance that they didn't see you. Wouldn't one of them have called your phone to double-check?" Alessandro asks, his logic making perfect sense. It almost makes *too* much sense.

"But what if they still saw me?" My brain feeling the need to make scenarios of me arriving home to both of my brothers finding me gone.

"Well, it's definitely possible. I'm not denying that. I *am* saying that it would be rather difficult from how far away they were."

"Do you think they saw us kissing?" I blurt, needing to know his answer.

"Absolutely. There's no doubt about that, but *who* I was kissing would be a little bit harder to figure out." Alessandro pauses. "And how would they even know that I'm me?"

"Well, you *do* drive this to school every single day, but other than that, I don't know what else would give it away."

"True. Let's just assume right now that they have no idea you're with me. If it does come out that you were with me, we'll figure something out." He sucks in a deep breath. "Besides, there's nothing we can even do right now. We're already taking you home."

"Out of sight, out of mind, huh?" I tease, offering Alessandro one of my french fries as he drives.

"Not exactly, but close. I mean, logically, what *can* we do?" He says as he takes the fry and pops it into his mouth.

"True, I guess. But I highly doubt that you're going to be the one that goes down for this."

"Oh, knowing your brothers, I'll be skinned alive before they even talk to you." Alessandro says with a chuckle before taking a sip of his milkshake.

"You think so?"

"I know so." He takes a breath before continuing. "You really don't realize how much Santiago—and Matteo—dislike me. I would go so far as to say that they *hate* me."

But why? The question is on the tip of my tongue, but I refrain from asking. Alessandro has already told me why.

There are always two sides to every story, and while I think that Alessandro has told me his side, if I were a betting woman, I would say that there's something else that really irks Santiago. Something that I just haven't figured out yet.

"I guess I don't know the extent of your feud, then. It doesn't seem like Santiago, and especially not Matteo, to just *hate* somebody."

Alessandro smiles ever so slightly as he listens. "There might be something that I don't know about, but sometimes us men are a little bit…hot-headed. I can say that I've had feuds and arguments for the smallest of reasons."

Ouch. I know he's not saying this to change my mind, but the protective part of me wants to defend Santiago. I mean, he's my *brother*. And, he's not here to defend himself.

"So you think he's just being unreasonable?" I blurt out, immediately regretting it. I don't *want* to be on one side of their argument. I want to be Switzerland. I don't want to have to choose between my brother or the boy I *really* like.

Well, Alessandro isn't exactly asking me to choose, but I feel pressure to choose, even if it's not intentional.

"I think…" He trails off for a moment. "I think that it's a bit more complicated than that, and maybe just a little bit unfair." Alessandro finally says, his hands gripping slightly tighter on the steering wheel.

"So, yes?" I press, feeling stubborn. Alessandro's silence is enough to give me his answer, and I bite the inside of my cheek in anger.

For the second time tonight, I wonder how I got here. Tonight was supposed to be fun, and most definitely was not supposed to end up with an argument between us.

Minutes pass by, and there's still silence suffocating us. The world whizzes by around us as Alessandro continues to drive, and I wish we could go back in time. To a moment just before I demanded for him to unpack whatever problems he and Santiago are having.

"When you get back inside, text me and let me know you're okay." Alessandro says as he pulls to a halt in front of the gates.

"Why wouldn't I be okay?" I ask, still feeling slightly bitter. Wow, that came out a lot more harsh than I'd planned for it to.

"I'm not saying-" He takes a breath. "I was trying to say that you should text me and let me know if your brothers found out you were gone." Alessandro finally says, sounding both frustrated and hurt.

"Okay, then. I will." I say, climbing out of his car, resisting the urge to slam the door shut behind me.

As I reach the wall, I do what I should have done in the beginning, and use one of the ivy vines and small crevices to quickly climb over the wall.

"Hey, wait!" Alessandro whisper-shouts, quickly climbing the wall to sit next to me. I can't help but notice how quickly he scales it, and I have to wonder just how muscled he is. You know, just out of pure curiosity.

"Why?" I ask defiantly, not forgetting our mini argument.

"Listen, I need to apologize. I shouldn't have said those things about your brothers. I'm sorry." Alessandro says, looking at me with sincerity in his eyes.

And that's when it hits me. *I'm* the one who's being unfair. I demanded an answer from him, one that I knew I wasn't going to like, and still got angry when he was honest, but still nice. Yikes. I don't want to be like this.

"I- You- I accept your apology." I say, taking a deep breath of fresh air before speaking again. "And you should probably get going, because I don't know if they're back home, yet. There's nothing more incriminating than you being at the scene of the crime." I say with a small smile before jumping down the side of the wall.

I turn back a few minutes later to see the silhouette of Alessandro still sitting on the edge of the wall, still watching me.

Why did he apologize when it was literally me who made the problem?

Why did he insist on checking on me, even when I'd been extremely rude to him?

Why was I so adamant on making him answer my question,

when he was so obviously trying to protect me?

Ugh, there it is again. *Another* boy trying to protect and shelter me. Even though I know it's wrong, another wave of hurt crashes over me.

Flopping down in bed a few minutes later, I pull out my phone and send Alessandro a quick text, letting him know that I'm back inside. I don't say anything about my brothers, which if I'm being honest, is super rude. He intentionally asked me to let him know if my brothers saw us, and I didn't tell him.

The part of my brain that wants to protect myself, tells me that I didn't do anything wrong. And the part of my brain that's honest with me, tells me that I'm being completely mean.

Either way, my brothers probably weren't home, because I didn't crawl through the window to find them waiting up for me.

So, basically, I've made a mess out of everything. At least, that's how it feels.

CHAPTER TWENTY-ONE

The sunlight that streams through my open window is the only thing that gets me out of bed, and only because the blinding rays are burning my eyes from behind my eyelids.

I reach to rub my eyes, and I wince at the pressure. They're swollen from my crying last night, and no doubt look worse than they feel. I quickly stand and look into the mirror, feeling angry with myself, and with the events of last night. Why did I allow last night to spiral so far out of my control?

Did I ever actually have control over last night? Do I have control over anything in my life?

I feel tears rising thanks to the direction my thoughts are going, and my throat begins to burn at the thought of last night.

I *really* messed things up. Even if Alessandro apologized, it wasn't his place to do so. *I* should have been the one apologizing for becoming so defensive and cold, when he tried to steer the direction of conversation from something so controversial.

"You look tired." Mother comments over breakfast, eyeing me as she takes a sip from her tea. Great. Just great.

"I didn't sleep well. I think I've been so busy with school that I haven't been sleeping enough." I quickly say, feeling my pulse beat in my throat as she hopefully buys my lie. To be fair, I wasn't near as tired until I started my mini argument with Alessandro, so it's not like sneaking out is the exact reason why I'm tired. Logic, right?

"Well, you'll want to freshen up before you leave. You look rather…disheveled. Don't you agree, Matteo?" Mother asks, bringing even more eyes to our conversation.

"Pardon?" Matteo asks, his eyes rising from his food, to Mother. Always the gentleman.

"I was just saying that Carmen looks rather tired and disheveled. Don't you agree?"

Matteo looks between us for a long second, as if deciding who he's going to have to upset with his response. Matteo has absolutely no reason to believe that I've been sneaking out, so I don't care if he thinks I look tired. And, while I've given Mother no reason to believe so, too, it would be much easier to convince Matteo that I'm just busy and stressed, rather than her.

Matteo always takes it easy on me, unless there's cold, hard evidence that I've done something I wasn't supposed to.

"I'm not sure. I think we've all been a little bit tired, recently." Matteo finally answers, his eyes looking just as tired as mine.

Well, I already know that he was out with Santiago last night, so it makes sense. I give him a sidelong glance, wondering just how much he knows. Does he know? What would his response be to the fact that I've been seeing Alessandro behind his and Santoago's backs?

"Carmen, I'm going to be driving into town in a few minutes, so I was thinking I should drop you and Santiago off at school. What do you think?" Matteo says after a few seconds of silence between us.

Oh no. He must know. Right? Why else would he be dropping us both off? If I had a license, I would *not* be in this predicament.

"I'm cool with it." Santiago says from behind Matteo, his school uniform pressed and fit to him. I look down at the fuzzy, cow pajamas that I'm still wearing and quickly stand.

"Yeah, I'm good with that. I'll be back down here in a few minutes." I say, hyperventilating as I take the stairs two at a time.

What am I going to do? Of course, I'll deny anything they ask me, but will that be enough?

After sliding my clothes on, I swipe a light layer of makeup on, hopefully concealing the 'disheveled' look that I seem to be wearing.

Once I'm back down the stairs and outside, I find both of my brothers already in Matteo's car.

Sucking in a deep breath, I climb into the back seat, setting my school bag down next to me.

"Everyone in?" Matteo asks, sliding the car into reverse.

"I don't know who would be missing, since you already have the two of us, but hopefully they're in their seat." Santiago says, teasing him, but also sounding the slightest bit annoyed. He looks tired, too.

Us Alvarez siblings have a whacky sleep schedule, I guess. All three of us sneaking out, and arriving home well into the morning hours? We're a mess.

"Nope, just my little Santiago and Carmen." Matteo replies,

teasing him back. Santiago opens his mouth to argue about the 'little' part, but Matteo hushes him with a finger. "No, don't even try that one, Santiago. You're always going to be my little brother, even if you're almost an adult." He says, accelerating his car as we reach the main road.

"Yeah, yeah, you've told me a thousand times." Santiago starts, not really trying to argue with Matteo. "But why don't you tell Carmen that every now and then?" He says, releasing a fake, exasperated sigh.

"Because Carmen never tries to tell me she's not my little sister." Matteo says simply.

"True." Is all Santiago replies with, before pulling his phone out of his bag pocket, and starts typing.

"Hey, this is family time." I tease, reaching forward in a joking gesture, acting as though I'm about to take his phone.

To my surprise, he immediately throws it into his bag, in an almost…desperate movement to remove it from my reach. "Chill out." I say coolly, surprised by his reaction.

"No doubt. What's got you so riled up, Santi?" Matteo asks from the driver's seat.

"Nothing. I was just replying to a message, and put it away when I was done." Santiago says, trying to sound nonchalant.

"Yeah, of course. We both believe you." I say, trying to stir him even more. Maybe it's rude, but he ruined my night last night. The least he can do is be uncomfortable for a little bit.

Last night.

Why have my brothers not mentioned anything yet? As if Santiago can read my thoughts, he starts speaking.

"Was someone awake last night? I could have sworn I heard

footsteps." Oh, this is *not* good.

"What? No. What did you hear?" Matteo answers immediately, sounding so innocent, as if he wasn't in the same car with Santiago last night.

"I don't really know. What about you, Carmen? Did you hear anything?" Santiago asks, turning in his seat to study me.

"No. I finished my homework and went right to bed. I slept through the whole night, so I heard nothing. If Matteo didn't hear anything, either, it's possible you were just tired." I lie, adding on the gaslighting at the end for good measure. If I'm already going to be lying, I might as well go all out and completely discredit anything he's saying.

My head whips to Matteo when he speaks, because I do not expect his response.

"Carmen might be right, you know. We *do* live in a big house. Are you sure you actually heard something?"

Weird. Shouldn't Matteo be agreeing with Santiago, that way I'll fess up over my whereabouts? I mean, it's good for me, but also confusing. I'm not going to be questioning him.

"Do you two really not believe me? Whatever." Santiago says, folding his arms and looking at his watch, presumably to estimate how much longer he has to be in the same car as Matteo and I.

"Come on, Santi, don't be like that. Neither of us heard anything, so we're just asking." Matteo says, trying to smooth things over with Santiago.

"It's fine. You don't have to believe me." Why is he so adamant that he heard something, when he obviously wasn't home for much of last night. I *saw* his car, and definitely saw him when I looked back for a second.

And Alessandro saw Matteo.

Alessandro.

I suck in a deep breath as I relive the events last night, and remember how I left things with him. I really need to apologize to Alessandro, today. He didn't deserve to be treated that way, even if I was upset or stressed out.

"Will you be picking us back up?" Santiago asks, looking curiously at Matteo as he waits for his response.

"I, um, I don't think so. I'm going to be working late, so I won't have time." Matteo says coolly. "I'll be sure to let your driver know that you'll need to be picked up.

Neither Santiago nor I say anything, and even though I was stressing over being in the same car as my brothers, I'm feeling slightly bummed. It's been a long time since we were all together, and he's already abandoning us.

"We need to talk." I say, breathless as I just ran down one of the long corridors, barely reaching Alessandro before he turned into one of the rooms.

"I know, but I don't think we should do it here. I'm supposed to be meeting a friend here in a minute." Alessandro says. His voice sounds both hurt, and a strange mix of tired control.

"Okay, but where should we meet?" I ask, my tone coming out slightly hurt. I know he's just trying to look out for me, but the feeling of being shut out is strong.

Alessandro seems to puzzle my question, almost as if he's trying to decide something. "My house. I know that no one will be there for a while, so we should be good."

Alessandro's house?

Like, his *house* house?

Footsteps sound down the hall, and without a chance to say anything other than "okay," I quickly slip into an empty classroom to avoid being seen.

"Hey, man, were you just with someone?" A boy says, sounding close to the door.

"No. I think you're wrong." Alessandro says, his tone a faux bored.

"Are you sure? I swear that I heard someone." The boy says, stepping closer to the door.

Oh no. This is not happening.

Thinking quickly, I lean against the wooden door, hoping the weight of my small frame will hold the door in the case that the boy just outside of the wall opens the door.

Seriously, why is he acting like a dog on the trail of some innocent fox? Just allow yourself to be gaslight and leave the door alone!

"Just leave it. We're going to be late all because you're convinced that you saw something that doesn't exist." Alessandro says, his voice sounding bored and condescending, something that I don't think I've ever heard from him before.

"Whatever, man. I just thought I heard something."

"It's an old building. There's probably ghosts here or something." Alessandro says, immediately cooling now that his friend isn't trying to open the door.

As their footsteps fade, Alessandro's words come back to me. Does he actually think there are ghosts here? Was he just saying that to let his friend off of the hook?

A creak sounds at the back of the room, and I stifle a scream.

It is *definitely* time to go.

Slipping out of the classroom door, I take off in a half walk, half jog, hoping that my class hasn't started, yet. I *really* don't need to be put on notice.

As the school day comes to a close, and everyone is starting to file out of the main exits, I stay by my locker for a few extra minutes, going over my story.

Just as I take in a deep breath, confident in my story, I see my brother. Perfect. "Santiago!" His head turns as he sees me, but doesn't say anything as he approaches.

"What's going on?" He asks, leaning against the locker next to mine as he waits for my answer.

"I, um, I'm not driving home with you today." I say, giving him an–what I hope is–easy smile.

"Why?" He asks simply. Luckily, I have an excuse, but I don't like how he's not agreeing with me like a few weeks ago.

"I'm going to run by a shoe store. I need to find something to match that red dress of mine." Of course this story is bologna, and I don't have any such dress, but he doesn't need to know that.

"Who's going to drive you? Since I'm going to be with our driver, of course." Okay, now there's a slight snag in the plan. Why didn't I think of that?

"My friend, Aless." I say, quickly improvising and

shortening Alessandro's name into a feminine-sounding one. I pronounce it exactly how I would say 'Alessandro' but I leave off the end.

"And she is?" Santiago asks, taking the bait.

"My friend." I say, unzipping my bag and rummaging around, trying to seem bored of the conversation.

"Okay, but make sure you're home at a reasonable hour. And if you need help or anything, you know Matteo and I are here." Santiago says, sounding dissatisfied with conversation. Like he's sure there's something off about my story, but he can't quite put his finger on it.

"You know I will. I need to run to the restroom, see you later. I love you." I quickly say, rising on my tiptoes to give him a quick kiss on the cheek as I turn for the women's bathrooms.

Of course, I don't actually need to use the restroom, but if I hang out in here for a few minutes, then Santiago should be gone by the time that I'm out. There's no reason for him to stay.

Ten minutes elapse before I make my way to Alessandro's locker. We previously decided a week ago that if we're going to meet at school, Alessandro has to wait at his locker. It's way less suspicious if I'm the one by his locker, instead of him at mine. Especially if there's a chance that Santiago is still on the premises.

"Ah, I almost thought that you forgot about me." Alessandro says as I approach. I smile at him, and immediately I'm reminded of why I love spending time with him. Even the shortest of sentences from him is enough to bring a smile to my face.

Everything from his slight Italian accent, to his brown-blond hair, to his lightly tanned skin, to his smile, brings me happiness.

"Never." I say, reaching down to take his hand. I clasp my fingers around his, and for a moment, I allow myself to believe that everything is right in the world.

Which, if I'm being honest, is kind of true as long as I'm with Alessandro.

"So, you were able to clear your afternoon schedule?" Alessandro asks as he takes my bag and slings it over his shoulder to sit next to his.

"Yeah, but I might have had to come up with a little lie to do so." I say sheepishly, looking up to watch Alessandro's expression as I speak.

"And what was it?" He asks curiously, our steps echoing down the empty hallways.

"I might have made it seem like I'm spending my afternoon with a girl named…" I take a breath in before finishing. "Aless." Alessandro just lets out a burst of laughter. It's not long before I've joined in.

"So, to be clear, it's spelled A-L-E-S-S?" Alessandro teases, sounding not the least bit fazed.

"Absolutely." I say, glad that he's making jokes over my quick thinking.

"I kind of like it, to be honest." Alessandro says, opening the passenger door, allowing me to slide into the seat. "No one has called me that before. It's usually Sandro or something, so this is new." He says as he places both of our school bags in the backseat, before sliding behind the wheel.

"You do? I just came up with it on the spot. I don't have to call you that or anything." I say, not expecting him to still be thinking about his new nickname.

"I wouldn't mind it, actually. You can still call me Alessandro, but Aless isn't bad at all." Alessandro says as he pulls out of the school parking lot.

I don't say anything in response, instead, I just watch as he weaves through traffic and takes the road back to my house. "Wait, aren't we going to your house? This is the road that goes to mine, right?" I ask, recognizing the familiar roads and structures.

"Yes. We really don't live that far apart, you know." Alessandro says with a grin, turning onto a road that's only three before mine.

"Oh, you really weren't joking." I breathe, realizing just how close Alessandro has been. "When did you move here?"

The large wall that surrounds his house and winding driveway is similar to mine, and the large, multi-story house is roughly the same size as my family's.

"Years and years ago. Probably around the same time you did."

"But I was still a baby. That would have made you, what? Maybe a year old?"
"Probably. I don't remember when we moved here, but I know that I wasn't born here." Alessandro says, pressing a button in his car to activate the automatic gate. "I don't know how our paths didn't cross before that night in the club, though."

"Maybe we did. You know, the red string theory, right?" I say, looking over with a smile as Alessandro drives into the large garage and parks his car.

"I think I'm familiar with the story, but it's been a while since someone mentioned it." He says as he closes his door and rounds the car to open mine.

"Do you think we've met before, though? It makes sense that we would." I ask, taking the hand that Alessandro extends.

"I'd like to think that I would have noticed you had I seen you before that night, but I don't know." Alessandro asks, opening the door to enter the house.

The entryway is spacious and welcoming, and I notice that while my family's house has a more Spanish feel to it, Alessandro's is more Italian.

A few maids breeze past us, and as an older man approaches us, I freeze for a second, wondering if he's Alessandro's father. I give myself a mental slap as I realize that I've literally met Alessandro's father before. Stupid nerves.

"Hey, um, Ruben, do you mind keeping this between the two of us." Alessandro asks, and for the first time, I've heard him sound shy. I'm sure Ruben is their head of staff–like Lindsey is for us–so I'm surprised to hear uncertainty in Alessandro's tone.

"Of course. Your business is none of mine, nor the rest of the staff." Ruben says with an easy smile, his words unbothered or strained.

I wonder if Alessandro and Ruben are close. While I'm not particularly close with Lindsey, she was the one I approached when I wanted to make sure any video footage of me sneaking out wasn't mentioned at any time.

"Thank you." Alessandro says, giving him a smile before leading me to one of the flights of stairs. "My wing is on level three."

"Hey, that's what my level is on, too." I say, noting the similarities between us. "Although, I *do* have to share the floor with my brothers. We each have our own bedrooms and bathrooms, but we share a common room." I say as we make it up one of the flights of stairs. We don't say anything as we walk, rather I just study the many family portraits that line the walls, some of Alessandro and both of his parents, some of just him and one of his parents, some of him by himself, and some of just his parents.

Do they do these often? Different groups of photos appear as though they were taken only a month or two apart.

We reach Alessandro's wing, and once he opens his room, my breathing hitches.

It's not from the amount of stairs, seeing as I make the same walk multiple times a day at home, rather, my breathing is slightly ragged as nerves catch up with me.

It will be the literal end of me if it ever comes out that I'm at Alessandro's house.

In his room.

If my brothers don't kill me first, Mother and Father will make sure that the next time I ever see the inside of a boy's room—especially a boy like Alessandro—it will be my ghost here.

"Wow." I breathe. His room is large, a king sized bed taking up room on the wall opposite to us, shelves of books taking up another wall, and the largest of all of the walls is filled with exquisite paintings. Afternoon light floods through all of the many windows, bathing his room in a hazy, golden glow. "Are these yours?" I ask, taking another step closer to the wall of paintings.

"Yeah, they're all mine. I know they're not very good, but I like hanging them up, and-"

"They're *amazing*." I say, studying the intricate designs of each painting. His paintings reach from the bottom of the wall, all the way to the twelve-foot ceilings.

It's beautiful.

"When did you start painting? Are all of these recent?" I ask, taking a deep breath in as my eyes roam over the various paintings.

"I think my first one was from when I was thirteen. It's that one." Alessandro answers, taking my hand and pointing it at a painting in the far corner. "Luckily, I was methodical enough to start in a place that would allow for the most amount of paintings to be hung." Alessandro says. He's rambling. I glance over to see the shy smile that plays across Alessandro's face as he finishes speaking.

"I can see that." I say, looking over the wall one last time, before turning my attention to the bookshelves that line the wall. "What are your favorites?"

"Um, I usually read school books, but I do like a few classic fantasy books." Alessandro says, running a hand through his hair. "What about you? Do you read?"

"Sometimes. I'm not as much of a reader as Matteo is, but occasionally he'll buy me a book that he thinks I'll like, and I read those." I take a breath before continuing. "Does 'reading' magazines count? I do 'read' a lot of those. The modeling ones, of course."

"I would say so." Alessandro says, turning to sit on the edge of his bed, his school bag landing on the floor. "Speaking of that, have you talked to your family about that?"

"Oh, um, not yet. I don't really think that there's a good way to, yet. You know what I'm saying?"

"More than you can imagine." Alessandro says. I sit next to him on the bed before speaking.

"Elaborate?" I ask, sliding off my shoes and pulling my feet on the bed.

"I know that I said it's a lot of pressure from my parents to be the best son ever, but it's more than that." He takes a breath. "They want me to have amazing grades, which isn't the worst thing, I know, but recently I've been pressured to help manage the business."

"I bet. Father has been on Matteo and Santiago recently. Of course he's always been that way, but it's at an all-time high."

"I know. That's what's even worse. I don't know if it was intentional or not, but Father is only now teaching me how to manage a company, and I'm millions of years behind them. He's so stressed about me being 'less than them', and I haven't a clue on what to do." Alessandro runs a hand through his hair before continuing. "And, he's getting pressure left and right from Mother, because she's trying to one-up your family by having this perfect son, and apparently I'm not good enough right now." Alessandro finishes. His voice sounds tired, and almost defeated. As though he's been battling these things for much longer than I'd previously imagined.

"That's…a lot." I say, needing a moment to figure out an appropriate response. I've had no idea what he's been going through, and he'd been covering it up all so perfectly.

"Yeah, tell me about it. And, I know how stupid I sound. I'm complaining because my parents want me to have a successful future, and all they're doing is requiring me to take a more adult role, but it's *so* much right now. It's like they didn't care about needing me to have experience in the business world, and now it's the most important thing ever." Alessandro adds, as if realizing how brutally honest he just was.

"I don't think that." I say, reassuring him. Alessandro flops back into his bed, his legs hanging off of the edge as his head lays in the middle of the bed. I copy his motion, our bodies only a few inches apart now. "In fact, I think I feel the same way, just with different things."

"You think so? It didn't just sound like a spoiled rich kid complaining because Mommy and Daddy are trying to set him up for life?" Alessandro says, a small laugh escaping his lips as he finishes his sentence.

"Not at all." I say with a smile, turning my body so we're facing each other.

"I feel like you should be judging me right now. That's what everyone else has done when I start to talk about these things." Alessandro says softly.

"Judging isn't really my style. Besides, how could I be judging you, when I spilled my guts to you the other night and you didn't even bat an eyelash?" I ask, genuinely meaning it. "I literally dumped all of my problems and worries on you, and you…embraced it."

"That was nothing. You were…struggling and I was there for you. That's what boyfriends do, right?" Alessandro asks with a teasing smile as he says the word 'boyfriend'.

"I guess so. I wouldn't know for sure though. I mean, you *are* my first ever boyfriend." I say as Alessandro reaches for my hand and threads his fingers through mine.

"Even if it wasn't–which I know it is–I would still be there for you. You're so different from everyone. I've never met anyone as…special as you, and I've definitely never felt this way before." Alessandro confesses.

"Never?" I ask, needing to hear him say it again.

"Never." Alessandro breathes. "And you?"

"I just told you that I've never had a boyfriend before. How could I ever feel this with someone else?" I ask, teasing as I squeeze his fingers.

"I don't know. I just…don't want to be the only one that feels this way." Alessandro finally answers.

"You're not." I say, smiling as I watch his eyes. There's a certain brightness to them when I say this.

"I'm glad. There-" He stops abruptly and sits up, his tone and demeanor changing.

"What's going on?" I ask sitting up, confused as to what is happening.

"I think you need to leave." Alessandro says, standing and reaching for my hand. "I mean, of course I'm going to drive you, but I just heard my Mother's car. She's home."

CHAPTER TWENTY-TWO

Oh.

That's the only thought that rushes through my mind as I realize what this means. If this ever gets out, I will be in hot water for the rest of my life. Literally, the rest of my life.

"What are you going to do?" I ask, placing all of the responsibility on Alessandro's shoulders. It's not my fault that his mom came home early, neither is it his, but since we're at his house, the problem is his. Great outlook, I know.

"Um, I haven't thought that far, yet." He says, taking a pause as he looks around the room. "Okay, never mind, I have. You're going to wait in here while I greet my Mother. Then, once I'm sure of her whereabouts, I'll come back to get you, and we can leave. Are you good with that?" Alessandro says, thinking quickly.

I give him a nod as I take a seat on his bed.

"Okay. I'll see you in a few minutes, then." Alessandro says, slipping out the door.

Well, this is quite the predicament, isn't it?

Minutes tick by as I wait for Alessandro, and just as I'm imagining him never coming back for me, the door opens.

"Carmen?" Alessandro whispers, taking a step in the room. "We're good to go, now. Mother is in the parlor, and should be there for the next few minutes. The coast is clear." He says, reaching for my hand.

I look up and smile, before taking his hand and allowing Alessandro to pull me to my feet.

Alessandro leads me through the winding hallways and stairs, stopping every few moments to listen for footsteps. For the briefest of seconds, it's like a game. The stop-and-go of our movements and the avoidance of any footsteps creates a pattern.

"Alessandro? Where are you going? I only just got here, son." A woman's voice calls out.

Alessandro freezes for half a second, turning back to me with a panicked expression playing across his face. This most definitely does not feel like a game anymore.

"I left my school bag with a friend. I'm going to pick it up." He calls back, continuing to walk, only with a much longer stride. One that I can hardly keep up with.

I trip twice as he weaves through another hallway, stopping at the door that enters the garage.

"Why on earth did you do that?" His mother asks, sounding closer to us. "And why are you moving so quickly?" She huffs.

Alessandro looks down at me as the shadow of his approaching mother appears. "Wait in there." He whispers, punching in the door code and opening it. I slip in easily, and he shuts it just as his mother rounds the corner.

"Well, why is your bag with a friend?" I hear Mrs. Valentino ask through the closed door.

"He was carrying it for me as I went to grab a book from my locker. He must have forgotten to give it back to me." Alessandro says easily.

"But you were so irresponsible to forget about it. Seriously, imagine that it was more important than just a school bag.

What if it was paperwork for the business?" His mother demands, any softness from earlier evaporating.

"I know, Mother. I won-"

"Don't tell me that, Alessandro. It's always something with you. You're so irresponsible for being seventeen years old. Go and fetch it, but don't let something like this happen again." She says, sounding annoyed.

Wow. Her words sting even me, and I have to wonder if this sort of conversation is normal.

I slip away from the door and stand by the car door, waiting for Alessandro. I can hear a few more words spoken, but I can't make them out.

The door opens and closes quickly, with Alessandro appearing in the darkness.

He doesn't say anything, rather he brings his index finger to his mouth in a 'be quiet' gesture. I nod as he unlocks his car, staying silent as he opens the door and allows me to slide into the passenger seat.

Once we're outside of the gate and on the road I see and hear a sigh of relief leave Alessandro.

"Home free." He says with a chuckle, one hand leaving the steering wheel as he rests it on his leg. Looking over, I see an easy expression playing across his face, and I wonder just how often he has interactions like the one I just heard. Maybe it's just me, but I would be upset if I was spoken to the same way he just was.

"That was close." I finally comment, watching his eyes to gauge his reaction. His eyebrow flicks as he listens, and I wonder if he's going to answer me.

"I know. I thought that for a second there, we were going to get caught." Alessandro says with a chuckle.

"Same."

The rest of the quick drive to my house is silent, and just before we pull onto my road, I come to the realization that since it's evening, and not dark, someone could look out one of the upper-floor windows and see his car.

"Wait, what if someone sees you drop me off?" I question, looking over with worry in my eyes.

Alessandro doesn't say anything, rather he just slows, presumably to give him more time to think.

"I'm sure no one will see us. And, if they do, who's to say that this is my car?" Alessandro says, sounding as if he's trying to convince himself.

"That's one way to look at it." I say, not sure of his answer.

He slows in front of my house, and I give him a sidelong glance as I reach into the backseat for my book bag.

"Sorry for all of the…commotion that happened earlier. I really didn't think that anyone would be home." Alessandro apologizes. My gaze softens before I speak.

"It wasn't your fault. And, besides, it was *maybe* a little bit fun to be sneaking around your house." I tease, giving him a smile as I reach for the door handles.

Alessandro doesn't make a move to open it for me, and I know that if he could, he would. If he gets out and someone sees him, we'll be done for.

"Have a nice evening, Carmen." Alessandro says softly as I close the door behind me. I turn my head to acknowledge that I heard him, and continue my walk to the gate. I use the password on the gate, knowing that the security team will see that the code was used.

"How was your friend, Aless?" Santiago asks as I round the top of the stairs. Darn. He didn't even give me a chance to put my bag in my room before he decided to start his interrogation.

"Good. We had a great afternoon." I say, giving him a smile before continuing to my room.

"That's fun. Did you get the shoes you needed?" Santiago asks, standing from the

"Shoes?" I ask, confused.

"That you needed to get. Isn't that why you left school with her?" He asks, his voice gaining traction as he realizes that I completely lied to him.

"Oh, um, I didn't find the ones that I needed. We ended up going to grab dessert." I lie, digging my grave down even deeper than it already is. Santiago doesn't say anything, rather, he just gives me a sidelong glance before muttering something and walking into his room.

Ugh. Why did I not even remember my own lie?

I close my door behind me and collapse on my bed.

This is *so* hard. How am I supposed to keep lying to my brothers, sneak around my family, *and* hide from Alessandro's parents? This is *not* what I signed up for.

Rolling over, I hug my pillow to my chest as I try to imagine what a life without Alessandro would be like, but I just can't picture it.

A knock on my door stirs me from my daydreams, and I call out a "come in" to whoever is at my door. Looking up, I realize that doing that was *not* a good idea.

CHAPTER TWENTY-THREE

"Carmen?" Matteo asks, his deep voice pulling me from my panic. This is *not* the time to be stressing. For all I know, he could just be asking me to come down for dinner.

Of course, that's absolutely not why he's here, but I do a good job of convincing myself, until he opens his mouth.

"I know that I dropped you both off, and then kind of left you hanging, after. Is that why you got a ride with your friend, Aless?" Matteo asks, curiosity in his voice.

"No, of course not. We made plans." I say easily. His expression changes as he takes in this piece of information, and I can tell he's debating on saying something.

"Well, thanks for letting me know. When Santiago said you were riding home with a friend, I was wondering if you were hurt or something." Matteo finally says.

Suddenly, a wild idea pops into my head, and my mouth doesn't hold it in as it fully forms in my head. "Will you drive me to a casting in a few days?" I blurt, reaching out to grab his wrist as he begins to leave.

"Casting? For what?" Matteo asks.

"Oh, you know, modeling. I saw that there's an open casting, so I was wondering if you would drive me." I ramble. "Of course you don't have to, and I can have the driver, but I was just wondering…" I trail off.

"Um, I'm not sure. Let's talk about it later, yeah?"

"But Matteo, please? You can't just say yes?" I plead, giving him my best baby sister eyes. It seems to be working, because his eyes soften ever so slightly.

"I mean, I can't promise anything, but I'm sure I can. When is it? You have permission, right?" He asks, covering all of the bases that a responsible adult would. Sometimes I wish that Matteo would be less adult-ish, but I can't ever remember a time that he wasn't. He's always been the third parent. Or, one of the many nannies that took care of us.

"Yeah, it's at ten in the morning, but we should be there kind of early, don't you think? Won't that set a good image for me?" I ask, dodging the 'permission' part of his question. And it's definitely not because I don't have permission. Obviously.

Who am I kidding? I totally *don't* have any sort of permission. Why on earth would Mother and Father suddenly agree with the fact that modeling is something I'm good at?

"Yes, arriving early is a good idea. You'll be the first person there, okay?" Matteo says assuringly, giving me a smile before gently tugging his wrist in a weak attempt to loosen my grasp. I immediately let go, now that I have what I need.

"Thank you, Matteo." I say as he strides to the door. "I love you!"

Another fire has been put out, and things might *actually* be going my way, now.

I smile as I lean back and allow my blankets to wrap me in their warmth. While today has had *plenty* of ups and downs, there've been so many wonderful ones, too. Matteo agreeing to drive me, Alessandro showing me his home, and Santiago not pressing on my obvious lie.

Alessandro.

My mind snaps back to our earlier encounter with his mother, and I feel guilty all over again. He took the heat for something that wasn't even remotely true. And while I was there because he asked me to be, I still feel bad that he had to deal with the consequences.

I need to be more careful. This isn't fun and games anymore. And while this instance was small, it could become much larger if we actually get caught together.

It pains me to think about pulling away from Alessandro, but I don't like him getting in trouble for spending time with me.

Besides, he won't even notice if I pull away slightly. It's not like I'm breaking up with him or anything. I'm simply going to be putting certain parameters in place, so that we never get caught.

Simple as that.

CHAPTER TWENTY-FOUR

"And you're sure that this is the place?" Matteo asks as we arrive in front of a large, well-kept building in the city. It's honestly not that far away from Father's business building, which is in the *very* expensive part of the city.

"Yes. This is supposed to be a very up-and-coming designer." I reply, opening my door, greeted by the sounds of the bustling city and the cold breeze.

"I'm not saying that they're not, I am just saying that this is a very expensive area of the city, so I'm surprised that this person can afford to rent out one of these offices." Matteo says, sliding off his sunglasses as he opens the building door.

I gasp as I step into the well-decorated room, because everything is just as I would have done. From the pink rug that covers the seating area, to the signs and photographs on the wall, it's perfect here.

Matteo walks over to the fluffy chairs that reside by the electric fireplace, and I take that as my cue to walk over to the main desk, where a woman of about thirty years old works at a computer.

"Hello, dear, what can I do for you?" The woman–Ashlee, judging from the nameplate in front of her–asks, looking over her reading glasses as she addresses me.

"I'm here for the modeling opening for Daniela Lozano.

Is this the correct place?" I ask, giving her my best professional voice. Ashlee looks me up and down before nodding.

"Yes, you are in the correct place. The castings are on the seventh floor, two doors down on the left. That's where you're going to meet Daniela. You'll receive further instructions from her." Ashlee says, giving me a smile before looking down at her work again, a crystal clear dismissal.

I look over to see Matteo watching me, and I give him a look that says, 'get over here', and thankfully he quickly stands and walks towards me.

"Level seven." I say as we step into the elevator, and Matteo quickly punches in the numbers. The elevator jolts as it begins upwards, but it stops on the second floor, and someone slips into the elevator with us.

"Hello. Sorry for stopping your ride up, but I just needed to grab a few papers." The woman says, giving me a businessy and friendly smile as she speaks. "I'm Daniela by the way."

No way. She's the owner of the brand. She'll probably be the one doing all of the castings.

"Hi, Daniela. I'm Carmen." I say, releasing a slightly shaky breath. "I'm going to be auditioning for your casting." I say, my voice steadier, now.

"Marvelous. I can't wait to see what you have." Daniela says with a smile. She seems to finally notice my hulking brother behind me, and looks him up and down before speaking. "And you are?"

"He's my bodyguard." I blurt out, before Matteo has the chance to say anything. There's no way I'm going to be looking like a child in need of a babysitter as I apply for this casting. Matteo does the smart thing and doesn't open his mouth, rather he just nods at me once I've finished speaking.

"Oh, of course. Sorry about that." Daniela says, quickly moving her eyes to the papers in her hands. I don't speak, rather I just fix my eyes on the numbers that let us know what floor we're on.

We get off on our level, Daniela, of course, following us as we walk into the appropriate door.

Inside, it's like stepping into Antarctica, because all around us is white. It must be where some of Daniela's photoshoots are done, because the whole setup is extremely professional.

"Wow." I breathe, doing a full three-sixty as I try to take in the whole room. It looks—and even smells—like what I previously imagined a photoshoot room would be.

"This is nice." Matteo comments. And while he's not marveling in the same way I am, he's definitely impressed.

"Isn't it?" I reply, taking one last look around as Daniela settles on a couch near the edge of the room. "I'm going to talk to her. You should wait…" My words trail off as I realize I have no clue where to put him, and more people will start arriving soon.

"Is this your way of kicking me out?" Matteo jokingly asks, taking a step towards the big open doors.

"No! Well, yes, but-"

"It's fine, Carmen. I'm going to wait in the hallway. I'll see you later." Matteo says with a reassuring smile before walking into the hallway.

Sucking in a deep breath, I exit the casting room. If Matteo weren't waiting for me, I might allow a few tears to slip down my cheeks.

That was…way harder than I expected. Just about every other girl who was auditioning for the spot in her new line, had *way* more talent than me. From they way they posed, to the confident aura that they possessed, everything those girls did was better than me.

"Carmen?" Matteo's voice calls out, and I look up to see him having a discussion with Daniela.

"Yes?" I respond, quickly righting my face as I lock eyes with him, then Daniela. There is no way that either of them will see me acting like a baby over the fact that I was one of the worst out of the girls who auditioned.

"Are you just about ready to leave? I think we need to get going." Matteo says, glancing down at his watch after he speaks.

"Yeah, of course. Let's get going." I say with a fake smile. Knowing Matteo, he can probably guess that I'm upset, but to his credit, he doesn't say anything. Rather, he just gives a polite nod to Daniela, and walks alongside me as we make our way to the elevator.

"So, how did it go?" Matteo asks once the doors have successfully closed and the elevator has started descending.

"Um, it went well. I won't know anything until later on, but I think that it was…good." I respond, avoiding eye contact with him as the elevator doors slide open.

"That's great. Why don't we stop by Father's office so I can pick up a few papers, then go home?" Matteo asks, opening the passenger door of his car, allowing me to slide into the seat.

"Sure. That sounds good." I say, faking my enthusiasm.

Matteo shouldn't have to deal with the fact that I'm in a sour mood, just because I deluded myself into believing that I would be good at this.

"Perfect." Matteo responds as he starts the engine of his car.

"Perfect." I echo, leaning my forehead on the window as the rumble of the engine drowns out my thoughts.

CHAPTER TWENTY-FIVE

"Make sure you wear that red dress that I bought for you the other day." Mother calls through my open door as she bustles down the hallway.

Tonight, she and Father are going to arrive early, in an attempt to place their bidding on the best items. The club is holding a charity auction and dance, and my mother is ecstatic over the idea of the Alvarez family name being listed as the highest bidder.

I slide on the deep, red dress, the color adding a nice contrast to my skin. I smile to myself as I apply my makeup, the thought of seeing Alessandro intoxicating. It's been three days since I've spoken to him, and I'm excited by the prospect of being around him again.

"Let's get moving. I know that we need to arrive early if we want to be in Mother and Father's good graces." Matteo calls out thirty minutes later, sticking his head into my room as he clasps his cufflinks.

"Okay, just give me a few minutes to put on my shoes." I say, leaning down from my vanity chair to slide on the black, stiletto heels that complement my dress.

Taking the steps two at a time is probably not the best idea since I'm wearing heels, but my excitement isn't allowing me to go any slower. What has Alessandro done to me?

I stop in my tracks when I notice that both Matteo and Santiago have their cars out, both of them standing next to

Santiago's as they talk.

What's going on? We're always driven to club events together.

"Ah, perfect. Who do you want to ride with? We both want to drive our cars, and we figured that you'd rather ride with one of us, rather than be alone." Santiago asks, looking down at his watch as he speaks.

I look back and forth between my brothers, and decide on Santiago. I've hardly spent any time–minus the time that we've argued–with him.

"I'll ride with you, Santiago." I say, giving Matteo an apologetic smile before sliding into the door that Santiago opens for me.

It's been a long time since I've been in Santiago's car. I almost don't remember the last time that I rode in here. Much less the last time I rode in the front seat.

"Are you going to be bidding on anything?" I ask Santiago a few minutes later, once we're on the road.

"Nah, I think I'll leave that to Mother and Father. It's all under the Alvarez name, anyway." Santiago responds, his hands sliding across the wheel as he weaves in and out of traffic.

"True. What are you going to do then?" I question, suddenly wanting to know what he does during club events.

"Um, I don't know. Hang around the old snobby people who have too many opinions. Same as always." He says, rubbing the back of his neck as speaks.

"Right. Of course." I say, noticing how his hand tightens on the wheel as he talks about the company we're around whenever there's a club event.

"What, you don't notice how much they intrude into everyone else's business?" Santiago asks, as if he's taking my response differently than how I wanted it to land.

"Oh, of course I notice. So many of the people there are

insufferable." I lament. I realize that he's only the second person I've had this conversation with. Alessandro is the only one who knows how annoyed I get with the people at the club.

"You could say that again. I mean, they're so concerned with what I'm doing with my life, that they don't even see all of the problems with theirs." He says quickly. "Who cares if I'm not the perfect person that the club wants me to be?" Santiago asks, sounding both defeated and angered.

I don't know what to say, so I just make a sound of agreement before fixing my eyes on the road ahead of us.

Occasionally, I glance in the rearview mirror to watch Matteo behind us, but mostly, I keep my eyes glued to the road, as if watching it will make us arrive sooner. It's silly, I know, but I'm so excited to see Alessandro.

It's been days since we've been able to interact, and with the promise of almost everybody being occupied with the auction, we'll be able to spend time together.

I peel my eyes from the road to eye Santiago, wondering what he'll be doing all evening, since he has no interest in the auction.

As Santiago drives through the large gates of the club, the small lights brighten from the car's motion, and the glowing pathway guides us.

"I'm going to put my car away, and then I'll be inside." Santiago says as he opens my door, offering me a hand as I step out.

"Why aren't you asking one of the valet drivers to put your car away?" I question. Santiago doesn't say anything for a second, and I have to wonder if he even heard me.

"Because this is my car, and no offense to anyone that works here, but the price of this thing is a little bit above their paycheck." He finally says, giving me a small wink before walking back to the driver's side. I huff at his answer, but I don't say anything.

Whatever.

Picking up the bottom of my red dress so it doesn't drag over the ground, I take the few steps to the doors, where a few members of the staff open them for me. I smile at them before entering, and once I've entered the main room, I realize what a large event this is.

The large windows have their curtains open, allowing the night sky to be viewed, and the large tables house objects and paper slips for bidders. Most of the room is being used for tables and chairs, but there are still small areas for groups to mingle.

Of course, I knew that this event is important, but I didn't expect something this large to come of this event.

I'm sure that when the dance rolls around, there will be some sort of intermission, where the staff will remove all of the tables and chairs, to give way to a dance floor.

Will Alessandro and I be able to dance together? Would it be so horrible if we were allowed *one* dance together?

Would anyone bat an eyelash? Or would our families charge onto the dancefloor and demand that we never even look at each other again?

"Miss Carmen, there you are. Come over here for a minute." An all too familiar voice says. I turn to spot Mrs. Valentino beckoning me over, and I give her my brightest smile before making my way over.

"Hello, ladies." I say as politely and confidently as possible, my smile never faltering as I take in the group of women that surround Mrs. Valentino. It's a few of the women that I've never really got along with, but one of the ladies in particular is the one that was demanding for Santiago to be removed from the premises when he and Emilio had their…whatever it was.

"Hello, sweet Carmen. You look so grown up in this dress." One of the ladies says, her smile looking less than genuine.

"I have to agree. It wouldn't have been my first choice if I had a daughter, but maybe I'm just a bit old-fashioned." Another says, looking me up and down as she speaks.

I smile back at them before looking down at the dress, taking in the beauty of it. The back is floor length, and has a small train, but the front cuts off right about my knees, blending into the long back.

"Oh, well I'm glad that the times have changed, then. I just love this dress." I say with my largest of smiles. "I'm glad you all love it, too."

Mrs. Valentino looks me up and down, and gives me a small smirk, as she listens. She surely heard how I stuck up for myself, and I wonder if her smirk has to signify that she likes how I told them off, all the while being sugary sweet. Even though these women seem to be her friends, she respects that I can hold my own in front of them.

I don't stick around them for long, since there's nothing more for me in their conversation, and I wander around the items that are up for bidding. I glance down at the papers that hold the names of the bidders, and the numbers they placed.

I hold in a gasp as I read my mother's bids, wondering just how many zeros are unacceptable for an event like this. Since this is a silent auction, I spot Mother's name every few lines, and I chuckle at her persistence.

Of course Mrs. Valentino's name is always before or after Mother's, their silent war making its way into their bidding.

"Placing any bids?" A deep voice says right next to me, and I jump slightly at the noise. Looking over, the noise is from Emilio, and I bristle at the sight of him. While I don't know what happened with him and Santiago, Santiago is my brother, and I'm on his side. No matter what.

"No. Just looking." I say with a fake smile, turning to find someone—anyone—other than Emilio to be around.

"Ah, I see. Well, I'm placing a few. Which do you think I should put my money on?" His voice says, carrying over to me. I stop, not knowing what to do.

If this were anywhere else, I would just ignore him and walk away, but if I do something wrong here, Mother and Father will lose their minds. How rude would it be if I just ignored him? Rude enough that I would get in trouble if it ever came to light?

The answer is yes. Most definitely.

I turn around with my fakest of smiles, and quickly look up and down the items. My eye catches on a painting a few feet away from me, and just a quick glance at the votes lets me know that this–if he does end up being the highest bidder–will cause a sore spot in his wallet.

"That painting." I say, motioning with my hand at the display.

"Well, that is a nice one. I think I will place a small bid on it." He says, stepping forward and writing his name and price on it, the number only slightly more than the previous bid. Way to really show off your money, right?

I give him a last glance before turning, and really leaving. Shuddering as I walk, I notice Matteo watching me from the far side of the room, his whole body still, his eyes never blinking. I meet his gaze, and instead of giving me a signal that we're having eye contact, he just continues to watch me.

Weird. I take a seat at the table labeled "Alvarez", unsure of what to do now.

A few lights dim as the auction slowly winds down, and people–including my mother and Mrs. Valentino–rush to the sheets to place their last bids.

A few men and women that I don't know start to sit at tables around me, and it's only a few more moments before my family arrives. As the table next to me fills, I make the mistake of glancing over towards the occupants.

CHAPTER TWENTY-SIX

Alessandro's familiar smirk is present as his eyes land on mine, and I have to force my eyes to rise from his lips.

The announcing of the items is going to be much longer, now that I'm going to be sitting right next to Alessandro.

What if there's a way for us to both slip away and spend the remainder of the evening together…

No.

Carmen, get yourself together. What happened to pulling away from him and creating some distance? A safety net to keep people from questioning us.

I risk another glance over, and see that Alessandro is still watching me intently, as if he's waiting to see what my next move is. Our eyes lock, and for a moment, it's only us in this room. The bustling of people in the background is all a blur, and the only thing that exists is Alessandro.

The dark room around me seems to swallow us whole, and the passing of time is irrelevant.

That is, until Emilio sits down at the Valentino table, completely obstructing my view of Alessandro. And maybe it's dramatic, but in a different setting, I might just scream.

Emilio has a bad habit of showing up when I need him the least. He has an especially bad habit–even if it was just once–of making my brother look crazy.

I still haven't figured out what went down, but that doesn't mean that Emilio gets my support.

A deep sigh releases from within me, and I turn my attention back to the tiny, gold statue that Mother must have bid on. She releases a small squeal and grabs Father's arm.

From behind, I can see the look that passes between Matteo and Santiago, and their faces are priceless. Their identical confusion over her excitement is almost enough to cause laughter from me.

While my brothers and I haven't ever verbally voiced that Mother and Father's obsession with being the perfect family is both draining and amusing, I know that we all think it.

Minutes tick by as more items are announced, a round of applause following each announcement. Just as I'm sure that I can't take any more of the boring event, the announcer calls out that the auction is now over, and if everyone could file outside to the gardens for a few moments, then the staff will remove the tables and chairs, allowing for a dance.

I wait a few extra moments for the rest of my family to start shuffling out, in hopes that Alessandro does the same. I stand, fixing my dress for much longer than what's necessary, but when I look up, it was worth it.

Here, under the low lights, Alessandro is standing a few feet away from me, patiently waiting for me to finish "fixing" my dress.

I don't say anything, rather I step past him, motioning for him to follow behind me as people shuffle around us. He stands directly behind me as people move and crowd for the doors, and when an over-eager woman knocks into me, Alessandro reaches his hand out to steady me, pressing his long fingers into my side.

Even though his hand isn't touching any exposed skin, every inch of my body feels electrified. I draw in a shaky breath as my feet cross the threshold of the main doors, the cold air a shock.

"It's cold out here." Alessandro says, falling into step next to me as we walk towards the gardens.

"You could say that again. And, you're the one that has a jacket." I say, rubbing my chilled arms, glancing over to see Alessandro's amused face.

"If it makes you feel better, you can have this." Alessandro says, sliding his tuxedo jacket off of his shoulders with ease. He wraps it around me within seconds, and when he does, the scent and warmth of Alessandro surrounds me.

I inhale the smell, before realizing what I've just done.

We are in a *very* public place, and literally anybody–including my family–could be watching us. Remembering my earlier vow to put a little bit of distance between us, I allow the jacket to slide off of my shoulders.

"Thank you, but I don't think wearing your jacket is good for our image." I say with a regretful smile, offering the jacket back to him.

Alessandro doesn't say anything for a second, rather he just takes it back and shrugs it back on "Yeah, I guess you're right. Sorry, Carmen." The words sound slightly dejected, but I try to not dwell on it. It's not my fault that we're not supposed to be together. I'm simply the one that's trying to keep us from getting in trouble.

"Hey, my father wants to see me for a few minutes. I need to go find him before he comes looking for me." Alessandro says after a few moments of silence.

"Of course. Have fun." I say, inputting as much enthusiasm as possible. It's not that I don't want him to see his father or whatever, but it's the fact that I can't even have him to myself, even on a night like this.

Around thirty minutes pass by before we're allowed to begin moving into the new dancefloor, the tables and chairs now removed.

I find myself in between people I'm not familiar with, and as I listen to the women ahead of me speak, my ears go on high alert. They're talking about Santiago and the event that happened between him and Emilio. I try to inconspicuously listen to their conversation, as curiosity brims within me.

"Well, did you see what happened, Grace? That Alvarez boy just…hit him." One of the women says. Although I can't see her in the almost complete darkness, I'm sure that if she had pearls, she'd be clutching them.

"You know that I wasn't over there. I wish I was, though. What was it all over? Too much alcohol?" The woman– presumably Grace–asks.

Hold up. Alcohol? I can't say that I've *never* seen Santiago with alcohol, it's never been enough to cause something like that. I know that for a fact.

"I simply don't know. I wasn't watching what *exactly* went down, I mean, how could I? I was talking to Ted. But I was close enough that when the Alvarez boy punched him or whatever, I *heard* it. Nasty sound, might I say."

"Well, next time you're at the scene of the crime, try to find the facts, Melinda." Grace says with a laugh.

I feel my insides burn as their conversation shifts to something unimportant, their casual discussion of my brother infuriating. These two women—Grace and Melinda—have no right to just discuss whatever happened so nonchalantly. Whatever Santiago did, it was for good reason. Whether I understand or not, he's not a complete hot head or stupid reckless.

Right?

I don't allow myself to question the trust I have in Santiago. Even if he's completely stupid for not liking Alessandro, that's just one instance. Otherwise, I agree with him on most things.

I walk up the steps, back in the entryway, the chill evaporating as the warm heaters blast onto me.

Upon entry, there's already a few couples dancing to the soft music that plays over the speakers. I step farther into the room, my feet unsure of where to go.

What should I do? Uneasiness floods my body as a man and woman brush past me. Arm in arm and chatting. Yet, here I am, alone and unsure of what to do.

I take another few steps, and then a hand takes mine, the comfort instant.

I look up to find Matteo, his smile enough to bring one of my own. He leads me to the floor, before placing my other hand where it should rest on his shoulder.

"Thank you, Matteo." I say, giving him a sincere smile, admiration in my voice. Matteo is a real lifesaver, and I can never tell him that enough times.

"For what? I'm just dancing with my little sister." Matteo answers, obviously knowing what I'm talking about.

"You know, for saving me from embarrassment." I say, squeezing his large hand with mine.

"Was that what I did? I just saw my sister and wanted to dance with her. Like old times." He responds, giving me another smile.

"Yeah, I'm sure." I say, leaning in and messing up the steps as I give him a quick hug.

"Absolutely." Matteo says, wrapping me in closer for another second. We must look rather foolish, like two children who were allowed to come to the adult party, but for a moment, I don't allow myself to worry what others will think as I hug my big brother. No matter how old we may get, Matteo will always be my big brother.

The song ends, and Matteo makes his way over to the drink table, and I find myself near the edge of the crowd. I'm just about to give up on the idea of dancing with Alessandro, but like a ghost, he appears next to me.

"Hello." I say as I look up through my eyelashes, my smile no doubt giddy.

"Hello, my lady." Alessandro says before raising a hand. "What would it take for a man such as myself to have this dance with a lady of your status?" He asks, a smile cracking through his façade.

"Let me think about that, sir. What are you willing to offer?" I ask, our joke endearing.

"My soul." Alessandro answers within seconds, his face unwavering. "My social status, anything you'd like. Take it." Again, nothing about him changes as he speaks, the genuine sincerity in his voice causing a reaction within me.

I have to wonder if he's continuing to play along, or if he's using this as a way to tell me that he doesn't care who really sees us.

"I'll have nothing of that sort. Let's just dance already." I say, placing my hand in his outstretched one.

"Of course." Is all Alessandro says before leading me onto the dancefloor.

I turn my head slightly to see who might be watching, and when I do, I have to do a double take. Is that Daniela Lozano? I make out her figure next to Matteo, and I breathe a sigh of relief over the fact that he's probably putting in a good word for me.

"How many people are watching us?" I ask as Alessandro's hand settles on my waist, the other firmly in my hand.

"Not many. I don't think we've really called too much attention, yet." Alessandro says easily. I almost pull away from him as I realize that he's not taking this as seriously as he should. While I had been planning on dancing with him, I never thought of letting my guard down.

Does Alessandro not care about the repercussions of us being caught in some sort of dating rumor? That will be it for me.

"Well that doesn't mean that it won't happen." I say through my teeth. Alessandro looks down at me, his expression confused. I quickly change my slightly cold face to something more polite, as I remember that being rude to Alessandro when he has no idea what he's done wrong isn't nice.

It's not fair to act as though I wasn't hoping that he would come find and dance with me.

We dance through the whole song without speaking,

neither of us able to find the right words. I know that there's no scientific evidence that points to time moving faster when you're having an amazing time, but I feel like it should be studied.

It feels like only mere seconds have passed, but instead, it's been the full six-and-a-half minutes of the song. I should be happy that the classical song has lasted this long, but I can't find it in my heart. I want more time without Alessandro.

Just as I'm opening my mouth to ask Alessandro to stay for another dance, a large hand presses on my arm, moving me slightly away from Alessandro.

CHAPTER TWENTY-SEVEN

"Carmen, won't you dance with me?" Santiago asks, his voice sounding slightly hardened. I turn in shock, the surprise of him being there, unexpected.

"I-" I turn my head to face him, my hand still firmly in Alessandro's. The look he gives me back is both curious and knowing. "Of course." I say, moving my arms from Alessandro's to Santiago. The feeling of Alessandro's hands on my body lingers, but I try to forget about it as I turn away from him.

A minute or so passes as we dance, neither of us saying anything. I want so badly to turn and find Alessandro's face in the crowd, but for the sake of keeping up appearances, I refrain.

"So, how did you come to be dancing with Alessandro?" Santiago asks, his tone cautious and curious, as if he's trying to hide his disdain for him.

"I, um, he asked me to dance when he saw Matteo leave." I improvise, knowing that while it's very close to the truth, it's not exactly the whole story.

"Wasn't that nice of him?" Santiago says, his question sounding more like a statement, and like he has more to say. I don't have to wait long for him to speak again. "Have you met him before? He's in my class, you know."

"Not really. I think I've said 'hi' to him once or twice at the parties here, but there's a lot of people here." I lie. Mentally cringing at the amount of lies I've fed to Santiago over the past few minutes, I focus on putting one foot ahead of the other as I dance.

"That's…" He trails off as he tries to find the right words. I've seen him do this many times, so I know that he's trying to find the best thing to say. "Do you know anything about him?"

"No." I answer quickly, realizing how non-convincing I must sound. Santiago's eyebrow quirks as though he doesn't quite agree with me, but isn't sure if I'm being honest.

"Well, anyways, thanks for dancing with me. I couldn't let Matteo be the only brother who danced with you." Santiago says as he clears his throat. What a topic change.

"I'm not doing you any favors. I'm still just your annoying little sister with a fancy dress and makeup." I tease, a small laugh escaping me. Santiago cracks a smile at this, a chuckle escaping him, too.

"I wouldn't necessarily say *annoying*, but something along the lines of it, though." Santiago agrees, his teasing smile enough to bring another burst of giggles.

"On second thought, you're welcome. You should definitely be thanking me for allowing you to dance with me. I mean, how many other ladies here would be dancing with you if I weren't?" I tease, knowing full well that Santiago–Matteo, too–has a whole entourage of girls and women alike that are vying for his attention. He never pays many of them any attention, but not because he's already with someone. He just doesn't find them interesting.

"I'm sure there's *someone* out there who would be more than pleased to dance with me." Santiago says, his eyes sweeping the room above my head, almost like he's searching for someone. *Does* he have somebody? No. There's no way that he would keep a secret like that.

"Maybe just one person." I finally agree. "But she would be old. Like, ninety or something. And the only reason would be because she'll be mistaking you for her deceased husband or something."

"Oh, now that's just rude. Come on, Carmen. There would be at least one other woman–half of ninety at least–who would be interested in dancing with me." Santiago says, sounding fake-outraged.

"Forty-five is still a little bit old for a boy of just eighteen, though." I retort, loving how his face morphs into another one of fake-indignation.

"A *boy*, now? Eighteen is an adult." Santiago says, opening his mouth to speak again, but the cut of the music is enough to stop him.

"I guess your one dance with the only lady that will tolerate you is over." I say, reaching up to pat his cheek before walking off of the dance floor. I turn back, giggling as I do so, and I see Santiago laughing, too. An older lady that was just dancing with her husband asks to dance with him, and over her shoulder, I give him an 'I told you so' look. He only shakes his head and presses his lips to contain laughter.

I can feel my smile as I take a sip of water in a dark corner, the interactions with both of my brothers refreshing. It's been too long since I actually enjoyed their company, and did things with them just because I love them.

"Would this be a good time to ask for another dance?"

Alessandro says, leaning his shoulder on the wall next to me. I almost cough out my drink at the surprise of him being here, but swallow just before that happens.

"If I don't die from a heart attack, then, maybe." I say, but my heart isn't really in the threat. I'm still happy to see him.

"Oops. Sorry about that, Carmen." Alessandro says sheepishly. He rubs the back of his neck as he says this, and I can't help but find it adorable.

"I'm sure." I say, taking his hand and leading him down one of the many winding hallways.

"I was, but if you're planning on killing me back here while no one is looking, then I might not be." Alessandro says, chuckling as he allows himself to be pulled along.

"Do you think that anyone suspects us?" I ask as we walk into one of the many empty rooms, only a sofa, bookshelf, and fireplace occupying the room.

"No." Alessandro answers too quickly.

"Aless, really. I'm worried that someone is going to see us and completely ruin everything." I say, sitting down on the sofa as I spill my worries. "That will be it for me. And you, too. I'm kind of already walking on thin ice with my family, and I haven't really been all that honest with them recently. This will be the literal icing on the cake." I confess.

"What do you mean? Of course I know that we can't be found out, but what about the other part? Where you're already on thin ice?" Alessandro asks.

"Well, I kind of made Matteo take me to a casting for a modeling thing…" I start, looking up as Alessandro nods, waiting for me to finish. "And I might have not told my parents. Also, I might have not really told him that I didn't have approval."

"Arguably, it could be worse. But that's not the point. How did it go?" Alessandro says, his curiosity seemingly taking the weight off of my shoulders. I half-expected him to be disapproving over the fact that I lied to my family again. Because, that's exactly what I would be doing to him if the roles were reversed.

"*Really* bad. Honestly, I wouldn't be surprised if she never calls me back." I confess.

"What exactly is 'bad'? Is there an exact definition of this in the modeling world?" Alessandro asks, genuinely wanting to know. Not like he's just trying to cheer me up. "And, let's just say that you somehow met the criteria for 'bad', it was still a learning experience, right? You still learned something?"

"You sound four times your age." Is all I respond with, small tears prickling at the edge of my eyes. Why am I getting upset with this all over again? I really need to pull this together.

"Maybe so, but you never answered my question." Alessandro says, gently tugging my shoulder, so it rests my head on his shoulder.

"I don't know. Not able to fit in with the other models is a good start. Have you seen how tall most of the girls are? I stick out like a sore thumb. A short one, at that." I say, moving my eyes so I'm looking up at him.

"I guess some models are tall, but there should always be space for..." Alessandro trails off as though he doesn't want to sound offensive.

"Just say 'short'."

"Okay, then. There should always be room for the short models, too. Not all of the market will be girls that are tall, right?"

"I don't know."

"Are you sure you actually did poorly? Or are you just telling yourself that?" Alessandro questions.

"I'm positive I did poorly. There's no way I didn't." I argue.

"See? You just proved my point. What if you actually did well, but you're just not allowing yourself to imagine that?"

"I highly doubt that. How is there any chance that I did well? I have no training, no experience, no…*anything*." I say, my words coming out much more raw than I'd expected.

"You're naturally good at those things. And, you don't not have anything." He says, taking a breath. "You have me. And your family. While some of them might not like you modeling, or not like…me, they still love you."

"Yeah, well-" I don't get to finish speaking, because Alessandro clamps a hand over my mouth and looks at me apologetically. He brings a finger to his lips and waits until I've nodded before removing his hand.

"There's someone back here." Alessandro whispers, gesturing towards the door for me to listen.

"Really?"

"Really. I swear I heard someone down here. It sounded like at least two people." My eyes widen in horror, the thought of not just one, but two people being able to find us terrifying.

I quickly stand, Alessandro following. We step near the door, where sure enough, two muffled voices could be heard. I look back in question, not knowing what to do now. Alessandro steps ahead of me and listens for a second, looking back and taking my hand in his.

"What are you-" Alessandro doesn't let me continue, because he brings his finger back to his lips in a 'be quiet' gesture, and gives my hand a slight squeeze as he quietly steps into the hall.

I follow, and instead of going the way that we came, Alessandro pulls me behind him as we grow deeper into the maze of hallways and flights of stairs. For minutes, I allow myself to be led by Alessandro, not worried about becoming lost or being caught, but after another few minutes pass, I have to wonder if we're even remotely close to where we started.

"Are we lost?" I question, worried about how far we've moved within these seemingly never ending walls.

"No. I'm just finding the exit to the balcony staircase, that way when we come out, it's not too suspicious." Alessandro says reassuringly, taking a step through an open door. "I'm sorry if you think we're lost. We're really not."

"I believe you, I'm just curious as to how you know all of the paths, and can remember all of them at a time like this." I say, now trusting that he knows his way. He doesn't respond, but I'm sure it's due to the fact that he's focused on getting us out. We walk through the door and end up on the balcony that overlooks the party room, and Alessandro makes a move to walk down the stairs, leading us down at the party, but I gently tug his arm and lean against the railing, watching the couples below move to a soft song.

The lights twinkling all around us bathe the room in a warm hue, and the scene below us looks like one of a movie. My eye catches on Matteo, dancing with a woman that I can't quite identify, a wide smile on his face as he listens to her speak, her dark hair shading her face.

My eyes scan the room for any other members of my family, and I spot Mother and Father dancing together, genuine smiles on their faces as they gaze into each other's eyes.

Now, to find Santiago. I search for at least a full minute, until my eyes long on him, as he speaks to a woman wearing a black dress. Her hair is pulled into a bun, and it bobs slightly as she nods her head at whatever he's saying. Again, I can't identify her, but her dress looks familiar, and that makes me all the more curious as to where I would have seen her, before.

"Who are you looking for?" Alessandro whispers in my ear. I shiver, his breath warm on my neck.

"My family. I was just curious as to what they're doing." I say, turning to face Alessandro as he keeps his gaze focused on the scene below us.

"Do you think they've noticed that you're gone?"

"No. I don't think so." I say, Alessandro still watching the couples. "Do you think your parents have noticed you're absent?"

"No. It won't be long before they do, though." Alessandro answers, finally turning to face me.

"Then we should get down there, right?" I say, taking a few steps toward the stairway.

"We don't necessarily *have* to." Alessandro says, following me and taking my hand in his. My breath catches as he raises my hand and presses his lips against my wrist. Even with my breath leaving me, and my mind becoming light-headed, I know better than this. I have to stop this before we lose track of time and get caught together.

Something about him not being as careful as he should be rubs me the wrong way, even when I know it's wrong. Alessandro shouldn't have to walk on eggshells when he's with me. If he were with someone else, this wouldn't be a problem. I know that I'm being unfairly harsh with him—and myself—but I can't find it in myself to feel sorry.

"Yes, we do. Come on." I say, playfully tugging him along as take another step towards the stairs. I try to keep all of my negative thoughts at bay when I speak, hoping that my voice doesn't sound as rude as my mind does right now.

Looking pained, Alessandro follows, falling into step with me as we walk. Neither of us speak, and as we reach the bottom of the stairs, I stand back on the bottom step, the height just barely making it possible for me to press a soft kiss on Alessandro's cheek.

Leaving Alessandro behind as I lead myself into the party room, and I don't look back. We're okay right now, and I need to be able to separate myself from him at this moment.

"Wow, what a stunning dress. I don't think I've seen you all night, dear." Renee, Mother's friend, says as I'm moving past her.

"Oh, thank you, Renee. I'm glad to see you here. I know you've missed the last few parties." I say, stopping to talk to the older woman.

"How did you know that, dear? Is someone here talking about me?" She asks, sounding half indignant, and half amused.

"Not that I'm aware of. I just remember Mother saying something in passing to me a while back. Don't worry." I assure her. Her hand rests on the cane that supports her, and I have to wonder how much effort this night must have taken if she's been having trouble attending parties recently.

"Camila." Renee says with a tsk of her tongue. "That woman needs to stop spreading rumors about me. I just came along to this one in case there happens to be another bout of excitement." She says with a laugh. And while I know that she sees my mother in a daughterly sense, I have to try so hard to not make a face when she mentions the 'excitement' part.

It took me a moment to realize what she was referring to, and now I'm way less inclined to want to continue a conversation with her.

"I'm glad you could make it, Renne. I have to get going, but if I don't see you again tonight, have a nice night." I say with a regretful smile.

What is with people being so worked up over Santiago and Emilio's little mishap? I *still* don't know what happened, and I'm less concerned about it than some of these people.

"Well, it was nice talking to you, Carmen. You have a nice night, and make sure to dance with plenty of pretty boys." Renee says, oblivious to the fact that I'm already past our conversation, and disinterested in whatever she has to say right now.

I take a few more steps, turning to view the dancing couples as I walk towards the drinks, when I bump right into someone. I freeze, feeling slightly frightened to look up.

"I'm so sorry." I say as I lift my eyes, my apology coming out before I've even identified the victim. It's…Alessandro's father.

"Carmen, isn't this just strange." He says with a small smile, sounding unbothered, but also curious, too. I guess it *is* a little bit strange that I've bumped into him *twice* recently. Not a good look.

"I- um- yes. I really don't know what's happening. I hope I didn't disturb you." I apologize again, hoping my voice conveys that it was truly an accident.

"There was no harm done. Feel free to go about your evening." Mr. Valentino says easily. Giving a smile in response, I continue my walk to the drinks, my throat parched from all of the talking I've been doing, not to mention, my little escapade with Alessandro throughout the halls of the building.

I don't see Santiago or Matteo, but I'm not too concerned about it. I do however feel strange, because I have nothing to do now. There's no way I'm going to be dancing with a stranger, and I'm not going to go exploring or anything.

Sitting down on one of the various chairs and sofas that line one area of the great room, I watch as people dance and laugh with their person, and wish that this could be Alessandro and I. What I would give to be able to show Alessandro off, To show that he's someone I care so deeply about.

Just how much do I care for Alessandro? The question pops into my head, demanding an answer that I'm not quite ready to give. I know that I *really* like him, but I also know that at this moment in time, I can't ever admit that to someone else.

Before my thoughts can continue to spiral any further, someone sits down next to me, the sofa sinking slightly under the person's weight. I turn, expecting someone I'm close to, considering whoever is next to me is rather close, but to both my horror and shock, it's one of the last people I want to be next to.

CHAPTER TWENTY-EIGHT

Emilio.

Every time I see him, my dislike grows. Admittedly, he's never done anything to *me*, but being involved with the Santiago altercation, and continuing to be everywhere that I don't need him to be, my dislike is growing.

"This evening has been so enjoyable, don't you think, Carmen?" Emilio asks, looking over as he speaks. I accidentally make eye contact with him, my instinct to face someone when they're speaking to me.

I force myself to nod, the annoyance in my smile surely visible. "Definitely."

"What do you say about–"

"Carmen, there you are. Remember how I said we needed to be leaving by midnight?" Santiago says, appearing out of nowhere, his hand outstretched. I glance up, both surprised and grateful for his sudden appearance.

"Yeah, of course. I'm sorry, Emilio, we have to be leaving." I say, latching onto Santiago's hand like it's a lifeline. Which, in this instance, it kind of is.

Once we're out of the crowds and on our way out, I drop Santiago's hand, still unsure of what he's playing at. "Are we actually leaving?"

"Of course. It's already super late, and you know I don't

like driving at night." Santiago replies easily, the jingling of his car keys on his finger as he rustles them is the only sound in the quiet night, since we're the only two people outside. Well, except for the sound of Santiago's scuffling shoes as he stumbles on nothing. Seriously, what is it with men not wanting to use a flashlight?

"But what about-" I bite my tongue before finishing my sentence, because I almost just outed myself to him. If I hadn't stopped just then, I would have asked about the time that he followed Alessandro and I that one night. I almost forgot about him being there, but now that I've remembered, the question burns within me.

"What?" Santiago asks, leaning slightly to listen. Even if it weren't cold enough to send goosebumps up and down my arms, I'm sure his words would. How could I be so stupid as to not think before speaking?

"Oh, nothing. I was going to ask about why you drove here even when you don't like driving at night, but I-" I fish for a good end to my sentence. "Um, remembered that you said you wanted some time behind the wheel." I say, proud of myself for the quick save. He doesn't say anything, rather we just make the walk to the parking area, and slide into his car.

The seats and air warm almost immediately, and I mentally thank Santiago for being so picky and fancy when he picked out this car. Any longer outside, and I'm sure that I would have frozen into a Carmen sized ice pop. And that's *not* an exaggeration.

Santi rubs his hands together before placing his hands on the heated steering wheel and sliding the car into drive.

"When will Matteo and our parents leave?" I ask after a few minutes of silence.

"If I were guessing, Matteo will be leaving soon. As for Mother and Father, I'm sure that they'll be there for much longer. You know how they are when it comes to events like this." Santiago says, all the while weaving through traffic and driving near the top of the speed limit.

"Yeah, I guess so." I say. And, because I just can't help myself, I ask him another question. "Why don't you like driving at night?" I can tell my question is unexpected, but to Santi's credit, he doesn't hesitate to launch into a long-winded explanation about how it's not really him, but how other drivers are more reckless. A few of his words catch as a few cars swerve around us, and I almost end up agreeing with him.

Almost.

If he really was behind Alessandro and I that night–which I know he was–then where was his concern for driving at night?

"I see." Is all I say, content to leave the conversation. Apparently, though, Santiago isn't.

"Why are you so curious? I don't think you've ever asked me about my driving habits before." He asks.

"Well, you know, for when I get my license and all. I should be aware of these things, right?" I question, bringing out my most innocent voice possible.

"Of course you should be aware of these things, but won't it be a while before you get a license?" Santiago inquires, sounding mildly suspicious. Oh great. With each lie I create, I seem to have to create ten more just to validate the first one.

"Maybe. I'm thinking about talking to Father about it more,

and if he approves, I want to be ready." I answer, the confidence in my voice much stronger than how I feel.

"Okay, then. If you get his approval, you know that I'm a much better driver than Matteo, so you should come to me for lessons." Santiago offers. I do a double take at him, because never in a million years did I imagine him offering me driving lessons. Who is this version of my brother?

"Are you okay?" I ask, genuinely wondering if he's going crazy or something.

"Yeah? Why wouldn't I be?" Santiago immediately answers, sounding slightly defensive. His tone isn't necessarily sharp, but it has more of an edge to it than before. His shoulders tense as he waits for my answer.

"You practically just offered me driving lessons. Normally, you would never do that." I say, and Santiago's shoulders visibly loosen as I speak.

"Well, I was just offering, you know. You don't have to accept my lessons or anything." He says, his voice cooler again.

"I never said I wouldn't say yes, I was just…confused. You've always seemed so against me driving or whatever. I don't know." I say, concluding that the conversation between us isn't going anywhere. Santiago doesn't even seem to be paying attention to me, his full focus on the road ahead of us.

School passes quickly, the event last night making everything today a blur. Who's making all of these events land on school nights?

After finishing all of my homework, I flop down on my bed, the glowing numbers on my clock reading eleven o'clock. My pajama shorts and button up shirt are soft as I roll over and open my phone, checking the bright screen for the first time in a few hours, and the chime of a notification declares a new message.

Opening the chat, I see that it's from Alessandro, and my heart picks up speed as I read the message. Alessandro…wants to come over to my house. It states that he's home alone, and he should come over to eat pizza. *Right now.*

Well, he didn't exactly say *right now*, but the message indicates that he would *like* to come over right now. My stomach grumbles, since I didn't eat dinner earlier–thanks to school work–and the thought of spending time with Alessandro in a calm atmosphere is rather enticing. It's been forever since I've been able to be myself around him, with no outside eyes watching our every move.

I contemplate telling him that him coming over would be disastrous, but just before I hit send, the memory of Matteo saying he'd be out for a while tonight pops into mind. And, Mother and Father are out at dinner with friends. Meaning, Santiago and I are the only members of the Alvarez family that are home.

Of course, there's security and a few of the maids, but not *that* many people. Wait, am I actually considering this?

Before I give it any more thought, I message back that he can come over as long as he doesn't alert *anyone* that he's here.

Alessandro quickly messages back that he'll do nothing of the sort, and that he's on his way over, now. I press the call icon next to his name, hoping that he'll answer before he gets any closer.

"Hello?" Alessandro's deep voice says through the microphone.

"Hi. Drive slowly so I can talk before you get here." I demand, both panic and excitement in my voice. Who is this boy that is making me throw out any logical thoughts?

"Yes, ma'am."

"Okay, when you get here, you're going to have to leave your car at the staff driveway, which has an entrance near the back of the property. Also, when you get there, if you see someone by the name of Lindsey, tell her that I know you're here, and that she doesn't need to alert anyone that you're here." I say, giving him rapid-fire instructions. "Oh, and you're going to have to be extremely quiet when you come in through the staff entrance. I'll be waiting for you down there."

"Sounds good. I'll be quiet and won't let anyone know that I'm here. Oh, and what's the gate code?"

I relay it to him, and once we've hung up, I slide on slippers, and slip out of my door. Leaving it cracked open, I step past Santiago's room, surprised to see a small light coming from under his door. Should I knock and see if he's still awake? No.

I don't hear any movement from his room, and as if my hand has a mind of its own, I reach out and knock on his door. What am I thinking?

There's no answer, so I knock again, louder this time. "Santiago?" I call through the door. No response. Feeling brave, I twist the knob, surprised that it opens with ease. Why isn't it locked?

Santiago isn't here. I'm not sure why I'm so shocked, but I am. Where is he? Calling out Santiago's name one last time with no response, I shut the door and rush down the stairs, realizing that Alessandro is probably almost here.

A thought dawns on me as I make my way down the stairs, and I take a calming breath. What if Santiago went with Matteo, to whatever thing he was going to? It's not too far-fetched, because they *do* go out to eat or to parties together. That's it, I'm sure.

I have no more time to worry about Santiago, because I see Alessandro's figure outside of the door, and I quickly open it and let him in. Alessandro looks me up and down, a strange smile on his face as he closes the door behind himself.

"What?" I whisper, taking his free hand—the other holds a pizza box—and tugging him behind me as I start moving back towards the stairs. The feeling of his hand on mine sends warmth up my arm, but I dismiss it as I continue walking.

"I, I guess I didn't think you'd be in pajamas. There's nothing wrong with them, of course, but I've never imagined or seen you in anything other than regular clothes or dresses." He whispers behind me. I trip on the step I'm taking, now slightly self-conscious. Why didn't I think to change?

"Oh." Is all I respond with, the hallway a welcoming sight after being in the wide open as we rushed up here. I push Alessandro into my room, closing the door behind us and leaning against it. That was…nerve-wracking.

"It wasn't an insult or anything. Gosh, I'm kind of bad at this." Alessandro says, running his hand through his hair as his eyes roam around my room.

"No, I was just…I don't know." I say, straightening and surveying my room. "You can sit on the couch or my bed, but take off your shoes if you want to step any farther." I say, my tone teasing, but truthfulness in my voice. Even *I* hardly wear shoes within my room, so there's no way someone else's germs are going to be tracked throughout my room. Alessandro raises an eyebrow in question, but slides off his shoes.

I finally notice what he's wearing, and it feels strange to see him in something other than a school uniform or club attire. Sure, we had our few late-night dates, but I wasn't really paying attention—nor could I see—his clothes. Right now he has on a pair of dark jeans and a sweater, the color perfectly accentuating his golden skin and hair.

"Can we just sit on the floor? I kind of don't want to ruin your sofa or bed in case the grease leaks through the box." Alessandro asks, sitting criss-cross in the middle of my floor. Reaching behind me to verify that the door is locked, I nod. After grabbing a blanket and wrapping it around myself, I plop down next to Alessandro.

"So, what's with the late-night visit?" I finally ask, taking a bite of the warm, pepperoni pizza. Alessandro shrugs.

"I just…miss you. I feel like I don't ever see you enough." He answers, looking up somewhat sheepishly.

While I want to feel flattered—I do—I can't help but feel worried. How long can we keep this distance between us when our feelings for each other grow every single day? How will we keep up appearances when we can't stay apart from each other?

"I, I missed you, too." I finally say, biting my lip. I *really* like Alessandro. I like him so much that it's scary.

How can I like him this much when I'm trying to find ways to put space between us? How can I like him this much when we're not allowed to be together? A prick of pain pulls me from my thoughts, and I realize with a start that it's the feeling of the inside of my lip starting to bleed.

As the night carries on, we talk about mundane things, neither of us feeling extremely upbeat tonight. I think that it's just lack of sleep–for both of us–but I can't help but feel that there's something else brewing under the surface.

"Do you think that if people found out about us that they would be angry?" Alessandro suddenly asks. I turn my head from where it is resting on his shoulder as we lay in the middle of the floor.

"What?" I ask, not because I didn't hear him, but because I seriously wonder if he's actually asking. He starts to repeat his question, but I stop him. "Sorry, I did hear you. I was just surprised that you asked me that."

"Why?"

"Because you've seen the rivalry that goes on between our families. And with you and Santiago…I think that it would have a lot of negative repercussions if people found out." I say softly.

Alessandro groans, rubbing his hand against his face. "I know, I know. I'm just so tired of not being able to show people that I care for you. Or interact with you during school. Or dance with you at club parties." Alessandro confesses, sounding frustrated. While I agree with him, a small part of me chimes in that it wouldn't be like this for us if we were with other people. If we didn't fall for the person that we're not allowed to have.

"I…I agree with you, Alessandro. But is it really that bad? It's not ideal, but we could not go to school together. Or go to the club. We *are* pretty lucky." I offer, knowing how weak my 'argument' is. It sounds pathetic to even me.

"Of course. I'm just complaining." He says quickly, as if realizing how his words must sound.

"No, you're right. It's stupid that we can't be together in public." I state, huffing out a breath heavy enough that it ruffles a few of the strands of hair that rest on his ear. I watch as goosebumps flood his neck where the air hit him, and I smile at this.

Neither of us speak for a while, the sound of our breaths coming in and out enough noise to fill the silence. That is, until I hear a sound that I've heard every day of my life. Santiago's door.

"Santiago is home." I whisper to Alessandro, my eyes moving to the door as if to say 'listen'. We both listen as the sound of shuffling around in his room continues, and finally, when it stops.

"I should be going home now. If I stay any later, It'll be morning before I leave." Alessandro declares, turning his gaze to focus it on me.

I don't speak, rather I just move even closer, allowing my lips to reach his. I'm not sure why I waited so long to kiss him, but I regret it. Alessandro doesn't move for a second, as if he's surprised by my actions. He quickly moves his hand to cup the back of my neck, rolling slightly to where he's leaning over me.

Only so much more time elapses before Alessandro pulls away, his hair ruffled from when I ran my hands through it, his eyes a little bit more wild than they were a few minutes ago.

"I… I should probably get going. Your family will probably be home soon." Alessandro says, running his hand through his hair as he sits up. I flop my body back on the floor, feeling defeated.

"Okay, just leave me here all alone." I say, closing my eyes as if I'm going to be sleeping on the floor. And while this is all absolutely ridiculous, I don't dare break character.

"Carmen, come on. I'm just trying to make an effort to keep our relationship a secret. Being here when your family arrives home–which we have no idea when they will–isn't the most responsible thing to do." Alessandro says, his voice saying that he wants to stay.

"I know, I know. I just wish things were different." I say, finally sitting up. Alessandro reaches for my hand and pulls me to my feet, the world swaying slightly as my tired body tries to right itself.

Alessandro wraps his arm around my waist, pulling me towards him in a hug. "I know." Is all he says, resting his head on my shoulder, a small area of skin exposed as his lips and nose press against it.

I wrap my arms around his neck, pulling him in tighter, and in response, Alessandro wraps his other arm around my waist. We stand in what feels like hours, unmoving as the undocumented amount of time slips away.

Finally, I step back, knowing that it is really time for him to go, and that we'll be lucky if no one else is home. Hours have passed since he first arrived, so surely someone is back. For once, I'm not the Alvarez on a midnight escapade.

"You should get going." I say, turning to move towards my bed. Something in me shifts and I turn back. "Thank you for coming over. I didn't realize how much I missed being around just you." And as if my body has a mind of its own, I place my hands on either side of Alessandro's face, pull him down to my height, and kiss him. It's a quick kiss, but I can feel the fire and passion in our bodies, so I pull away.

"Good night, Carmen."

"Good night, Alessandro."

The door closes softly behind Alessandro, and I flop down in bed, wave after wave of tiredness crashing down on me. But before I can pull the blanket over my body, a knock sounds on my door.

CHAPTER TWENTY-NINE

"Carmen? Are you in there?" Matteo calls through the closed door. Oh my gosh.

Panicking, I jump to my feet and my eyes scan around the room, searching for any evidence that Alessandro was here, in the case that Matteo comes inside. Just as I'm about to call back to him, my eyes land on the sweatshirt of Alessandro's that he must have taken off earlier. Quickly shoving it under my blanket, I take a step towards the door, Matteo calling my name again.

I open the door to see a fully dressed in everyday clothes, his attire not at all reflecting the hour. It's two-thirty in the morning, and he's not even in sweatpants or something?

"Yes?" I ask, my voice coming out only slightly sharper than intended. I mean, I was *just* laying down to go to sleep.

"Were you just outside?" He asks, not even bothering to wish me a good morning.

"Outside of the house?" I ask, feigning confusion. I want to know what he thinks he has me for before I start answering 'yes' or 'no'.

"No. I meant in the hall. I heard a door close, and assumed it was you. It didn't close for a second time, though." Matteo says, as if this is supposed to make sense to my sleep deprived brain.

"Okay?"

"So were you out here?"

Just leave it, Matteo. "No, I wasn't. But you should ask Santiago." I say, momentarily forgetting that he must have just been with him.

"I guess I could do that. I thought he was asleep though?" Matteo says, his words coming out as a question. Asleep? But shouldn't he have been with Matteo? "Has he been awake?" Matteo asks, looking down as he waits for an answer.

Thinking as quickly as I can, I start speaking. "I don't really know. Listen, you just woke me up, and I'm super tired. You should get some sleep, too." I say, patting his arm and closing the door. I need no more interactions for at *least* twelve hours.

"Good night." He calls through the now-closed door.

"Good night." I whisper back, knowing that he can't hear me. It's the thought that counts.

CHAPTER THIRTY

I stare at the email in disbelief. There's no way I'm reading this correctly. Leaning against my bed frame as I read the message again, I can't contain the excitement that bubbles within me.

Daniela wants me to be one of the models for her new collection that drops in a week. *A week.*

Thank goodness today isn't a school day. Rushing through my morning routine, I get dressed and do my makeup in efforts to show my parents that I'm taking this seriously. I've formed a game plan to ensure that they'll allow me to accept this.

Since I'm unfortunately still a minor, I can't sign a contract, so, now, the rest of my life is at their mercy. I just need to convince them that this will be a step up in the business world, and the sum of money that will accompany it should be enough to convince them. Hopefully.

Taking the stairs two at a time, I manage to catch both of my parents at the breakfast table, an assortment of pastries on the platters in front of them. The aroma is enough to make my stomach grumble, but I have a main objective right now, and becoming distracted by foods sweet enough that they should be qualified as desserts are not going to derail me.

"Good morning, Father, Mother." I greet, kissing both of their cheeks before settling in the chair across from Mother, diagonal from Father.

"Good morning, Carmen. You're quite chipper this morning." Father comments, looking over as he places a bite of pastry in his mouth.

"Oh, well, that would be because I have some amazing news." I say, knowing that my version of 'amazing news' is much different than theirs.

"Oh? Do tell us, Carmen." Mother says, looking interested.

"So, a while back, there was this casting for models, which I applied to, and today, I was alerted that I've been selected." I say, my eyes flicking back and forth between Mother and Father. Their expressions are…not promising.

"And why did you apply?" Mother finally asks, sounding hesitant.

"Well, it was for a large brand, and I know that this will really help me pursue a career. And the pay is exceptional."

"And what is this pay? Who is the designer?" Father asks, sounding less against the idea than I previously imagined.

I relay the numbers to him before telling him the brand. "It's for Daniela Lozano." I say, now turning to Mother. "You've probably met her before. She's a member at the club."

"She is? Goodness, I don't think I've met her." Mother says, finally sounding impressed.

"Yes. And her clothing is of superior materials, so it won't be like I'm modeling for an inferior company." I offer, knowing that the gears are spinning in my parents minds.

"So if we agree to this, what are we expected to do? You know how busy I am right now with the business. And your Mother can't be bothered to be keeping tabs on all of this."

Father asks. Yes! He's actually considering this.

"All you would need to do is sign the contract. I'll have either Matteo or the driver take me to and from the company building." I state earnestly.

"Matteo? Why him?" Mother asks. Oops. I probably shouldn't have said that.

"Well, he was…kind of the one that helped me with this. So I was thinking that he could continue to be there." I say, looking up to watch their expressions change with this new information.

"Matteo…helped you with this?" Mother questions.

"Yes. But it was only because I asked. And, he seemed to think it was a good idea." I say, watching her reaction.

"Well, if Matteo thinks that this is a good idea and has already been there to see this all happen, then I don't see why not you can chase this little endeavor." Mother says dismissively. I want to argue that she's wrong about this being a 'little endeavor', but I know that since she's basically on my side, arguing probably isn't the best idea right now.

"I agree. Since Matteo helped get you into this, he can be the one that manages it all." Father says, looking back down at his food.

Great. When I finally get permission, it's because Matteo can help 'manage' it, and I'm only being permitted because they don't think my passion for this will last.

I can't argue, though. If I have the chance to do this, all it takes is me being able to prove that I am passionate about modeling. And by then, I'll have already received permission.

"Thank you. I'll have everything for you to sign for you by tonight." I say, standing and rushing up the stairs.

Printing all of the paperwork I compile it all into a file and place it in a folder for Father. Knowing him, he'll have his lawyers overlook it before he signs. They'll surely approve it.

Rushing over to Matteo's room and knocking on the door, I wait for him to respond, but after a second of no response, I knock three more times, the excitement apparent in my erratic knocking.

"I'm coming, I'm coming." Matteo's low voice calls out. He opens the door, and before he can fully view me, I've launched myself into him, wrapping my arms around him in a hug.

"Matteo, guess what." I say, not peeling myself away from him yet.

"What?" He asks, gently wrapping me into a hug before he even understands what's happening.

"Mother and Father agreed. And Daniela said yes." I say, my terms vague enough that if someone just overheard us, they wouldn't understand what I'm saying.

"About the modeling thing?"

"Yes, Matteo! About the 'modeling thing'. They said yes." I say again, finally stepping back. "I'm going to be a part of this new clothing launch. Can you believe this?" I ask, excitement shining in my eyes.

"I'm happy for you, Carmen. I know how much you want this." Matteo responds, giving me another quick hug.

"Thank you." I say, suddenly remembering why I'm here. "Oh, and the main reason I'm here is because you're kind of going to play a large part in this."

"What? What is my part?" Matteo asks, half curious, half skeptical.

"Well, I kind of told Mother and Father that you helped me come this far so they said that you're going to *manage* this whole thing." I confess, looking up with an innocent expression.

"What did they think when you told them I was an accomplice?" Matteo questions.

"Not much. I think they were almost relieved that you understand what's going on." I answer honestly.

"Well, I'm glad that I could be of service. I guess most models have managers?" He teases, his eyes playful.

"I guess so. You'll need to add that to your résumé, you know? When I'm a big deal, it will look great for you."

"You're already a big deal, Carmen. This is just a job. You know you can't tie your self-worth to something like a job." Matteo says somewhat seriously, his playful voice gone.

I study him for a second, wondering what caused the sudden change in his attitude. "Yeah, I guess I know that." I state, the excitement partially drained from me. This *is* doing to define me. I've been working so hard to get here, and now that it's finally here, this is *my* moment. How can this not define me?

Matteo retreats into his room a few moments later, and I return to mine. As the hours pass, the memory of Alessandro being in here last night resurfaces when I pull the sweatshirt out from my blankets, and I hug it to my chest. How did things go so south last night?

When Matteo knocked, I was sure that it was him catching Alessandro leaving my room. It's a miracle he only heard my door, and not the conversation that was happening within my room.

That conversation.

I remember saying something like 'I wish things were different', and that rings so true right now. I wish that I could just call him and tell him that I got my dream offer, and that my parents are actually approving of it. But I can't.

The pain that washes through me is sharp as a knife and painful as one.

What if I hadn't become so attached to Alessandro? What if I just chose someone that I'm allowed to be with? Why must every time a breath leaves my body, I feel thankful that I haven't somehow spilled my secret with everybody?

The thoughts plague me for hours, and by the time that it's dinner time, the thought of eating makes me feel nauseous. I'm going to have to sit with my whole family and pretend that I'm not betraying all of their trust.

I was *just* allowed to start modeling. If they figure out that I'm dating Alessandro and keeping my relationship from them, I'm sure that I can kiss that goodbye. What do I do now?

Is this what Alessandro is going through every day? The burden of something as important as his future hanging on by a thread just because of his relationship. Taking a shaky breath, I make my way to the dinner table.

There's no way I can do this. How can I sit here and lie, and be excited about my career, when the weight of my forbidden relationship is pressing down on my chest so hard that it's difficult to breathe? I can't.

"Santiago, it was great to see you being…yourself at the dance the other night. I was worried that you and that boy, whatever his name was, would have another altercation." Mother says only a few seconds into the meal. My eyes move to

Santiago, and I watch as his hand tightens on the spoon.

"Thank you, Mother." Is all Santi says, his jaw never unclenching.

"Of course, dear. And did everyone see Carmen's dress? I felt like it was just the perfect dress for her." Mother says, taking a pause as she takes a bite of food. "I can't believe there weren't more people lined up to dance with her. It was only you boys and the Valentino kid. What's his name?" Mother asks, her rambling trailing in an awful direction.

I can't believe she just brought that up. How could she have brought up the *one* thing—person—that I absolutely didn't need to be thinking about during dinner?

"Yeah, Mother, it was great." Matteo says, his message intended for her, but his eyes fixed on me. Oh, great.

"What was his name, though? I always forget it. It's something so-"

"Alessandro." I blurt. Oh my gosh, I'm really just digging this grave even deeper, aren't I?

"What?" Mother asks, confused.

There's no retreating now. "His name is Alessandro. He's in Santiago's grade at school." I say, turning my head back to my plate. The meal here is much more appealing than having a conversation with my mother about Alessandro. I mean, have green beans ever looked this appealing?

"Oh, that must be it. I can't believe I forgot. I'm usually so good with them. I guess it might be the fact that it's such a popular one." Mother says, shaking her head as though it's a sad fact. "You know, with you three, I made sure to give you something that would also be less popular, that way your name would always stand out in a group of people. It was all strategic." Mother states, as if this is a normal conversation for the dinner table. As if naming your child so that they have a leg up in a public setting is a normal thing to admit.

"I'm glad that you thought that far ahead. It's really helped us out in public settings." Santiago says dryly, the sarcasm in his voice seeping.

"Santiago…" Father warns, his voice more annoyed than anything.

"What, Father? I was just pointing out how helpful it's been that our names are unique. It really has helped." He says, not even trying to hide the sarcasm now.

"Well, I'm glad." Mother says, finally picking up on the conversation. "Carmen? Matteo? Don't you think that since you have unique names you've been able to be the most watched in a room?" Mother says, her eyes flicking over us three. My eyes flit over to my brothers, as we all seemingly consider that our names are rather popular.

"I'm sure that it has." I say to her, just saying what she wants to hear so I can leave later without feeling guilty.

"See, Santiago. Carmen agrees with me." Mother says, giving him one of her best side-eyes. She's dangerously good at those.

"Yes, of course she does." He says before looking up with a humorous expression on his face. Oh no, Whatever he's about to say won't be beneficial to me.

"What's that supposed to mean?" Mother asks, skepticism in her voice as she eyes him.

"I'm just saying that it's convenient for her to say that,

because you *just*…" Santiago trails off as he seemingly realizes that whatever he's about to say is just going to drag me down further in this conversation that's not mine. He glances over as if to apologize for bringing me into whatever dispute he seems to be having with our parents.

What is the problem he has with them? I know that their opinions don't normally match with his, but if he's being this… bold at the dinner table, I have to wonder what exactly is going down between them.

"What were you going to say, son?" Father asks, not letting Santiago off the hook. My eyes flit between Father and Santiago, and I feel bad for watching their argument. I *really* don't want to watching this. It's not like they've had horrible arguments in the past, but I don't like seeing strife in my family. It's…unsettling.

I know that we all love each other, but sometimes I wonder if we're all *too* different. That if we weren't family, if we would even be friends.

Mother is so involved in social things that she's hardly ever home, and with Father managing his business, I don't think any of us have ever spent *that* much time with either of them.

And while Matteo and Santiago are great older brothers—not that I have much experience with other ones—we're still all wildly different. Matteo is so dedicated to his future that he graduated college by the age of twenty. Santiago is… I struggle for a word to describe him as the sounds of his and Father's voices carry around me. They're not necessarily arguing anymore, rather Santiago is getting lectured, and Mother is keeping a steady conversation with Matteo.

Santiago doesn't quite fit in. That's the only way that I can think of to describe him. It's not like I see him differently, but I know that's what Mother and Father see. He doesn't fit the mold of what a son that comes from them should be.

While Matteo is 'perfect' in their eyes, Santiago is opinionated, maybe a little bit more reckless. And the largest thing of all, he doesn't seem to care about what others think of him. Whenever Mother compares him to someone else—besides Alessandro, of course—he doesn't care about what they think.

My attention returns to the table as dessert is served, and I try to be present in the conversation. Staring off into space isn't going to help my 'I'm not seeing anyone' act that I'm trying—and failing—to pull off.

How much longer can I do this for? How much longer can I lie to my brothers and parents? How much longer can I just ignore everything that my family wants for me?

The thought is painful, but I have to question these things. Does Alessandro care this much about me? Is Alessandro wrestling with these thoughts, too?

"Carmen, did you hear me?" Matteo asks, tapping my shoulder to gain my attention. There goes my attempt at being present in the conversation.

"Sorry, what did you say?"

"I asked if you want to come with me to the office tonight. I need to send an email that I forgot about yesterday."

"And you need to do this from the office?" I question, the whole thing seeming strange.

"Yes. That's the problem. The computer there has the whole document and everything on it. I need to send it from there."

He says sheepishly, running his hand through his hair as he seemingly waits for my disapproval.

"Yeah, I guess I'll come. When are we leaving?" I ask, looking around the table to see that everyone is finished, and apparently I've just been staring into space as conversations flowed around me.

"Now." Matteo says, pushing away from the table and pulling out my chair.

"Okay, just let me grab my shoes." I say, turning from him and starting the walk to my room. I also grab my purse and phone, but the few seconds that it takes me to do that shouldn't matter to Matteo.

After sliding into the passenger seat, Matteo starts to shift the car into drive, but the sight of Santiago running towards us stops him.

"Let me in. I need a break from the house." He says at Matteo's window, a half pleading, half joking expression on his face.

The doors click unlocked. "Get in."

"Thanks, Matteo." Santiago says as he climbs in behind him.

"This is kind of nice, you know. Riding up front for once." I tease, looking back at Santi as he buckles.

"Yeah, it is. Good thing it's only happening this one time." He teases back, leaning his head on the headrest.

"Okay, you two. Let's remember who owns this car." Matteo says as he accelerates down the road.

"And let's remember who hasn't said-"

"Point taken." Matteo quickly calls out, silencing whatever Santiago was about to share.

"That's what I thought." Santiago says smugly, folding his hands behind his head.

"Oh, be quiet. You're just jealous." Matteo says, obviously knowing that Santiago won't reply to this. Whatever their conversation is about, it's clear that both of them won't say any more about it.

That doesn't mean I'm not going to ask, though. "What's going on? What does he know?" I ask, looking over to Matteo.

"He doesn't know anything. He's just trying to act like he does." Matteo says dismissively.

"Yeah, I'm sure." I huff.

"Exactly. Besides, if we're sharing anything with each other, why don't we share why you were dancing with Alessandro Valentino?" Matteo suggests, curiosity and something else in his voice.

I freeze, not a breath coming in or out of me as I realize what a predicament I'm now in. Why in the world did he bring that up?

"Yeah, that *is* a great question. The floor is yours, Carm." Santiago chimes in, leaning forward in his seat.

"I, I hardly know him. You know that, Santiago. You already asked me this." I say, turning on the defensive. What am I going to do now?

"Yes, but you never really said why he just approached you." He says.

"Yeah, I did. I told you that he saw Matteo leave and offered so I didn't flounder in the middle of the floor."

"But why was he so worried about you 'floundering'?"

"Because he's nice." I snap back.

I did not just say that. I narrowly stop myself from clamping my hand over my mouth, because there is no way that I just passionately defended him when I was trying to prove that I don't know him.

"How do you know that he's nice?" Matteo pipes up. I whip my head over to him, momentarily forgetting that he's here.

"I assume that he's nice." I amend, hoping that I sound convincing enough.

"Yeah, well, he's not." Santiago says from the backseat. If this weren't such a bad situation for me, I would be reveling in the chance to pick Santiago's brain concerning Alessandro.

"Why not?" I ask, taking the bait.

"Well for starters, he's a complete jerk. He's always competing with me, and can't ever take a loss. Never. He always needs a leg up." Santiago says, his knuckles cracking as he pops them.

"And?" I press.

"And he's the reason that I was caught when we were breaking into the club." He blurts, pressing his face into the palms of his hands.

"*What*?" Matteo and I blurt out at the same time.

"You're telling me that he was there?" Matteo says, his voice hard.

"When did this even happen? How did I not know about this?" I question.

"When we were sixteen. Don't you remember when I was completely grounded?" Santiago asks, answering my question before Matteo's.

"No? When was this?" I say, completely confused. "How

would I have remembered that? I was, what? Twelve? Thirteen"

"Yeah, I think that it was right before your thirteenth birthday. How do you not remember this?" Santiago says skeptically.

"I don't know? Maybe my head was buried in fashion magazines and not my brother's problems?" I snap, frustrated that he keeps asking the same questions.

"To be fair, since it was staff that found us, there never was any police involvement or anything. But still, how did you forget about that?"

"Listen, before you respond to Santiago, remember that this is my car and I'll send you both on your way if you keep arguing in it." Matteo says, his voice raising ever so slightly. "Now, Santiago, tell me how you failed to mention that you had an accomplice to that little escapade of yours. Why did you never stand up for yourself?"

"Well, it was a little bit more complicated than that. I couldn't just out him, without him outing myself."

"What do you mean? You were *literally* caught. Newsflash, you were already outed." Matteo says, frustration clear in his voice.

"Well, I mean this wasn't exactly our first…escapade." Santiago says sheepishly.

"Tell me what exactly went down with you two. The whole story, and nothing less." Matteo says, his grip tightening on the wheel. "Now."

"Okay, okay, guys. You'd think I'm some sort of criminal by the way you two are acting." Santiago says.

"Isn't breaking and entering a crime?" I ask, pulling my

best innocent face as I watch both Santiago and Matteo's faces morph into what I can only describe as 'this is funny but I shouldn't be laughing' expression.

"Santiago, talk." Matteo says.

"Yeah, well, anyways. Basically, we were also the ones that scattered all of those tennis balls throughout the whole club, and we might have had something to do with the suspiciously empty gas tanks on those golf carts a few times. Also, the golf course being spray painted red was us." Santiago says, pressing his lips before speaking again. "Oh, and we were kind of, maybe, involved with the stained glass window that shattered in the back of the club. And possibly also associated with the fire alarms that got set off during the exams. There are a few other things, but those are the main ones."

"You…did all of that?" Matteo asks, his voice level. I can tell that he's trying hard to get us to our destination in one piece.

"Yeah…" Santiago says, ducking his head as he realizes just how much this is disappointing Matteo.

"Why?" I ask, Matteo speaking at the same time.

Santiago shrugs. "To blow off steam? I don't know. We were just…having fun." He takes a breath. "Alessandro was the only one who understood what I was going through."

"And I didn't?" Matteo asks, both hurt and angry. We near the parking lot, and I'm thankful for the distraction. When Santiago doesn't answer, Matteo steps out and opens the back door. "You're coming with me. Carmen, please stay here." And with that, I'm left alone in the car, watching the receding figures of my brothers.

Is it bad to say that I'm glad I'm not in the hot seat right now? I guess the only plus to this whole revelation is that Matteo and Santiago aren't asking about Alessandro and I.

Alessandro.

A wave of fury rushes through me as I realize how he lied to me. Why didn't he tell me about his and Santiago's past? Why did he keep that from me? How did he keep that from me?

When was he just going to say 'oh yeah, your brother? Well, I'm part of the reason he's seen with so much disdain'?

I know that Santiago has always made a reputation of himself for being reckless, but this is different. Alessandro could have at least told me that he really did know why there's been a feud between him and my brother.

My brother. Another wave of fury washes over me as I picture him lying about this, too. Even if he was the one who took the heat, he still lied. How would I have known to not trust Alessandro when we met?

Do I trust Alessandro now? I wrestle with the question for a few minutes, and I finally come up with an answer that breaks my heart.

I don't trust Alessandro.

How can I after he lied to me?

CHAPTER THIRTY-ONE

Matteo and Santiago return to the car thirty minutes later, much longer than it would have taken to send an email, but I don't say anything. There is no way I'm going to poke one of these angry bears.

I doubt that Matteo will tell our parents about this, but I know that he's going to hang on to the disappointment of knowing that Santiago did all of those things behind his back. While I understand that this is bad and all, there's nothing that can even be done. Like Santiago said, the law was never involved in any of this, so technically all of this coming to light will do nothing.

Well, except for having every single person look down at him even more than they do now. I don't want that, and I know that Matteo definitely doesn't. While I've never seen him directly confront anyone for bad mouthing Santiago, I know that he hates it. I do, too.

The drive home is silent, but my brain isn't. I need to talk to Alessandro. Tonight.

Slipping out through the window that I've used so many times before to meet Alessandro, I promise myself that this is the last time I'll do this.

I make it to the wall and climb over, my body used to this by now. Of course, Alessandro's car is waiting for me like normal. I slide into the passenger seat without looking over at Alessandro, and only once he speaks, do I glance over.

"So, what's going on?" He's referring to the stream of texts that I sent earlier, demanding that we meet tonight.

"Can you drive just a little bit down? Not too far, but close enough that it will only take a few minutes to get back home."

"Sure." He says, parking us maybe a mile down the road. "Now, are you okay? What's going on with you?"

I turn to face him, my throat already tight and burning. "Yes. There's absolutely something wrong." I take a breath. "But it's not with me. It's with you."

Alessandro's face morphs into confusion. "What do you mean? I- I think I'm okay?" He says it like a question, and the pain in my throat persists.

"No, you're not okay. You *lied* to me!" I say, my voice rising as the words finally free themselves from my mouth.

"What? When? Carmen, I-"

"Don't do this to me, Aless. You lied about what happened with Santiago. You let him take the fall for something that you *both* did. And you lied to me when I asked why you didn't like each other."

"He…he told you that?" Is all Alessandro asks, as if he can't imagine that the truth actually came to light.

"Yes, he did. And he told me about all of your other escapades together. You lied about…all of it." I say, a tear slipping down my cheek. "*You lied.*"

Alessandro doesn't even try to defend himself, and I almost

wish that he would. That he would prove Santiago wrong, and not put this burden on me. "I did." He breathes, looking up before continuing. "I did all of that. We were best friends, you know. No one knew that we were hanging out during all of the parties, and sneaking out of class so we could fool around and then study afterwards. He was the brother that I never had." Alessandro confesses.

I scoff. "So I'm not the only Alvarez that you played? That you *lied* to?" I hiss, feeling even more angry now that he's confessed this. Alessandro reels at this, and it takes him a moment before he responds.

"I never meant to lie to him. We promised each other that whatever happened, we would stick together. That didn't happen when he took a risk that was far past what I was comfortable with. Santiago was going through something, and was reckless. When he suggested breaking into the club to raid the liquor, I didn't want to do it." Alessandro says, his voice picking up speed as he talks. "I *really* didn't want to have a part in that. Yes, we did dumb things before that, but that was different. That was going to be punishable by law if it ever came out that we were involved in it."

"So you just decided to betray my brother?"

"It wasn't like that? You don't-"

"I'm going to stop you right there. Because while I may not understand exactly what went down, I understand that it's over for us." I say, tears spilling down my cheeks as I say this.

Alessandro doesn't speak, and when I glance over at him, his jaw is clenched so hard that I wonder if he's going to break it.

"Please drive me home. I don't want to be here anymore." I say, turning to look out the window and crossing my arms.

"Carmen-"

"Take. Me. Home." I say through my own clenched teeth.

He doesn't try to speak, and as soon as the car is in park in front of my home, I swing my door open. Unsurprisingly, Alessandro jumps out and follows me.

"Carmen, please don't do this. I don't know what you want me to do, but-"

"I *wanted* you to be honest with me. I didn't want to be lied to." I say, scrambling to where I'm sitting on top of the wall. This isn't about Santiago taking the blame anymore, rather just that he never told me the truth.

Alessandro watches me, and for a moment, I wonder if he's going to climb up here, too. I want him to. I want him to be right in this situation. I want him to tell me that this is all a big misunderstanding, and that he was never involved with Santiago.

"Carmen, I'm sorry. I don't think I'll ever be able to tell you that enough, but I am." Alessandro says, looking up with guilt heavy in his eyes. I can tell that he's being sincere, but that doesn't take away the pain of the betrayal I feel. "And I know that being sorry doesn't fix this, but I want you to at least know that I never wanted to hurt you."

And with that, I jump down the wall, placing a whole world between us.

CHAPTER THIRTY-TWO

I go to sleep crying, and wake up doing the same. I spend all day at home, giving Mother the excuse that I'm sick. And I guess, I am sick.

Lovesick. Sick over the fact that Santiago *and* Alessandro have been lying, sick over the fact that I broke things off with Alessandro.

I know that we haven't been with each other for very long, but I know that whatever we had was real. I know that I *really* care for him. And as horrible as it sounds, I still love him.

Love him?

More sobs escape me as I realize how true that statement is. I *do* love Alessandro.

As I bury myself deeper into the blankets, Alessandro's sweater on my body, all I can think about is how betrayed I feel.

It's not like I'm angry about Alessandro letting Santiago take the blame—yes, I'm somewhat angry about that—but it's really about how I asked, and he lied. Alessandro told me that the only thing was school. Not that he was involved with breaking and entering, and my brother taking the blame for a literal *crime*.

All he ever said was that it was about something small. And I believed him.

I believed him.

He lied to me, and I believed him.

CHAPTER THIRTY-THREE

"Okay, Carmen, can you come this way, please?" Daniela calls out from her directing chair. I look down at the floral dress that I'm wearing for the photoshoot and nod, stepping off of the white background and flooring that I've been on for the last thirty minutes.

"Honey, I know that this is your first time doing something like this, but I really need you at the top of your game." Daniela says, giving me a sympathetic smile. She must notice the small wince that I release, because her face softens. "Hey, Karina, please just move on to the next one, right now."

Karina gives her a nod and moves on to the next, much more experienced model. "So, what's going on? This isn't the confidence or excitement you displayed when we were casting. You were like…a different girl, then." Daniela asks, looking me up and down as she speaks.

"I," I suck in a deep breath. "I have some stuff happening right now, but I never wanted it to bleed into my modeling like this. I promise that I'm not trying to bring my problems into this." I apologize, giving her my best apologetic face.

"And that stuff is enough to completely change your confidence and shift your light?" Daniela questions. I wince again.

"Maybe?"

"That's not a good answer, you know. I'm going to take a wild guess and say that this has something to do with a boy, and I would suggest that you reexamine what your relationship was." She takes a breath of air as if she's reminding herself of this, too. "Usually when this happens, it's one of two things. Either he was horrible for you, and you're coming out of a relationship, or he was the best thing ever. Am I right about this?" She asks understandingly. I nod, feeling seen by her words.

"Then I would ask yourself if he was worth keeping, or if this is what needed to happen. People don't just lose their spark like this, Carmen." Daniela says, reaching out to pull me into a hug.

"I'm sorry." I whisper, feeling like an even bigger failure.

"I'm not the person to be apologizing to. I feel like you need to be forgiving yourself for feeling this way. And maybe someone else." While I know that she has no idea about anything to do with Alessandro, for a second I wonder if she does. How would she know that I just broke someone's heart?

"Now, go get back up there and let's follow this dream of yours. Don't ever give up your dreams just because of a boy." She says, patting me on the back as I step away from her.

It's been two weeks since the photos from the shoot were released, and Daniela's brand–if it's even possible–has exploded even more. Her business has already been featured in one of the largest fashion reporting companies ever, and I was lucky enough that one of the photos that was used was of me.

The only downside that has arised since the release of the photos has been the amount of people that have been prying into my personal life. And while I don't want to say that I have 'fans', I'm not sure what other word to use. There have been people who stop me in public and ask me if I was one of the models in Daniela Lozano's new launch, and if they can get a photo with me.

I'm not sure that I realized wearing clothing in a line would make me almost as popular as the actual designer of the clothes, but here I am. I also can't say that I wanted this level of attention, but if I were to give it up, it would mean leaving modeling behind.

I still think about Alessandro every day, and when I see him at school, it takes all of my self-control to not go up to him. I still want him.

So badly.

It's ridiculous how much I still want Alessandro, but ever since I realized that I love him, it's impossible to just forget about him.

As I slide on an outfit to wear to the dinner party that the club is hosting, I prepare myself to see Alessandro. I've seen him occasionally in school, but whenever one of us catches the other staring, we've made it a point to completely avoid each other for the rest of the day.

Even with the success of the clothing launch and my photos in it, nothing has dulled the ache of leaving Alessandro. It's stupid. He shouldn't have this much of an effect on my life. Especially since I broke up with him.

I should be celebrating and excited over how my life has

completely changed for the better with this modeling deal.

Another wave of piercing pain runs through me as I finish buckling the straps of my heels, the rose gold sparkles complementing my skin tone. If I were still with Alessandro, I would be excited to show him the colors, and he would watch me and smile as I talked.

If is the key word, because I broke up with him. Because he lied.

Shoving away the thought of being with Alessandro, I straighten, grabbing my purse before exiting my room. There's no time to be pining over Alessandro, when I've already broken up with him.

I slide into the backseat of the limousine, Santiago and Matteo following soon after. Oh, did I mention that as well as Alessandro and I being done, my brothers are still giving each other the cold shoulder. Whatever went down that evening in Father's office when Santiago confessed that Alessandro was with him when he was caught, there's been visible tension between the two of them.

Do I want to know what happened? Yes.

Do I want to ask? No.

And that's about where I'm at with those two. If Alessandro weren't a part of any of our lives, then this would have never happened. I wouldn't be heartbroken, and my brothers wouldn't be fighting.

I know deep down that this isn't his fault, and that I would never give up my memories with Alessandro, but the part of me that's hurting can't help but feel this way.

The ride passes in silence, and as I watch the dusk lighting fade away into a cool night, I can't help but remember what it felt like to be alone with Alessandro as we drove into the night.

How we laughed, how we talked, how we kissed. Everything was perfectly imperfect. There were bumps in the road and small disagreements, but we still embraced it. We struggled through not being able to be together, and made it work.

And now, that's all gone. Gone because Alessandro couldn't just tell me the truth. Gone because he was too worried about his reputation to even care that he was lying to me. Gone because all he was looking out for was himself. Not the girl that he successfully charmed and made believe that she had a future with him.

Stepping out of the car once we arrive at the club makes me feel nauseous, knowing that both of our families will be here and that we're going to be within mere feet of each other for the rest of the evening. What am I going to do all evening? I can't look weak and torn up over this, even though that's exactly how I feel.

"Carmen?" Santiago says my name from beside me, alerting me to the fact that I'm just standing here, not taking any steps to go inside the warm building.

"Yes?" I reply, taking a step forward.

"Nothing." He says, taking my hand and squeezing it as we walk through the doors. As I slide off my light shrug, I intentionally drop Santiago's hand. It's not that I'm angry with him, rather I just wish that he was honest, too. None of this would be a problem if Alessandro and Santiago would have just been honest to begin with.

To be fair, not being honest about my previous relationship

wasn't exactly what I would call being truthful either, but it was different.

Different? I stop myself from questioning my crazy logic, because deep down, I know that none of this was right. Nothing I, Alessandro, or Santiago did was right or honest.

Was it really that bad if you love Alessandro? A small part of my brain questions.

I don't have time to mull over these things, because we're being escorted into the large dining hall, where the chandeliers are all lit, and the tables are set with the finest of china.

It's breathtaking.

Only a few other people have been seated, seeing as it's still a little bit early in the evening. Out of those that are seated, there's Mother and Father, a few of their friends…and the Valentino family. I gasp for air when my gaze catches on Alessandro.

His hair is styled to perfection, and his tuxedo is fitted to his exact measurements. In more ways than one, he looks like the boy that I locked eyes with on my very first night at the club. Then, I was haunted by the look of the beautiful boy who so easily captured my attention. And now, I'm haunted by the boy that broke my heart.

"You're right here." The waitress says, motioning at the seat across from Alessandro. Of course. I slide into the seat, desperately trying to keep my eyes off of Alesandro. If I thought that I didn't have a chance of holding it together before, now I'm really screwed.

"Carmen, Santiago, Matteo, you're finally here." Mother says from a few seats down, Mrs. Valentino across from her.

"We were just talking about how you three are becoming so successful. Especially with your modeling, Carmen." Mother brags. While she *is* bragging, I can hear a hint of actual proudness in her voice, and that makes me smile.

"I saw some of the photos. You looked lovely in them." Mrs. Valentino says, genuine admiration in her voice. That surprises me.

"Thank you. I'm really grateful for the opportunity that was given to me." I say, smiling at her. Losing the battle to keep my gaze off of Alessandro, I shift my eyes to him for a split-second, and the look he's giving me isn't anything like I was expecting.

The world stops around us as our eyes meet. All of the conversations happening around us fade into the background as our eyes lock.

His eyes are…proud. There's sadness in them, but pure proudness seems to be bleeding from his gaze.

Why? Is he proud of me? Why would he be proud of the girl that just broke up with him?

Alessandro gives me a small grin, but a few seconds later, he moves his eyes off of me to listen to his father describe a business strategy with Father.

Keeping my eyes to myself and only glancing around the room—and not looking in Alessandro's direction—I watch as the rest of the dinner crowd arrives. Soon enough every seat is filled, and the appetizers are being brought out.

The salad is okay, but mid-bite, a shoe jostles against my own under the table. I resist the urge to raise my eyes to the only person who could have done that, and swallow the leafy greens that are in my mouth. Alessandro is not going to be doing anything to distract me tonight. Tonight isn't for thinking about him or reminiscing on our days and nights spent together.

As the main course is served, I spend way too much time taking careful and conscious bites of my food, reminding myself to not bring my eyes to Alessandro. Besides the fact that I still desperately want him, we're still at risk of being noticed.

It hasn't been that long since I broke up with him, and more than ever people are watching me. Even the slightest gaze could give people the wrong impression of us. I can't do that to myself.

And if I'm being honest, I don't really want to ruin Alessandro's public image, either. Even though he wasn't honest with me, it's not my job to fix or punish him for that. I've already broken up with him. He's not a part of my life anymore.

I almost laugh at that. Alessandro is definitely still a part of my life. He might just be the person that I think about the most. I think about him when I'm angry, and I think about him when I'm happy. When I'm reminiscent, and when I think of the future.

Alessandro is literally everywhere in my mind. There's not a part of my brain that's not thinking about him twenty-four hours of the day. It's not fair, because he doesn't seem that heartbroken over it.

Was our relationship worth as much to him as it was for me? Was that why he lied to me? Did he just not care that much about our relationship and the future of it? These questions burn in my mind all over again, and I feel my throat start to burn in the tell-tale sign of tears.

I can't cry right now. I've done that too much in the past few weeks. I'm surprised that no one in my family has noticed the swollen and puffy eyes that are now a part of my everyday life. I'm even more surprised by how well they were hidden by the makeup that Daniela's staff applied to me.

In the photos that were released, I look so happy. Even I can't tell that I was sobbing ten minutes prior to the shot that single-handedly exploded Daniela's business. Under all of the makeup there was a girl who was torn up and broken inside, but above was the picture perfect photo of a smiling girl that looked like she was on cloud nine.

I know that the makeup and facial cleansing routine that I did covers all of the puffiness and sadness from my face, but I can't wrap my mind around the fact that while I look happy and beautiful from the outside, people can't see the girl that's heartbroken on the inside.

Alessandro's foot jostles against mine again, and I resist the urge to look up and demand an answer from him. Why is he doing this right now? There's literally no reason for him to be trying to mess me up.

I feel his foot on mine, and instead of ignoring him like the last two times, I stomp my heel against the toe of his shoe. It's not loud enough for anyone else to hear, and I feel a sense of satisfaction with myself. That will show him.

Glancing up to view his reaction, Alessandro is looking directly at me with a small smile on his face. This boy. He seriously thinks he's so funny.

I know for a fact that my shoe was painful, and probably left a small mark on his shoe. I don't care, though. Alessandro shouldn't be pulling stunts like this when we're not together.

The memory of Alessandro passing me his jacket when we

were walking to the gardens pops into my head, reminding me of just how brave we were getting together. Of just how much we were starting to lose the constant panic of being caught together.

If we were still together, I know that I would be reveling at the chance to interact with Alessandro, even if it were something stupid like our feet knocking against each other. Now, I'm actively trying to push him as far as possible away from my brain.

It's funny how just a little bit of time can make the largest difference in the way that we see someone else.

"Carmen, do you have any plans for any future photoshoots this year?" Mrs. Valentino asks, curiosity in her tone.

"Yes, I do. Daniela has a few more pieces that she's going to release this year, and I'm signed to participate in all of them." I say, looking down the table to see her a few people past Matteo. I hope she doesn't mind that I'm telling Mrs. Valentino this. She's already hinted at having a few more clothing drops this year, but she hasn't revealed what models that will be participating. Oh well. It's not like I'm world famous or anything, yet. My photo simply did better than the other ones in the shoot, and now I'm having my five minutes—or two weeks— of fame, and it will blow over soon.

Mother has warned me against thinking this way, but I'm pretty certain that my fame will be gone just as soon as it came. It's been silly to be recognized as much as I have been. As my social media profiles have been actively gaining followers, Matteo took it upon himself to add my profiles to his phone to monitor it all.

I haven't ever been too interested in social media, since it was pretty much not allowed in my house—when your father is an extremely rich business man *and* you're encouraged to act like an adult, social media isn't looked well upon—and now that I've gained popularity, I'm not too interested in what people have to say about me.

I have to hand it to him, for being new to this all and being thrust into this new world of mine, Matteo has fully taken on the role that Father gave him. I haven't asked him in a while how anything on the business side of this has been going, because I know that he has it under control. I'm not sure that I would have been able to handle all of this myself, and while I'm still frustrated at him for being part of the reason there's tension between us three, I'm grateful for his help.

As he continually handles all of the extra things that comes with being a model, I wonder if this is just for my sake, or if he might just be enjoying being by my side.

While I imagined that there would be a business side to modeling, I don't think I was ready for it. I feel as though I've aged years in just a few short weeks, and I feel silly for thinking that I could have handled it all myself.

Daniela has been an amazing 'boss' to me, and although I don't necessarily consider her a friend, I trust her. She put faith in me when I had no experience in the modeling world, and created a pathway for me in this industry that so many have to work much harder for. I don't think that what she's done is ever repayable, but I'm happy to continue to appear in all of her upcoming photoshoots for as long as she'll have me.

Which, according to our contract, is a very long time.

I glance down to see her making conversation with people double and triple her age, smiling and chatting with them, as though she belongs here. Of course, she does, but I've seen the expressions she wears whenever she thinks no one is watching. As if she doesn't quite think somewhere like this is for her. While I don't know much about her life before she was in the fashion industry, I know that she's young. Twenty or twenty-one, I think.

Since just about everyone here is a business owner, it makes sense that she'd be a member here. The only catch is that everyone here just about has children her age, and she sticks out like a sore thumb at times. It also doesn't help that she just became a member here only recently.

It's strange for me to see her look uncomfortable at times, because that's not her personality at all. Daniela is outgoing and brave, and a complete professional. She's the owner of a successful business, and is very hands-on when it comes to her business. I respect her a *lot*.

"Excuse me, ma'am, but we're taking dessert orders. Would you like our menu?" A club staff member asks, breaking me out of my trance. I scan over the menu and decide on a molten lava cake, and give her my order as she moves on to Santiago.

I notice her dark hair that's tucked into a bun at the base of her neck, wondering how long it must be when it's let loose. Santiago orders, and she moves on to Matteo and the rest of our table.

While I don't pity her or anything, I wonder what my life would be like if my parents weren't who they are, and if Daniela hadn't taken a chance on an untrustworthy new model. Would

I be working a job like this? Not that working here would be terrible, but I wouldn't have the same opportunities as I do right now.

My dessert arrives a few moments later, and I make the stupid decision to glance in Alessandro's direction. Why, oh why, did I do that? His gaze is unwavering as he watches me, and based on the look he's giving me, it would seem that he's been watching me for a long time.

I shiver under his piercing gaze, knowing that he couldn't have heard my thoughts about him, and that he still believes that I'm just a heartless girl that he dated for a short time.

That must be what he thinks whenever he sees me. I'm sure of it. Who wouldn't think that about the girl who broke up with him pretty much out of the blue?

I'm not saying that I didn't have good reason, but Alessandro didn't have much of a warning. I found out about his deception and then broke up with him the very same day.

Again, the feeling of betrayal rushes through me. Why didn't he just tell me the truth? Why did he have to give me trust issues? Was anything he said to me true?

Spooning out a bite of my cake, the middle spills out onto the white and gold plate, and I watch as it cools on the plate and hardens ever so slightly.

If there's one thing that I can always rely on, it's desserts distracting me. As I slowly eat the rest of my lava cake, the conversation around me shifts into less formal conversations, and when I look down, I can spot Mother next to Renee, having traded seats with Father as he talks easily to Alessandro's father.

I look down at my hands that are folded in my lap as I

listen to conversations flow, and wonder how much longer I can just sit here. When would be an acceptable time to go home? There's literally nothing more appealing than just cozying up in bed, under my comfortable duvet, with nothing but my tears for company.

Okay, I'll admit that last part is a little bit dramatic, but I'll definitely be going home sad. As hurt as I am with Alessandro, I still want him. I still want him to wrap me into one of his hugs and kiss my forehead and tell me that everything will be okay.

It's shameful how much I still want him. The problem is that I still love him. I can't just change how I feel. Change what I know to be true.

I want to believe that he loves me, too, but it's hard to believe. Was I just someone that he chose to charm just because I was 'untouchable' because he and my brother had a falling out?

Carmen, you need to stop! My brain screams out. How many times have I done this already? How many times have I told myself to forget about Alessandro? Too many to count.

"Come on, Carm. We need to get going." Santiago says, his voice close to my ear.

"What?" I ask, dazed and unsure of what I've missed.

"We're going to get going back home. There's school tomorrow, so we need to be asleep pretty soon." He says, gesturing at the clock on the far wall. The hands read eleven-thirty, and I choose to not even argue with him.

This is a better escape than what I'd imagined when I pictured getting back home. "Okay, let's go. Is Matteo coming?"

"No. He's going to stay until Mother and Father leave. Mr Adult can't be seen leaving the party before it's over."

We're exiting the room before I speak again. "And you don't want to leave right now?"

"Of course not. I'm not a child, and I hate being treated like one. It's so tiring to be told to act like an adult, but then have to be sent home so that I don't miss my 'bedtime'. Seriously, it really gets to me." Santiago grumbles, handing me my shrug before opening the door for us. "Don't you feel that way?"

"I don't know. I guess I was happy to leave. Sometimes I think that, but at this point, I don't really care." I answer, my feet freezing as we walk to where the driver is waiting for us.

"You weren't enjoying it in there? Are you feeling okay?" Santiago questions, his voice changing from annoyed to concerned.

"No- well- yes. I'm just tired and…upset. I have a lot going on and this wasn't particularly helpful." I say, tripping over my words.

"Why? Is there something going on that you're keeping to yourself?" Santiago asks, sounding suspicious.

I wish there were something going on that he doesn't know about, because that secret would be Alessandro. Instead of admitting that, I speak as truthfully as possible without giving away the fact that I do have a secret that I'm hiding from him. "No, there's not. I'm just busy with school, modeling, and just… life. You know what I mean." I say, sliding into the door that our driver opens for us.

"I do know, but I also think that you're being secretive. Maybe I'm wrong." Santiago says, sliding in beside me.

I look him up and down before responding, hoping that my disapproving look is enough to make him reconsider his guess.

"You're right about one thing, and that would be that you are wrong. I'm not…keeping things from you or whatever you said." I say, about to tune him out. But, for some reason, I feel like letting him know how I really feel. "And besides, let's say that I am hiding something from you. So what? I should be able to have my own personal life that you and Matteo don't need to be meddling in. Don't you think that it's a little bit funny how I know just about nothing concerning your personal life, but you're both so invested in mine?" I say, folding my arms and shifting in my seat to face him.

Santiago doesn't speak for a long moment, but I keep my gaze on him, not giving him the chance to slide out of this conversation. "I guess so. I don't really think that Matteo and I are really meddling in your life, rather we're just looking out for you. Don't you think so?"

"I completely think that you meddle. I think you're so concerned with 'looking out for me' that you forget that I'm also my own person. I'm not your responsibility." I say, my words coming out quicker and quicker. "While I like having you and Matteo there for me no matter what, I think that you're both a little bit controlling at times."

"Oh. Well, thanks for telling me, I guess." Santiago says, sounding shocked at my sudden outburst. "I don't think I realized that I was doing that. You're my—our—little sister, and it's kind of our job to look out for you. I can promise you that I've never wanted to be controlling or anything." Santiago says, sounding hurt and confused.

I try to not feel bad, because I know that he's saying this not to change my mind, but to see his point of view. The only problem is that I *do* see his point of view. I *know* that neither he nor Matteo wants to be controlling. It's not just who they are.

"I know that, but maybe you should look at it like *you're* the youngest. You were just saying that you don't like being treated like a child, but you're unknowingly doing that same exact thing to me." I confess, my continued honesty surprising me.

"You really feel that way?" Santiago questions, curiosity in his voice.

"Absolutely. How can you not see that that's the way you both treat me? It's like with the driver's license thing a while back–which you never helped me with by the way–when you said something like I didn't need to be driving myself. That literally sounds like something someone in the eighteen hundreds would say." I say. "I know that you don't mean it like that, but imagine how hard it is to be me when you both don't see me as anything close to an adult."

"Wow, I've kind of been a horrible brother." Santiago says, wrapping his arms around me and pulling me into a hug.

"No you haven't. You've just been…unaware." I respond, leaning into his embrace. It's been a long time since we've just hugged, and it feels nice. It feels nice that we're talking through our problems and I'm not just keeping it all inside.

"Being unaware doesn't mean that I get a free pass, you know? I'm sorry. I'll make an effort to be less…controlling. I really don't want to be like that." Santiago says, a firmness in his voice that lets me know that he's taking this seriously.

I bite my lip, knowing that he's serious, but also knowing that something isn't exactly right with Santiago right now. I can't place it but something just feels off about him.

CHAPTER THIRTY-FOUR

Pulling into the drive-through for a coffee shop, Santiago orders me a hot chocolate. Morning came too soon, and I'm paying the price for thinking about Alessandro long after I got home last night after the dinner party.

As we arrive at the window, the girl behind it squints her eyes as she passes Santiago the cup, her eyes meeting mine for a split-second. "Oh my gosh, you're Carmen Alvarez! From the Fashion Ins-and-Outs magazine!" The girl exclaims.

I smile at her, unsure of what to do. I'm not good at this whole 'getting recognized' thing. "Yeah, that's me." I say, giving her a quick wave Santiago drives forward.

"Miss Popular has made a public appearance." Santiago teases, glancing over before he pulls on the road.

"Yeah, yeah. You know that it's weird." I say, taking a sip of the hot chocolate.

"Not really. I believe you, but I don't think that being recognized is the worst thing in the world."

"It's not the worst thing in the world, but it's weird. Going out, I've been looking over my shoulder because I feel like people are watching me all of the time. I don't want to disappoint anyone by not being professional or something." I confess, taking another sip of my drink.

"I guess I can see that. But I don't think people will be

disappointed with you if you're, I don't know, laughing too loudly." Santiago says, pulling into the school parking lot.

"What's going on here?" I question, as the vans that have news channels splayed across the sides of the vehicle crowd the front of the school.

"I think that the daughter of someone important is attending her last year of high school here. Her dad is a member of the club, but I can't remember his name. All I can remember is that he's very famous." Santiago replies, sliding into a spot near the front of the lot.

Thanks to him being a senior, he gets his own parking spot. I've never been more grateful for his spot than I am at this moment.

"I'll see you later, Santi." I say, slipping out of the door and making my way to the front doors. Santiago stays in his car for a bit longer, and as I step around the news crews and cords that line the walkway, I feel like everyone is watching me.

Turning, I realize that the news crews *are* watching me. I direct my eyes to the path ahead of me, and ignore the flood of questions and cameras that start impending my sight and hearing.

"Carmen Alvarez, I didn't know that you attended school here! Tell us, how does it feel to be the most popular model at this moment?" I'm the most popular model right now?

"Carmen, look this way! This is the perfect photo! Your outfit is so preppy!" Preppy? What is that supposed to mean? This is my mandated school uniform.

"How do you feel, knowing that you're going to school with one of the most up-and-coming actresses? You and Brooklynn

Carmine need to be friends!" Is that the girl that just started attending here?

I don't have time to ponder these questions, because I'm finally within the building, which the paparazzi can't legally step foot within. Taking a deep breath, I step towards my locker, feeling defeated already. This is exactly what I *didn't* want.

"Did those crazies get you, too? I'm seriously *so* tired of them." A girl says, leaning against the locker next to mine. I straighten immediately.

"Oh, um, yeah. I guess they're here because there's an actress starting school here?" I say, my words coming out more of a question rather than a statement. "At least, that's what I caught when I was trying to come in."

"Yeah, that's true." She says, her hazel curls bouncing near her shoulders as she considers something. "That would be me. Brooklynn Carmine at your service." She says, extending her hand.

"Wow, sorry about that. They said your name like I should recognize you, but I've kind of been trying to stay offline recently." I say, clasping my hand around hers.

"Don't worry, I *completely* get that. I mean, when a young girl such as you or I starts getting media attention, it's kind of hard to stay on the safe side of the internet." She says, her manicured nails ruffling her hair as she speaks.

"I agree. What movie are you in? I'm guessing it's a new release?" I ask, starting the walk to my class. To my surprise, she falls in step next to me.

"Yeah, it's new. Our Story is the title." She says, chewing her lip before speaking again. "It's a teenage love story. What about you? Aren't you kind of famous right now?" She inquires, sounding genuinely interested.

"I think I've heard of the title, but I haven't seen it. I'll have to watch it." I say, stopping at the classroom door. "People tell me I'm famous, but I haven't been online enough to know the extent of it. I was featured in Daniela Lozano's new line, and I guess people see potential." Opening the door, I step inside, followed by Brooklynn.

"Maybe we can watch the movie together? And maybe we can be friends?" Brooklynn asks, sitting down in the open chair next to me. "Yeah, you're pretty famous, girl. Don't downplay that. Also, I know I sound like a complete loser asking you to be my friend, but you're seriously so nice." She says with a giggle.

"I'd like that, although, I'm just like any other girl." I say, glancing over her features again. "The longer I'm around you, the more familiar you look. Have I met you before?" I finally ask, the question gnawing away at me.

Brooklynn smiles at this, the freckles that are scattered across her caramel skin standing out even more on her cheeks. "I don't think we've met, but the paparazzi didn't catch wind of me starting here until today. My family also goes to this club that I think you might know? We only became members a few weeks ago. It's called The Enchanted Ivy or something? I don't really know, they just call it the 'club'."

"Yeah, my family and I are members there. I'm surprised that we haven't run into each other there." I say, pulling out my textbook and opening it.

"I think I've seen you, but you always seem to be with that one boy." Brooklynn says nonchalantly as she pulls out her own book. I freeze, my hands hovering over my book.

"What?"

Brooklynn looks over, surprised at my sudden change in tone. "Oh, sorry, I guess I thought I saw you with that boy. He goes here, right?" She asks, confused.

"I-"

"Class, please quiet down. We have to be paying attention to learn, don't we?" Mr. Sanchez asks, looking over his glasses as he moves towards his computer. Thankfully, I don't have to respond to Brooklynn now that class has started.

Looking over at her out of the corner of my eye, I feel bad for completely switching up on her. Brooklynn noticing me being irresponsible isn't her fault. She just…saw through the cracks of the secret that I'd been hiding.

Class flys by, and as I'm walking to my class–Brooklynn going to a different one–I take comfort in the old hallways. Even though the air is slightly mustier here, and the walk less-bright, it's easier to breathe. That is, until the alarms signaling a school emergency start blaring.

CHAPTER THIRTY-FIVE

What in the world? I take a few unsteady steps as I try to remember what all of the safety drills taught us, and then it clicks. I need to be moving towards the back exit that funnels into the school grounds.

Taking off in a jog, it's not long before more students are around me, all of us heading in the same direction. The loudspeakers all around us blare the alarm, and it only fuels my desire to exit from the building.

What's happening? It's been ages since we've had a school emergency. As smoke begins to fill the hallways, my chest heaves in effort. Less and less people are around me, and it's almost too dark with smoke to see.

I lean against the cool wall for a moment, my senses unclear and disoriented. Where am I? Shouldn't I be outside by now? I suck in another breath of the smoke, and my lungs and throat scream in protest.

My eyes feel heavy as I struggle to continue forward. At this point, I'm just trying to find the nearest door, in hopes that it will be the exit. My eyes, throat, and lungs are burning due to the smoke, and it takes all of my effort to put one foot in front of the other.

This can't be healthy, but I'm almost too tired to care.

"Carmen!" A familiar voice screams out to me, a figure

approaching in the smoke. I lift my eyes to see Alessandro running towards me, panic clear on his face. "Carmen, what are you doing? Why are you still in here?" He shouts over the still-blaring alarm.

I don't respond, the sight of him enchanting. In the hazy walls and the loud noise, Alessandro is like a beacon of light.

"I, I got lost." I say, leaning against the wall. I can't give up, but the thought of taking a nap is appealing.

"What are you doing? Let's go!" Alessandro says, taking my hand and pulling me towards him.

"No, I need to rest. Go ahead, I just need to catch my breath." I warily say.

"Catch your breath? Where? In this smoke? Carmen, you're crazy. The smoke is getting to you. Come on." He says, wrapping his arm around me, coaxing me to walk.

"I need to rest. I need a nap." I say, feeling frustrated that he won't listen to me. "I'm tired."

"Listen, I know that. But I know that it's because of the smoke. You're coming with me right now." Alessandro says, seemingly making a decision as he speaks. I don't have a chance to say anything more, because suddenly, my feet aren't on the ground anymore.

Alessandro has me in his arms as he begins jogging–yes, jogging–in the direction of the exit. Well, what I hope is the exit.

As he moves, the headache that was at the back of my mind before is now pounding. I squeeze my eyes shut as the pain pulses.

"Carmen? Don't pass out or something!" Alessandro says

close to my ear. Opening my mouth to respond, I'm suddenly met with clean air. I throw my eyes open, and the blinding sunlight hits my skin.

Alessandro leans against the school wall, allowing me to take in my surroundings, and allowing me to see the approaching figure of Santiago.

"What happened? Carmen? Are you okay?" Santiago asks, his words coming out demanding and upset.

"Yes? I think I'm okay? There was so much smoke and I think I got turned around." I say, moving in a motion that signals to Alessandro that he should put me down. As he begins to set me down, I notice the camera crews that were here earlier, and notice the cameras that are being pointed directly at us from over the wall.

"No. No, no, no." I say, leaning against the wall in defeat.

"What's wrong?" Both Santiago and Alessandro ask at the same time.

"Look over there. They just the perfect shot of us, and probably a few of…" I trail off suddenly losing steam.

"Of what?" Santiago asks as he spins, facing the cameras that are still flashing, the lenses just over the wall.

"Of my…skirt." I say sheepishly, not needing to explain any more. Looking down in embarrassment, I focus my eyes on my smudged shoes.

"I'm going to go handle it. Breathe in some fresh air." Alessandro says, his face turning cold as he strides toward the school grounds exit.

"What happened back there?" I finally ask Santiago as we sit in the grass. The air is cold, but it's refreshing on my burning throat.

"The heating system malfunctioned, and since there was a small fire that broke out, the smoke was being blasted through all of the vents." Santiago explains slowly. "Why didn't you come out? I ran out, and as soon as I realized you weren't out here, the security guys wouldn't let me back in. I'm sorry I wasn't there."

"What? It wasn't your fault. At all." I blurt out, horrified. "I got turned around, and then Alessandro was able to come get me. The smoke was really starting to disorient me." I confess, upset that he's blaming himself.

"I know. He realized just as I did, and was able to slip past the security." Santiago says, watching me closely before speaking again. "Why did he go back in for you?"

I'm startled by his question, and I speak before thinking. "Why wouldn't he? Am I not important enough to be saved?"

"Carmen, you know that's not what I meant. I was asking why he ran completely fearlessly back into the building that everyone thought was on fire." Santiago's frustrated words echo in my ears before I respond. "When he and I don't like each other. Don't you think that would translate to him not paying attention to my little sister?"

Wow, there's a lot to unpack there. "Maybe because he knew I was still in there? Maybe because he decided to put you stupid war in the past to *save* me? And maybe he looked past the fact that I'm your little sister, and at the fact that I'm a human, too?" I argue, looking up with fire in my eyes. "I would hope that you would do the same if he had a little sister that was in *danger*." I say, emphasizing the 'danger' part.

"You're right. I'm sorry for acting like that." Santiago says, as if realizing that he's doing exactly what I told him I didn't like him doing.

"Thank you." I say, giving him a quick smile. "Can we go home? I don't want to be here anymore, and I'm sure that we will all be dismissed soon." I ask, desperate to get out of here.

"Yeah, let's go." Santi says, standing and offering me his hand. I gladly take it and stand on wobbly legs.

"Can you walk out?" Santiago says, concerned.

"I'm fine. Let's just get home." I say, my knees feeling weak as we walk to the student parking lot. "Fair warning, your car is going to smell like smoke." I say as Santiago opens the car door for me, allowing me to slide into the seat.

"I can always get it detailed. Don't worry, Carm." He says, walking around and sliding into his own seat. "You could have died, and you're worried about the smell of my car. I think you *might* need to reconsider your priorities."

"Maybe, but I know how you and Matteo are. You're both freaks about your cars being absolutely perfect." I retort with a shrug, letting him know that I'm only half-kidding.

"That's true, but I think you need to remember that your life wasn't previously in danger all of those other times I was frustrated with you dirtying up my car." Santiago says, turning on his car and pulling on the road. We drive for a few minutes before I speak.

"It could have been. What if all of those other times I almost died because I was too hungry?" I question.

"Yeah, I'm sure those times were really life-threatening." Santiago says with a roll of his eyes.

"Exactly. What if this time was less important than those?

What if I had more of a chance escaping the smoke than I did hunger?" I tease, looking over with a twinkle in my eyes.

To my surprise, Santiago doesn't look pleased. "Carmen, let's not joke about you being in there. It wasn't a joke to me, and I was truly panicked when they wouldn't let me go back in." Santiago says, his eyes firmly planted on the road. "The security was physically holding me down, because I was fighting so much. Nobody knew what was happening. All we knew was that there was a lot of smoke–" He takes a breath in. "–and that you were still inside."

I sober as I realize how I would feel if I were Santiago, and clear my throat. "Sorry, Santiago. Trust me, I was scared, too." I chew the inside of my cheek as I realize that I never thought of Santiago during my escape. I never worried about him being in there.

While I know it's because subconsciously my brian knew that he would escape somehow, I still feel guilty. Why didn't I worry about him as much as he worried about me?

"Don't apologize. I'm just worried. You really scared me in there, and I just need a while before I start joking about how scary that was. It's me, not you." Santiago says, sounding even more frustrated than he did before.

"No, you're right. I was just trying to lighten the mood." I say, turning my head and facing out the window.

Why *did* Alessandro turn around and come back for me? Why did he risk his life–or at the time think he was risking his life–to rescue the girl that broke up with him?

It's probable that he was just doing what any decent human would do, but I have to wonder if it's because he still has feelings for me.

I'm seriously deranged. There's no reason to be looking this deeply into Alessandro coming back for me. He did what any good person would do, and went back into danger to save me. Right?

The image of his receding figure as he went to go 'deal' with the reporters is still in my mind, and I wonder what he's going to do about the photos. I don't particularly want photos of my skirt…and everything else online. Especially when I just escaped a building that was flooded with smoke.

While I'm still slightly nervous about the photos that were taken, I know that without a doubt Alessandro will handle it. How do I know? I'm not sure. I just know that if he said he was going to handle it, Alessandro will handle it.

Just before we arrive home, I remember Brooklynn. How did I forget about her? She wouldn't know about the safety drills and where to exit, right? "Oh my gosh, Santiago, I forgot about Brooklynn!" I exclaim, slapping my forehead with the palm of my hand.

"What do you mean? Were you supposed to pick her up or something?"Santiago questions.

"No, well, maybe? She hasn't been going here for very long. What if she got turned around in school like I did, and wasn't able to get out?" I worry, chewing the inside of my cheek.

"I saw her outside, she got out. You were the last person inside." Santiago reassures, tapping his fingers on the steering wheel. "And, it was almost all smoke. They had the fire out by the time you got out, there was just a *lot* of smoke."

"Yeah, but what if she didn't get out, and I just left her? I just met her. I should have been taking care of her since she's unfamiliar here." I say, running my fingers through my hair. "If you're right, then she's safe, but what if she wasn't?"

"Hey, she's not your responsibility." Santiago says firmly, reaching over to gently remove the hair out of my hands. "And if you don't stop this, you're going to be bald within the hour. Brooklynn was outside and safe when we left. I know that for a fact."

I don't respond, and I'm grateful for the distraction of getting home. Matteo is sliding into his car as we pull up, panic on his face.

"Oh my gosh, you two! Why didn't you answer my calls? We've all been trying to get a hold of you. Father is in a meeting, but he's still been trying to call you. And I've been trying to get through to you, but *neither* of you picked up." Matteo says, worry and concern obvious in his voice as we get out of the car.

He pulls both Santiago and I into a hug, and instead of resisting like I might have a few days ago, I allow both of them to wrap their arms around me.

"Now that I know you're both safe, please enlighten me on why you didn't answer my ten billion calls." Matteo says against my head.

"I don't think either of our phones had the sound on. We got out and immediately started driving home. They were probably still on silent from when we were in class." Santiago says sheepishly.

"Well it's nice that you were trying to follow school rules— for once—but when you're in the middle of an emergency, try to remember that you have an older brother who is freaking out."

"For once? Come on, now!" Santiago teases.

"I'm glad that's all you retained from my little lecture." Matteo says, pulling away and tousling Santiago's hair.

"I for one, am I sorry about that." I say, keeping my face straight for as long as possible. "Does that mean I'm your favorite sibling, now?"

"You two are insufferable. I'm going to have gray hair early. I'm too young for this."

"Um, I think you need a reality check. You're ancient, and it's a surprise that your hair doesn't reflect that already." Santiago laughs, knocking his shoulder into Matteo's as we walk inside.

"At least I don't smell like I just came back from a week in the woods, and the only thing I bathed in was campfire smoke."

Santiago's jaw drops. "You're going to make jokes about our near-death experiences? Really," he clicks his tongue before continuing. "I'm surprised with you, brother. How insensitive."

They continue their little argument, but I slip into my room as soon as I reach my door.

Matteo is right, I *stink*. After showering for at least a half-hour, I'm certain that I've removed the smells of smoke and smell from me.

I decide to just wear pajamas, because there's no way I'm doing anything other than relaxing for the rest of the day, and I sit down on my window seat, curling my legs beneath me.

I power on my phone to see there's a *lot* of missed calls and messages. I call Mother and Father and fill them in on what happened, letting them know that we're both okay, and then I move on to the texts. There's a bunch from Matteo, and one from Alessandro.

In the message, he asks me to call him. Without thinking, I

open the app, about to press the dial button.

CHAPTER THIRTY-SIX

What am I doing? Somewhere in my brain screams out, and I drop my phone next to me.

I almost just called Alessandro! What's going on with me? I haven't talked to him since I broke up with him–excluding today–and I can't just start now, right?

What if it has something to do with the photographers? The part of my brain that wants to talk to him argues. Deciding to go with this, I press the button before I have the chance to use logic against myself.

"Hello?" Alessandro's voice says clearly through the microphone.

"Hi?" I say, stammering for the right words. "What's going on?"

"I-" Alessandro takes a breath before speaking again. "I was able to ensure that the photos won't get released. If any of the reporters go against their word, then they'll have a nice lawsuit against them."

"Thank you. Really, thank you." I reply, feeling grateful that he handled that messy situation.

"Carmen, you don't have to thank me. You know that I would do anything for you." Whoa, this is straying into dangerous territory.

"You- I-" Struggling for the correct thing to say, I lean back against the pillows. "Thank you, Aless." I don't know why I just called him by the nickname that I gave him, but it feels fitting for the moment. Listening to Alessandro's breathing hitch for a moment lets me know that he caught on to that, too.

"You're welcome." He takes a breath before talking again, his voice sounding measured and deliberate. "Can we talk?"

The question I've been dreading. It's my gut reaction to say no, but something inside me pauses. What if we just… talk? "Alessandro, I *want* to talk to you, but you have to know that nothing could come of this. If we just talk, would that be enough?" I ask, preparing myself for him to decline.

"Of course. I just want to talk." Alessandro says earnestly. "When do you want to talk?"

I scrunch my eyebrows. "Isn't that what we're doing right now?"

Alessandro chuckles from the other side of the phone, and I can imagine his smile as he does so. "Well, yeah, but I was hoping that we could talk in person?"

"Fine. We can, but remember that today was abnormal and my brothers are still…unaware of us." I warn, a smile rising on my face. Us. As much as I miss 'us' I know that I have to be responsible when it comes to whatever our conversation leads to. I can't just be blinded by my feelings.

"That's not a problem. Do you have time tonight? School is obviously out for the rest of the day, and I'm guessing it will be the same for tomorrow."

Pulling my phone away from my ear, the clock on it reads one in the afternoon. "Tonight is good. What time?"

"Whenever you'd like. I'll pick you up and we can figure out where we want to go from then."

"Meet me at midnight?" I ask, already regretting this whole thing. I'm seriously going to be regretting this later.

"I'll be there. Thank you, Carmen."

Why, oh why, did I ever commit to this? As I'm slipping into a sweater, tights, and a skirt, I'm seriously questioning my mental stability. Why did I think that meeting up with Alessandro to talk about our breakup—in the same car that I fell for him in—was a good idea?

I can't cancel on him now, seeing as he'll be here within ten minutes, but the thought is appealing. What if I just decide to lose my resolve and I end up pushing all of the hurt and betrayal to the back of my mind?

The logical part of my brain argues that I won't do that to myself, but the over-anxious side isn't so sure. I know that Alessandro won't do anything to force his opinions or side of the story on me, so all I need to worry about is myself.

Without any more time to worry, I slip out of my room and tiptoe down the hallway. There's no way I'm going to be trying to sneak all of the stairs and out the back entrance. This method is tried and true.

Stifling a laugh as I think this, I realize just how much I've changed in these last few months. How do I have a preferred method of sneaking out?

After crossing the lawn and wall, the familiar sight of Alessandro's car waiting is enough to tighten my throat. Nostalgia rushes through me, but I push it away as Alessandro opens the door for me. Still the gentleman.

"Instead of just parking somewhere? Can we just drive for a while?" I ask, glancing over at Alessandro's shadowed face. The sight of him sparks all of the memories I've been keeping at bay, and I swallow as I imagine just forgiving Alessandro so that I can have him back.

I'm seriously ridiculous, I know.

"Carmen?" Alessandro whispers softly. I blink furiously before responding, realizing that I've been staring at him for much longer than necessary.

"Yes?"

"This is going to sound like a weak apology, but this isn't everything I have to say. I just need to say this before we're in here any longer." Alessandro says. "Carmen, I'm so, so sorry for lying to you. I never wanted to lie to you, but I had to."

"You had to?" I question disregarding the apology.

"Yes. I want you to know the full story, not so you change your mind, instead, so you don't hate me. I promise that as soon as I realized I was going to have to lie to you, I regretted even being there with Santiago all of those years ago."

"Go ahead, tell me the whole story." I say, crossing my arms and glancing over skeptically.

"Starting from the beginning, I guess you know that Santiago and I were close. We were practically brothers, actually. You know that I don't have siblings, so having a good friend like him was like having a brother." He takes a pause. "And that's why I was able to be persuaded to be an accomplice in most of his bad ideas. That's what they were, really. Bad ideas."

Alessandro takes a few breaths before speaking again. "At

some point, we were both in too deep to just forget about all of the things we did together. And while some of it wasn't too bad, remember that Santiago kind of sees himself as the outcast out of you three. And me…you know what it's like with my family." Alessandro flicks on the blinker as he passes someone. "So I was pretty much down to do whatever he wanted. That was until the stained glass window broke. While that was an accident–I swear–it still scared me. The other things were a little bit more explainable–well, except for the golf course–and this was the first *big* thing. We would have been in serious trouble with not just our parents, but the club, too."

"Sorry to interrupt, but how did you get from accidents and harmless pranks to breaking and entering?" I ask, genuinely curious as to what their downfall was.

"Honestly, it was Santiago. I know that sounds like me placing the blame on him, but really, it was the pressure he was being put under from your father. He was upset with how he was supposed to be perfect, but how he felt like he was being cheated out of the business that he wanted." I'm guessing that he's talking about Father's business, but I don't want to interrupt. "So when he hatched this plan to break into the club for the fun of it, and maybe find drinks in there, I was against it. But me being the follower I was, I still agreed after some pressure and blackmail. Genuinely, it's the stupidest thing I've ever done." Alessandro says, sounding regretful.

"I'm glad you can at least see your past mistakes." I comment, not wanting to derail the conversation for too long.

"When we were…breaking in–I hate saying that–I went ahead of him. Santiago wanted to be the one to watch out for us, because, according to him, he was more aware of his surroundings." Alessandro takes a breath before continuing. "Once we were in, I was a few hallways ahead of him and was so turned around that I was lost. That's one of the reasons I vowed to memorize the hallways, by the way." He comments, referencing our conversation from a few weeks ago when I asked how he knew every little twist and turn of the club.

"Oh."

"Yeah. Anyway, I got so turned around that we were completely separated. That's when I heard the club alarms going off, and I freaked out. I guess I was too lost for even the staff there to find me and since they didn't know I was in there, no one was looking." Alessandro reaches down and takes a sip of water. "And while I don't know if Santiago thought I was caught or not, but either way, he didn't mention to anyone that I was there."

"Okay. What happened after that?"

"So a few days after everything went down, we met up and were talking, and apparently *I* was the reason he was caught. I triggered one of the alarms without knowing."

"Oh my gosh."

"Yeah, tell me about it. I felt horrible. The good news was that the police never got involved. The problem was that Santiago was mad at me. So I did what any reasonable person would do and apologized a million times, even though I'd practically been blackmailed into doing it."

"Blackmailed?"

"We'd already done all of the other things, so Santiago was pretty convincing when he was asking me to come along.

I wouldn't say that he was exactly trying to blackmail me, but when he was trying to get me in on it, he said things like 'we've already painted the golf course' and stuff like that. I felt like it was blackmail, even if that wasn't his exact intention." Alessandro confesses.

"So then how did you get here? Where you don't talk to him, and you…lie about why you don't talk." I say, hurt brimming in my voice as I speak.

"Eventually, after he kept saying 'we both should have been caught' I was freaked out. I was a nervous wreck, and I'm not too proud of what I did next." He takes a breath. "I told him that if he didn't stop saying things like that to me and sending me on edge every time we talked, that I was going to tell somebody about all of the other things we did together."

"But wouldn't that literally put him in the same place as you?"

"I told Santiago that I was going to say he confessed those things to me, and I was in no way associated with him. And since he had *just* been caught breaking and entering, who was going to be believed had any of it ever came to light? It was wrong, I know, but I felt so angry at him for pressuring me into going with him, and then getting angry at me when it wasn't my fault."

"You…*what?*" I question, feeling for both Santiago *and* Alessandro in this situation.

"I know, I know. It was horrible, but I was scared. Why was he trying to dredge up the past when it wasn't my fault? That was the only thing I could think. Well, besides the fact that I was going to be the biggest disappointment to my family."

Alessandro looks over his shoulder before switching lanes. "And that's when we decided that we were going to part ways and never speak of or to each other again. We both knew that we had too much to lose, and that we were both liabilities. So we swore to never tell anyone what happened, and to never talk about why we aren't friends." As he finishes speaking, there's a sadness to his voice that I've only heard a few times before.

"So that's why you just say that you're vying for the top student?"

"Yes. And, to be fair, that's the truth. We've had a silent war in school since that night." Alessandro says with a small smile.

"That's kind of sad, you know." I say, truthfully feeling it.

"I know. We were brothers at one point, and now we can't even speak to one another." Alessandro takes a deep breath. "But none of that is a good excuse for lying. I should have told you at least some of the truth. I shouldn't have expected you to be okay with me lying to you. I'm truly sorry, Carmen. I never wanted to hurt you, and I hope that you know that. The only reason that I did it was because if I ruined our friendship, the least I could do was uphold the deal that we swore on." Alessandro says, taking his eyes off of the road for the first time this evening, and glancing into mine for a split second.

I press my lips together as my throat tightens. This wasn't supposed to happen. Coming here was supposed to make me want him less, not more.

"I…" I take a deep breath. "I accept your apology, but I don't think that this can change things between us, yet. I'm not angry with you, but I'm still hurt. I know why you did what you did, but imagine if the roles were reversed. Imagine that I lied to you and kept you in the dark about something that you should have known about."

"I know. I completely accept responsibility, and understand that I was wrong for lying. I can't change the past, but I can hope that you'll at least see that I'm truly and sincerely sorry." Alessandro looks like he wants to say something else, but he closes his mouth. Somehow, we've ended up a few miles from my house, and Alessandro begins to slow.

"Did you just do a big loop around the city?" I ask, looking over at the clock that reads one-thirty.

"Yes. I didn't want to drive too far this late at night." Alessandro says, biting his lip before speaking again. "Do you want to keep driving?"

The question hurts, because I want to yes, but I can't. Not right now. "I think it's time for me to get home. I'm sorry." I say, intentionally looking out the windshield as I speak.

"Don't apologize. It's late, I completely understand." We reach my place, and just as I'm about to step out of the car, Alessandro rests his hand on my arm.

"Carmen, I don't know if there's ever going to be a chance to say this after tonight, so I'm just going to tell you. I promise that you don't have to look at me differently, and that you can go the rest of your life with me just being someone from your past." Alessandro sucks in a breath before looking me right in the eyes. "I love you. I understand if you don't feel the same way—and I don't expect you to—but I just needed to tell you. I needed to tell you now, before you move on, and I never get the chance to tell you. You don't have to do or say anything—nor do you have to feel even remotely the same—I just had to tell you." Alessandro says, pulling his hand back to his leg.

I stare at him with my mouth slightly open, the reality of what he just said sinking in. "You- you love me?"

"Yes." Alessandro says it with so much conviction and sincerity that if I were standing, I would most definitely fall over. His eyes burn holes into my own, and I remember all of the times that I looked directly into them before kissing him.

What about not falling for him all over again? That plan is currently being thrown out the window. "I, I need to go inside. I'm sorry." I say, bolting out of the car and racing to my house.

My stomach twists in knots as I scramble into my room. That didn't just happen. There's no way Alessandro told me that he loves me.

Loves me. Present tense.

Alessandro loves me.

Without even changing into pajamas, I flop down in bed. The conversation that we had did not go the way that I planned. Not in the slightest.

What am I going to do now? I *want* Alessandro. And now I know that he wants me.

Tears slip down my cheeks. I can't just say 'I want you' to him right after he explained what happened. I need to think all of this over when the words *I love you* aren't fresh in my mind. When I've had a chance to rationally review his story.

CHAPTER THIRTY-SEVEN

"Will you come with me to the office today? It's been so long since you've come down with your brothers." Father asks me at breakfast. I glance over at him, surprised at the offer. "Matteo and Santiago will be there, too, but maybe you want to come?"

I nod. "Sure, Father. When are you leaving?" I have dark circles under my eyes, and I'm sure that my hair is a mess. If almost dying from smoke inhalation wasn't enough to leave me sleep deprived, the whole Alessandro situation was the cherry on top.

I'm not mad at him anymore, but I'm still trying to sift through my feelings. *I* know that I love Alessandro, and I know that Alessandro loves me, but he doesn't know that I love him. I don't want to keep it that way, but I need to figure out exactly what I'm going to tell Alessandro.

I want to tell him that I love him and that I want our relationship again, but I also can't just come outright and say that. We need to regain our footing in our relationship before we just start dating again. Right?

"I'll be leaving after breakfast. You might want to…" Father looks me up and down before continuing. "Freshen up a bit before we leave."

I smile at his words. "Don't worry, I will."

"I'll meet you in the car in twenty minutes?" Father asks, standing from his seat.

"Yeah, twenty minutes." I say, making my way up to my room. I slip into pants, a shirt, a sleeveless sweater, and pull on shoes. Spotting my purse, I grab it and walk to Father's car.

I slide into the passenger seat, and as he shifts it in reverse, I try to remember the last time I rode in his car.

"So, I know you told me that you're okay, but how are you really? I heard from Santiago that it was more smoke than fire, but it must have been scary, right?" Father asks.

"It was scary, but I'm fine. I was able to get out before I inhaled too much smoke." I insist, not wanting to bring up the Alessandro part.

"Is that so? I'm glad you and Santiago are safe. I got word of the emergency when I was in the middle of a meeting, and couldn't leave."

"No, you're fine. Santi and I are safe, so there's nothing more to it." I say, giving Father a smile. A few more moments pass before I speak again, and while I'm not sure exactly why I'm bringing this up, I decide to give it a shot. "Father, I know that originally, you and Mother didn't think it was a good idea, but I was just wondering, when will I be able to get a driver's license?"

I glance over to watch Father's expression, and I'm surprised to see actual consideration on his face. "Well, I don't think that it would be horrible, but you also have to remember that driving isn't very safe. We'd have to get you a super safe car…" Father muses, listing off a few of his requirements. I can tell that they're not exactly for me to listen to, rather he's sorting out his brain.

"So, what do you think?" I ask after a few moments of

silence.

"I think I'll talk to your mother about it, but you're getting older, and with you proving how responsible you are with that modeling thing, I think that it might be okay." Father finally says, sounding like he's calculated it all out.

"Well, I would agree with the responsibility part." I agree, beaming from ear to ear. Life is starting to *really* look up.

"Of course you would, Carmen." Father says with a chuckle, shutting the engine off as we arrive at his office. Well, his building. Since Father owns the whole company and building, technically the whole building is his office.

"When will the boys be here?" Father asks as we walk the short distance inside. Thanks to his status, he has a special spot permanently reserved at the very front of the lot.

"I don't know. I barely saw them this morning." I say, giving the woman behind the front desk a smile.

"Of course those two are running late the one day I have a meeting set up with them scheduled to be present." Father grumbles, punching in the numbers to the elevator.

"We're going to a meeting this morning?" I ask, slightly worried. I wasn't prepared for this.

"Oh, well, your brothers and I are. You'll be able to just hang out in my office, don't worry." Father says, motioning for me to step out of the elevator ahead of him.

I nod, following him to his office. I'm not really sure why I came, then, but I don't really care. At least I'm a step closer to a driver's license.

"So, who is your meeting with?"

"Mr. Valentino. We've been discussing a trade in materials

for a while now, but we want to sit down and really go over details." Father says nonchalantly. "You've met him, right? He's a regular at the club."

"Yeah, I've met him. It's nice that you're doing business… things with him." I say, fumbling for words. If Mr. Valentino is here, then surely Alessandro is, right?

"Perfect, it looks like he's already here in the lounge. Won't you go ahead and sit with them while I gather my things and call your brothers. Those two really know how to deviate from schedule." Father says with a disapproving shake of his head.

Go in there and sit with them? And even worse, as a distraction? When I turn to decline Father's request, his office door is sliding shut behind him. You've got to be kidding me.

"Hello, Mr. Valentino." I say, walking into the lounge and stopping near the chairs that Alessandro and his father are occupying. I extend my hand for a handshake, and let out the breath I didn't know I was holding when Alessandro's father stands.

"Hello, Ms. Alvarez. I don't think I was expecting to see you today. Your father mentioned that your brothers would be here, but I'm sorry I don't remember him mentioning you."

"I'm not going to be attending the meeting. I'm just here to spend the day at the office." I say sheepishly, realizing how silly I must sound.

"No problem." Mr. Valentino says, sitting back down and bringing his coffee to his lips. "Alessandro, greet the girl, please. Where are your manners?"

Alessandro stands, his eyes gazing deeply into mine as he extends his hand. "Hello, Ms. Alvarez. It's good seeing you today." As soon as Alessandro's large hands wrap around mine, it feels like I've been shocked. Electricity shoots throughout my body, and goosebumps flood my arm. What's wrong with me?

"It's good to see you, too." I say, allowing Alessandro to hold my hand much longer than necessary. As if Alessandro realizes what's happening, and that his father is a mere four feet away from us, Alessandro pulls his hand back.

"Ah, sorry about the wait. My sons were driving a few things from the other office over here." Father says, stepping into the room. I know that he's not telling the truth, but it's not my place to tell everyone else that.

"Of course, of course. I know how they are. Sons, am I right?" Mr. Valentino says, standing and clapping Father on the back.

I allow them to walk ahead, deliberately hanging back so I can be near Alessandro for a few more moments.

"Fancy seeing you here." Alessandro says with a smirk, looking me up and down as we walk.

"Me? You're practically intruding upon my home." I tease back. A sense of rightness settles upon me, and it feels just like all of the times that Alessandro and I joked back and forth. When it was just us, and we could be ourselves.

"Fine, fine, but it's only business." That sobers me, because suddenly, I'm brought back to the present.

"Of course. And, speaking of that, you should get going. I don't think my father needs another boy slowing down his meeting." I say, gently pushing his shoulder.

"Ah, I knew that they were just late." Alessandro says with a wink, slipping into the door that leads to Father's personal conference room.

I eventually end up in Father's office, and I seat myself on the couch that lines one of the walls. If this meeting is going to take a while, then I might as well get comfortable.

Forty-five minutes later, I'm walking out of his door, in search of a bathroom. As I'm walking down one of the carpeted halls, I turn the corner and bump right into Alesandro.

"Carmen? I'm so-"

"Oh my gosh! I'm-" We both start to apologize, and then laugh at the absurdity of it.

"Is your meeting over already? I thought that it would last much longer." I ask, clasping my hands behind my back and leaning my shoulder against the wall.

"No, not yet. I needed to take a break from the tension in that room. It's a battle of 'who's son is better' right now." Alessandro says with a chuckle.

"How intriguing. Maybe you should go back and stick up for yourself?"

"I don't really care about the son of the year award that seems to be up for grabs right now."

"And why not?" I ask, looking up through my eyelashes and Alessandro steps closer.

Alessandro's voice lowers as he speaks. "Because I only care about-" I clasp my hand over his mouth before he has the chance to continue speaking, because the sound of footsteps echoing down the hallway captures my attention.

I quickly drop my hand and rush round the corner to enter the women's bathroom, listening for whoever was walking down the hall.

"I know, I know. I'm sorry, but I have this meeting that I need to be present for, and there's…" The sound of Matteo's voice is a surprise, but I'm even more interested in who he seems to be talking to on the phone. He doesn't come close enough to be heard again, and I wait until he's finally left this hallway before slipping out of the door and into Father's office.

What was Alessandro going to say before my brother ruined our conversation? There seems to be a common thread of my brothers messing up my love life.

Curiosity burns at me for the rest of the day, and since school won't be open for another week, I'm grateful for the party that's going to be held at the club tomorrow night.

I just need to contain my curiosity until then. I'll be able to talk to Alessandro and sort out my feelings.

CHAPTER THIRTY-EIGHT

Arriving at the annual Autumn party that the club hosts, I look down at the maroon dress that I pulled out specifically for this occasion. Everything about my outfit says autumn, but without having cheesy leaves or pine cones on my clothes.

Both of my brothers arrived early, so as I walk inside, it feels like I belong. Not like one of them walked me inside, and that's the only reason I'm allowed inside.

"Hello, ma'am. Do you need help with your coat?" A club staff member asks, extending his hands to help me out of my puffy jacket. While it doesn't necessarily match the aesthetic of my outfit, I did what I had to do to stay warm. Being warm is worth more, in my opinion.

"Yes, please." I respond, allowing him to help me out of the jacket. I thank him and continue my walk into the party. The sounds of music playing from the speakers as couples dance and gather in groups together creates a warm ambiance.

"You're here! Perfect." Mother says, breezing past me as Father leads her onto the dance floor. I watch as they dance, and smile when Father leans and gives her a peck on the cheek.

"Do you want to dance?" I whisper to Alessandro, walking right up to him and standing on my toes to reach his ears.

"I'd love to." He answers. If Alessandro is surprised by my question, he doesn't show it.

With the most amount of light coming from the candles that are light around the room, it feels safe to be so close to Alessandro.

He pulls me close, wrapping his hand around my waist, and clasping the other around my hand. I feel every nerve in my body as our bodies press together, moving to the rhythm of the music.

"Alessandro, I want to talk to you." I say, quietly.

"Okay. Do you want to talk here?" Alessandro responds.

"Yeah, this is fine. I just really need to tell you that-"

"Alessandro, please come over here. I need you to meet-" Mrs. Valentino's voice fades out of earshot as she turns from us to face whoever she's speaking to.

"You should go. I don't want you to keep your mother waiting." I whisper, wrapping my arms around Alessandro in a quick hug.

"I-" Alessandro looks conflicted, so I save him the trouble of trying to stay.

"Alessandro, really, go talk to your mother. I'll be here when you get back." I say, giving him a quick smile before gently pushing him in the direction of where his mother stands with another older woman.

"Okay, but just know that I'll come back."

After a few moments, I wander down one of the hallways as I wait for Alessandro, and I end up coming across a stained glass window at the end of the hall.

Is this the one that Alessandro and Santiago broke all of those years ago?

"Lovely seeing you here, Carmen." An all-too familiar voice

says, sounding extremely near. Emilio. Taking a step back, I give him a small smile.

"Yeah." Is all I manage, suddenly feeling very uncomfortable. While I've always felt strange around him, something about being all alone with him intensifies the feeling.

"Why would a pretty girl like yourself be all alone back here?" He asks, taking a step closer to me. That's when I smell the faint smell of alcohol under his breath, and I stiffen.

"I'm waiting for…someone to meet me. In fact, he'll be here in a moment, so I'd appreciate it if you wouldn't mind excusing me." I say, taking another step away.

"No, I think I'll stay back here." He says, taking a step closer.

Mustering up all of the courage I have, I take another firm step backward. "No, I really must be leaving. Thank you for your time." I say, trying to keep an air of politeness in my voice, even if it's the last thing I feel.

"I don't think so." Emilio says, jostling forward and reaching out to grab my arm. Just before his slimy hands can touch me, a shadow appears from behind me, and a hand is making physical contact with Emilio's face.

I whirl around just as Emilio's head thumps on the wall, and Santiago's body is in front of me.

"Carmen, get back." Is all Santiago says before not so gently pushing me behind him, just as Emilio lands a punch on Santiago's ribs.

Santiago lets out a yelp of surprise before landing another direct punch on Emilio's jaw. I watch helplessly as their fight persists, and when I start to run back and get help, I run directly into Alessandro's chest. "Aless, what?" I say, stepping back. "Go help him!"

Alessandro takes one look past me, and starts running. Just as I'm getting back to the horrible scene, Alessandro lands a hard punch to Emilio's side, and then another.

I suck in a breath, unsure of what to do. Santiago stands from where he was on the ground, and just as he's about to punch Emilio in the jaw, Alessandro does. The sound that follows is sickening, and I hear myself let out a yelp.

"Now stay away from Carmen. You're going to leave this place and never come back." Santiago says, grabbing a fistful of Emilio's bloodied jacket. "Do you understand me?"

Emilio only nods in response, unable to speak due to the damage Alessandro and Santiago just inflicted upon him. Santiago drops his jacket, and Emilio leans against the wall, weak and defeated.

"Now, does anyone care to explain to me why I just beat that guy up?" Alessandro asks, wrapping his arm around Santiago. Santi's face is only a little bit less damaged than Emilio's, and his hand is pressed against his rib.

"Yeah, because he's a creep, and just tried to grab my sister. I knew he was a piece of-" Santiago swears under his breath. "-but I didn't think he was this horrible. Are you okay, Carmen?" He asks, concerned only for me when he's the one who was just in a fight.

"I'm… I'm fine. You need help." I say, stepping forward with tears in my eyes. I wrap my arms around his neck, and pulling him into a hug. "I love you." I whisper into Santiago's ear. Santiago wraps his arms around me, and hugs me just as tightly.

"I love you, too, Carm." Pulling back, I notice the bruising on one of his cheeks, and the lip that's been cracked.

I turn to Alessandro, who's making sure that Emilio is walking out of the exit near here, and step towards him. For once, I don't care that Santiago is watching me. It's as though now that I've realized how easily something can slip from my grasp, I know to hold on to what I have tightly.

I clasp my hands on either side of Alessandro's face and pull his lips towards mine.

"What in the world!" Santiago exclaims from behind me. To his credit, he doesn't do anything other than mutter under his breath.

Alessandro doesn't hesitate to kiss me back, and he wraps his hands around the back of my neck and pulls me even closer. It feels like a live wire has been set loose in my body.

Pulling back only a few inches, I rest my forehead against Alessandro's. "I love you. That's what I was trying to tell you earlier." I confess, opening my eyes to meet his.

"I love you, too."

"You love each other?" Santiago exclaims from behind us. "Step away from each other and tell me what in the world is happening here. Right now." Santiago says, limping forward and standing right next to us.

I pull back even more from Alessandro, but wrap my hand around his. "I love Alessandro." I say boldly, unafraid of whatever Santiago will say.

"And you love Carmen? How long has this been going on? Since when do you love each other?" Santiago demands of Alessandro, not exactly angry, but not pleased, either.

"We've been dating for a while in secret, and we love each

other." Alessandro answers truthfully, meeting Santiago's cold gaze.

"You're dating my sister? And you, you're dating him?" Santiago asks, disbelief in his voice.

"Yes." We both answer at the same time.

"Wow, just when you think you're finally getting a grip on your life, you end up beating some jerk and find out that your sister is dating the one person you swore to never speak to again." Santiago says, his voice even calmer than the last time he spoke.

"You're not angry?" I ask.

"I'm trying to not be. Hurt? Yes. Confused? Yes. In a lot of pain? Yes." Santiago answers, his jaw clenched as he speaks.

"Oh, let's get you back home or something. I'm sorry!" I exclaim, realizing that Santiago has been in pain this whole time, and I've just been ignoring it.

Alessandro and I walk with Santiago to his car, having slipped out through one of the back exits, and Alessandro slides behind the wheel when we start getting in.

"Hey, hey, this is my car." Santiago says, his heart not really in the argument. He must be in *really* bad shape.

"Yeah, which is why I'm going to make sure we get back in one piece and don't total it. Just get in." Alessandro says with a chuckle.

Santiago silently climbs into the back seat, and I follow behind him.

CHAPTER THIRTY-NINE

"Thank you." I say, leaning against Alessandro's chest as I walk with him to the door. We arrived back at my house, and promptly fixed Santiago up, before he said he needed to be alone, and closed his room door behind him. I won't be surprised if he doesn't talk to me for a few days, but not because he's angry. From what he's said this evening–and that's not saying much–he's hurt and needs to deal with the shock of this. He did, however, hug Alessandro a few minutes ago, something tells me that they'll be friends again in the future.

"No, thank you. All I did was help Santiago. You forgave me, and quite possibly got my best friend back. I'll never be able to repay you for either of those things, you know?" Alessandro says, stopping at the top of the stairs and sitting down on the step. "While I hoped that you were going to tell me that you wanted me back earlier, I wasn't allowing myself to think that. And then when I saw you walk down that hallway, all I could think was that I blew my chance and you changed your mind." Alessandro confesses as I sit next to him.

My dress is torn near the bottom, and there's dried blood on Alessandro's jacket.

"Alessandro, I've always wanted you. Even when I was

breaking up with you, I still wanted you. All of the time when we were apart? I still wanted you. When you told me the full story, it was like a weight had been taken off of my chest. That was the go ahead to continue wanting you." I admit, looking up into his beautiful eyes as I speak.

"You really still wanted me?" Alessandro asks, sounding as if he never considered this a possibility.

"I really *do* want you."

THE END

Epilogue

"It would be rather inconvenient for us to be late, you know?" Alessandro says from behind me, wrapping his arms around my middle for a hug.

"It would, but it might be worth it." I reply, leaning my head back to rest on his chest.

"It would be worth it to be late to our own wedding?" Alessandro teases, stepping away from me and so he can pick up his shoes that wait by the door.

"Well, when you put it like that." I say, brushing my hands down the silk pajamas that I'm wearing. "Maybe you *should* be getting over to your dressing room. I know that the girls will be here in a few minutes to help me get my dress on." I say, mentioning my three friends that I chose to be my bridesmaids.

"You're right. I can't wait to see you walk down the aisle. Although, I can't promise that I'll be able to focus on the dress that I still haven't seen, because my eyes will be on you." Alessandro says, kissing me once more before stepping out of the room and into the hallway.

I smile even after the door is closed, because there's no way that bright-eyed, sixteen year old Carmen would believe that in eight years, she would be marrying the love of her life, at the place where it all started.

Stepping back in front of the window, I stare out at the lush gardens of The Enchanted Ivy, and picture the very first time I saw, spoke, and kissed Alessandro, replaying all of our firsts, as a new chapter in our life opens.

A knock sounds on my door, and before I open it, I take a breath and remember that whatever comes after this, Alessandro and I will face it together.

REVIEW

If you enjoyed Dances and Delegations, let others know!
I would love it if you shared a review or your thoughts on the
platform(s) where you purchased Dances and Delegations, social
media, or even with your friends and family!

STAY CONNECTED!

Wait! Have you followed me on social media and signed
up for my newsletter? I want to hear from you! Also, be sure to
check out my other books! All of my books are available on all
platforms, and are waiting for you to pick them up!

Jenevieve Hernandez

ACKNOWLEDGMENTS

Thank YOU for picking up Dances and Delegations! This book wouldn't be where it is without you. Maybe you're reading this because you need a pick me up, or maybe it's because someone picked it out for you. Maybe you're reading this for the first time, or maybe the hundredth. Either way, thank you! You mean so much to me, and you're so loved and appreciated!

Thank you to my family for supporting me as I wrote and published this book with a crazy deadline! I know that the many late nights that I spent on this book were worth it, and I'm so thankful that you worked your schedules around my crazy one, so I could finish Dances and Delegations! I'm eternally grateful for your support and excitement, and for listening to my constant book ramblings! You're all the best!

And last but not least, thank you, God, for continuing to give me the passion and talent for storytelling. I'm so grateful that this is my job, and that I can do this for a living. You've blessed me beyond belief, and while I can't see every path You have laid out for me, I know that Your plans will go above and beyond my wildest dreams.

ABOUT THE AUTHOR

Jenevieve Hernandez is the author of sweet and swoony romances, filled to the brim with the feeling of falling in love. She loves portraying character growth, unique plots, and, of course, romance in her books. Her books will never contain any explicit content, and are always guaranteed happily ever afters.

She enjoys spending her time in the pages of books, traveling from one story to the next, or outdoors, exploring the world around her.